☾ ☾ ☾

Moving quickly, Whit scrambled back from the cliff face, sending a few loose rocks rolling toward the edge. She raced to her motorcycle, jumped into the saddle, and snapped the kickstand up with her boot. As she reached for the starter, a sudden blow across the back of her head sent the moon and stars into a swirling black sea. She felt herself tumble from the bike, roll onto her back. She lay there, insensible, paralyzed.

In the moon bright night, another motorcycle was visible at the edge of the forest, and a woman clad in black leather pants and jacket was suddenly standing at Whit's feet. Through slitted eyes, Whit watched the woman kneel down, grip her boot, and with a grunt, begin dragging Whit toward the cliff edge.

Other Books by Jean Stewart:

Return to Isis

Isis Rising

Isis
Rising

ISIS RISING

JEAN STEWART

RISING
TIDE
PRESS

Rising Tide Press
5 Kivy Street
Huntington Station, NY 11746
(516) 427-1289

Printed in the United States on acid-free paper

Publisher's note:
All characters, places and situations in this book are fictitious and any
resemblance to persons (living or dead) is purely coincidental.

Publisher's Acknowledgments:
The publisher is grateful for all the support and expertise offered by the
members of its editorial board: Bobbi Bauer, Beth Heyn, Harriet
Edwards, Pat G., Adriane Balaban, and Marian Satriani. And a special
thanks to Harriet and Adriane for their excellent proofing and criticism,
to Edna G. for believing in us, and to the feminist bookstores for being
there.

First printing July, 1993
10 9 8 7 6 5 4 3 2

Edited by Lee Boojamra and Alice Frier
Book cover art: Evelyn Rysdyk

Stewart, Jean, 1952
   Isis Rising

ISBN 0—9628938-8-9

Library of Congress #: 93—083668

Great thanks to
Deborah Pursifull and SJH
for the laborious proofreading.
And Gaea's blessing on Lee Boojamra and Alice Frier, of
Rising Tide Press

For
Henrietta Leager Stewart
who read me fairy tales
and showed me the magic
of a well told tale.

I love you, Mom.

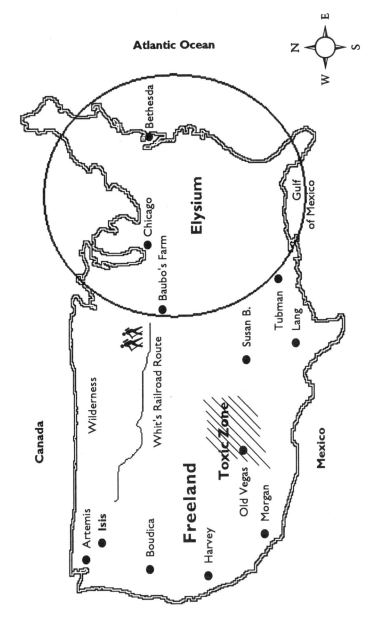

*K*ali wasn't exactly sure where she was. She was standing in bright moonlight, on the edge of some high promontory, surrounded by fir forest. The place was at once both mysteriously familiar and completely unknown. In the silvery light, the forest seemed eerily alive, shifting with black shadows and danger.

Where am I?

And then, as her eyes swept across the edge of the forest, the shadows beneath one particular tree gathered together—denser, darker. Suddenly, the shadows were human shapes, moving quickly, relentlessly toward her. As they entered the full illumination of moonlight, the uniforms on the men became shockingly distinct. Involuntarily, Kali gasped.

Regs! Oh Mother, they've found me!

There were at least twenty of the fascist soldiers, all of them huge and menacing, all of them laughing that harsh, bone-chilling, mirthless laughter that Kali remembered from Elysium.

One Reg separated from the group, rushing forward—without seeming to actually run—as if he were some demon spirit thrusting through the air like a blast of foul smoke. She tried to turn, tried to run, and with a wail of terror realized she couldn't move.

In the blink of an eye, the Reg closed the space between them. Seizing the front of her shirt, he ripped it apart in one savage tear. His cruel laughter became a roar of lust. She was screaming as his weight dropped fully on her, fighting with all her might as he grabbed her wrists and wrestled her down.

"Kali!" a husky voice cried in her ear.

Her heart slammed frantically in her chest, her back and scalp prickled with ice-cold sweat, and for a moment she did not recognize Whit's handsome face hovering above her, framed in dark, tousled hair.

Not a Reg—Whit.

Confused, Kali glanced around herself. Rosy, dawn light poured through the window, clearly revealing the section of the lab that had been converted into their bedroom.

Whit's gray eyes watched her, concerned. "Nightmare?"

Kali took a deep, ragged breath, almost unable to believe that she was in bed, safe in the temporary quarters she and Whit had made in her mother's lab, in the Isis Cedar House.

Pulling her into a comforting hug, Whit asked, "Want to talk about it?"

Kali breathed, "No."

"Sure? Your frightening scream...."

Shuddering, Kali whispered, "Just a crazy dream." She quickly resolved that she didn't want to confront the terror again by trying to talk about it. "Sorry I woke you up."

Whit lovingly pushed shoulder-length, golden hair away from Kali's face. "It's okay," she soothed. "I have to get up anyway. In another hour I have to fly over to Artemis and report for the Council Meeting."

Puzzled, and anxious for a distraction, Kali commented, "I still can't figure out what they want with you."

Whit shrugged. "What with it being Beltane tomorrow, Lilith due for retirement, and Isis ready to be declared an active colony again, the possibilities are endless. Lilith just told me to be sure and wear my dress uniform. Why don't you duck Lupa's work detail and come with me?"

"Can't. Tomorrow's the first of May. There are still too few workers and the hostel has to be finished before June—Lupa says that's when most women will make up their minds and move in on us. The meal hall is ready, so at least we'll all eat better, but we can't have everyone in tents...."

Whit interrupted, snuggling against her. "Lupa says you're a great plumber." Tenderly, Whit sent her hands across Kali's nakedness, repeatedly lingering over what she knew to be sensitive areas. "...So I suppose she really does need you," she finished with a sigh.

They fell silent for a moment. Kali realized she was reluctantly preparing herself; in another moment, Whit would let go of her and roll out of bed. They would each begin a day of meeting separate and very different demands.

Grimly, Kali accepted the reality of their roles in Isis. Whit had become the undesignated administrator of this new colony, sought out continually for advice, direction, dispute management. Kali, in contrast, had merely gained a reputation as a hard worker. After ten years of internment in Elysium, struggling to avoid starvation and the random cruelty of the Regs, Kali felt uneducated and uncertain of her place in Freeland. She was good with her hands, but she was years behind everyone else in any sort of worthwhile technological knowledge.

As expected, Whit moved back from her, then flashed a lazy grin and crooned, "Want to bring me luck?"

"How?" Kali returned, as usual, ready to do almost anything this woman asked.

"The Goddess's gift," Whit answered, laughing softly. "If I have to wear my warrior uniform, whatever's going on is important. Send me into action bathed in love."

With a pleased growl, Kali crawled on top of Whit and kissed her deeply, luxuriating in the feel of that strong body tensing beneath her. She was more than happy to comply with Whit's request.

☾ ☾ ☾

About ninety miles northwest of Isis, the morning was unfolding with unusual fanfare in the older city-colony of Artemis.

Her rows of black braids gleaming and her deep brown skin glowing in the soft, amber light, Cimbri Braun stood among a crowd of about nine hundred women, watching the off ramp of the small transport ship extend to the tarmac of the airfield. Cimbri nervously smoothed the sleeves of her salmon-colored jacket, admiring the satiny material that also made up the form-fitting pants. Lilith had told her to dress well, but would not disclose anything else.

In the distance, the peaceful scenery provided the same spectacular backdrop as it had for centuries. Puget Sound was a smear of many blues, luminous in the slant of northern light. Beyond the Sound, the Olympic Mountain Range rose like a jagged, purple wall. Cimbri noted that it was a beautiful morning for the end of April, and was thankful that the rains seemed to have ended early this year.

A baby started crying somewhere nearby, and a soft mother's voice began to croon a comforting tune. Then the door of the transport ship slid open. The crowd hummed with excited comments and gossip as everyone jostled for a better look.

An officious looking woman, her skin a lovely light brown and her long hair the wavy silk of mixed race genes, walked slowly down the carpeted metal incline that led from the ship. Her intelligent green eyes sparkled as she looked around, smiling.

"That's Arinna Sojourner, from the colony of Tubman—you know, Old Louisiana territory," announced a gravelly voice behind Cimbri. "I recognize her from the comline news reports. She's only about twenty-six, but they say she's a brilliant computer scientist. She's created some innovative communications designs for Tubman, and she's an influential member of the Tubman Council." The elderly voice dropped to a whisper as the speaker admired the flowing, beautifully embroidered dress Arinna wore.

Next, a woman with marked Chinese features paused dramatically in the door of the aircraft, then began descending the ramp. At once, the murmuring crowd grew louder, and Cimbri could see why. This was a devastatingly attractive woman—and she clearly knew the impact she was making on the hundreds of Artemisians gathered around the transport. Slender, but smoothly muscled, the woman moved with pride and an easy arrogance. Her stylishly cut black hair was complemented by the clinging orange of the revealing bodysuit she wore. The shoulder of her black, knee-length jacket sported a Deputy Leader's emblem.

"And that's Loy Yin Chen, of Boudicca," the same voice was announcing self-importantly. "Apparently, she's done an amazing job in her secondary role as Deputy Leader. My cousin Phoebe says everyone is kind of surprised, because Loy's the type that wants to be in charge of everything. No one thought she could endure being number two to anyone else's number one, but I suppose some people will do *anything* if it involves grooming themselves for power."

Stifling a smile, Cimbri turned around to see who was providing all this information. She recognized Marpe and her friend Samsi, a couple of genteel clothing merchants who were rumored to be readying for relocation to Isis. The two venerable, elderly women smiled back at her.

Emboldened by Cimbri's attention, Marpe asked, "Do you know why these illustrious personages are visiting us, Healer Braun? I don't think it's merely Arinna and Loy coming to celebrate Beltane with us, do you?"

No, I don't, Cimbri immediately thought, but aloud she responded, "We'll just have to wait and see what the Council Meeting is all about." And then Cimbri began to move forward, gently pushing between women until she could get a view of the reception party.

Lilith, the current Leader of Artemis, stood a short distance away. Tall and slender and dignified, she was leaning forward, embracing first Arinna, then Loy. Lilith's silver-white hair was swept back into a chignon, and her eyes seemed more blue than usual accented by the royal blue of the long jacket and pants set she wore.

Captain Nakotah Berry, Cimbri's partner, stepped forward from the ranks of the warrior patrol arranged around the ship's off ramp. Proudly, Cimbri noted how distinguished Nakotah looked in her short-waisted, wine-red warrior's jacket. Introductions were made and Nakotah's long, black hair shifted between her shoulders as she placed a hand over her heart in salute.

Arinna cast another disarmingly enchanting smile. Hand over her heart, Loy returned the salute, aiming an aloof scrutiny into the tall Sioux's dancing eyes.

Not only was Arinna lovely, she was smoothly in charge. "Lead on, Captain Berry." Arinna seemed intent on steering both Loy and Nakotah from the ramp of the transport.

But before Arinna succeeded in maneuvering the departure, Lilith said with surprise, "I thought there was to be a third member to your party."

With a baffled glance, Loy looked behind her. "Where is she?"

Just then, a redhead came staggering purposefully through the door and down the ramp, precariously balancing the weight of three duffel bags. This one was very young, possibly seventeen, but no more, her rangy adolescent body clad in well-pressed brown trousers and a billowing, white shirt. Wavy, red-gold hair curled about her expressive, freckled face.

"Apologies," the girl panted. "Thought I'd save someone the trouble of dragging out our baggage." And with that, several Artemis warriors leapt forward and relieved the girl of the load. She took her place beside Loy, while the younger warriors in Nakotah's patrol openly looked her over, obviously intrigued with this mixture of youth and tenacious will.

Grinning, Loy introduced her. "Danu Sullivan, apprentice architect from my home colony of Boudicca."

Bemused by the warriors who ringed her, staring, Danu merely stood there, the sky blue eyes wide.

Loy shot the girl an impatient look and prompted, "Follow the protocol."

As the girl continued to stand there, clearly awed by the size of the crowd before her, Loy shook her head and laughed. Flustered, Danu glanced at Loy, then went beet red with embarrassment.

Into the gap stepped gallant Nakotah. "Well, I, for one, admire a woman who will carry her own load," she quipped, and clapped Danu reassuringly on the shoulder.

Lilith gave Danu an affectionate smile. "May the young continue to lead us by their good example."

And with that, Lilith came forward, took Danu by the arm and turned to the crowd. "Let the welcoming procession begin!" she declared, her strong, compelling voice ringing through the crisp spring air.

The crowd parted, and Lilith and Danu began moving through the hundreds of women, across the tarmac, followed by Loy and Arinna, then Nakotah and her company of fifty warriors. The schoolgirl band waiting nearby burst into a melodic song on their flutes and drums. A long column of women and girls began to form behind the last of Nakotah's patrol, moving with the rhythmic step of a march. Cimbri strode along, her strong contralto rising to join the other voices as the procession burst into singing the Artemis anthem.

As she walked, Cimbri lifted her eyes and felt a rush of love for the eighty-year-old city-colony, gleaming like a jewel in the strong morning sunlight. The two and three-story houses were laid out in a jumble of styles and colors on streets hugging the hillsides all around her. In some areas, brightly painted Victorian clapboards dominated, while other streets, closer to the water, were crowded with stone cottages. In the business district, the structures were mostly sleek, titanium-sheeted designs. Between neighborhoods, flowering patches revealed the location of numerous gardens. Shade trees lined the streets, their spring greenery riffling in the breeze.

Artemis is a wondrous place to live, Cimbri thought once again, as she took a grateful breath of the fresh morning air.

(((

Still fastening her gun belt around her waist, Whit was charging out of the Isis Cedar House. She knew she was late, but it was hard to keep any awareness of time when she was making love with Kali. Clambering onto the big motorcycle she kept parked by the outer door, Whit gunned the engine to life and pointed the cycle toward the airfield.

The machine bumped along a narrow, winding trail and Whit felt thankful for the decibel-squelch device mounted in the engine cavity, which reduced the engine noise to a faint, barely discernible hum. She loved feeling the peaceful unity with the land as she rode over the earth on her way somewhere.

Broad valley grassland swelled into a great hill, providing Whit with a panoramic view of Pacific Northwest splendor. Timbered mountains spanned the horizon in blue-gray humps, like furry whales, far into the distance. Above the timberline and emerald green alpine meadows, ancient glaciers glittered brightly in the sunshine. Below, almost hidden by forest, lakes flashed a milky aquamarine blue.

And to the southeast, magnificent and huge and white, Mount Tahoma towered above everything.

The trail Whit followed left the ridge and forged upward into the forest. Riding easily, leaning forward in the saddle, she wrestled the handlebars over ruts and gullies. All around her, dark, glistening evergreen boughs waved, the needles singing whispery songs in the steady, sweeping wind. The cool air was sharp with pine scent, Whit's favorite smell.

The trail banked downward as Whit crested the hill. Shifting gears, she crossed the vast meadow to the airfield, already noting that there was no sign of the silver transport ship that carried settlers in and out of Isis each morning and evening.

Mother! I've missed the shuttle!

Exasperated, Whit glanced around. Beyond an open hangar door, a sleek, metal wing caught her eye. As Leader of Artemis, Lilith was furnished with her own plane. Called a Swallow, the machine was a small four-seater, tilt-rotor that could fly both vertically and horizontally. Since they had no Healer in Isis at present, Lilith had lent them the aircraft for use in the event of an emergency.

An emergency, Whit reflected, then gunned her cycle toward the hangar. *This was definitely an emergency.*

☾ ☾ ☾

In Artemis, the welcoming procession continued through the town, its hundreds of voices rising, resounding against the houses. All around Cimbri, framed in open windows, leaning on deck railings above, women waved greetings and joined in the singing. Weaving through the market place, up and down the main streets, the procession at last marched down the broad avenue toward the blue waters of Puget Sound. There, on a spacious plateau of grass above the beach, the Artemis Cedar House sat in all its rugged grandeur.

All the while, the crowd sang harmonies about sisterhood and the sun rose higher and warmer in the sky. As Cimbri joined the hundreds gathering before the large, cedar-log building, a warrior on either side of the entrance pulled the huge, oaken doors apart. Lilith led the way inside. Loy, Arinna, Danu and Nakotah followed after her. The rest of the crowd shifted impatiently before the building, waiting for Lilith to re-appear with Nakotah on the balcony above the Cedar House door.

Lilith raised her arm, announcing in her clear, musical voice, "By order of the Seven Leaders Council, the ruling body of Freeland, I summon the Council of Artemis."

There was a clamor of noise as everyone began to talk at once. Mothers, who had been carrying babies papoose-style upon their backs, gently removed their packs and handed their children over to self-important adolescents in the child-care squad. Toddlers were taken by the hand or swung up to ride upon strong, youthful shoulders, while the older children pushed through the crowd, seeking their favorite care-giving teenager.

Meanwhile, Council members, the fifty elected legislators who represented the roughly fifteen hundred women of Artemis, advanced through the opened Cedar House doors. Instinctively, Cimbri knew this would be an unusual session. Rarely did any colony Council meet on the order of the Seven Leaders.

Originally, the U.S. Constitution, which they still followed in Freeland, used an elected president to operate the executive branch. Artemis had modified that concept so that now, seven leaders, the heads of the city-colonies, shared the power that had formerly resided in one person. Since the second civil war—the Great Schism—had torn America into Freeland and Elysium, most free citizens had come to distrust the good intentions of a single, powerful ruler.

The Seven Leaders met daily by comline, the satellite-enabled visual telecommunicator that linked all of Freeland as the telephone had once linked all of Old America. Cimbri knew the Seven Leaders met to vote on decisions of national import, and rarely concerned themselves with individual colony politics. But for the Seven Leaders to be calling this session of the Artemis Council, meant something of herstoric significance was underway.

Lilith was shouting above the crowd noise. "May it be known to all that the nation is summoned. This Council Meeting will be telecast on the comline and all the citizens of Freeland are being urged to access and participate."

Cimbri moved toward the door, slithering through the women pressed closely together all around her. She was, as ever, ready to represent her district, but this time, she was not dreading the windy, off-the-topic debates that often slowed the function of democracy. This time, she was feeling her excitement crest in a wave of gooseflesh. *What on Gaea's sweet earth is going on?* she wondered.

❨ ❨ ❨

From her vantage point on the balcony, Lilith stood beside Nakotah, searching the crowd for a tall, dark-haired woman in a burgundy warrior's jacket.

Turning to Nakotah, Lilith fretted, "I can't imagine why Whit's late."

"I can," Nakotah returned with a sly grin.

Lilith looked at Nakotah blankly, then suddenly registered the innuendo.

Nakotah cocked a thick, black eyebrow, regarding Lilith with a slightly wicked smile.

Oddly discomfited, Lilith glanced away, remembering that she and Styx had also started the morning rather joyfully. *But it didn't make me late for my duties.*

Still, to be fair, Lilith reminded herself that Whit was technically just a reservist, and for the moment, her duties were her own to choose.

She recalled how upon leaving active duty status the previous November, Whit and Kali had successfully petitioned the Seven Leaders Council for permission to use the Isis Cedar House as a temporary residence. The two lovers had been living there all winter, assisting a crew of Artemis construction workers they had employed to build their new home on Whit's family property.

For a moment, Lilith contemplated the significance of what was occurring in the spectacularly beautiful mountain valley. Since the March thaw, women had begun venturing up into the Cascades, determined to be part of the herstoric re-settlement of Isis. Within the last month, a small tent city had sprung up in the meadow by the Isis Cedar House. Now, to house the several hundred women who had followed Whit and Kali into the ruins, Lupa Tagliaro's construction crew was engaged in building a hostel. The current settlers had pooled their resources to sow the seeds of a new society. Complete with a rudimentary meal hall and the latest in eco-system plumbing, a three-winged, two-story, pine barracks was being erected under Whit's competent supervision.

Lilith shook her head, laughing ruefully. As much as Whit claimed to dislike politics, she always seemed to end up in charge of things.

An odd, thudding sound broke through Lilith's thoughts. The crowd of women gathered before the Artemis Cedar House all raised their arms, pointing excitedly. Turning, following the enthusiastic gestures, Lilith discovered the reason for the pandemonium breaking out below.

Lilith's own Swallow aircraft floated over the back of the Cedar House, the two tilt-rotor engines at the end of each wing pointed up in the helicopter mode. Thoroughly soundless due to the decibel-squelch device within the engine cavities, the only noise was the thud of the short, curved blades chopping through the air as the plane hovered.

Without even scrutinizing the ample, plexiglass front of the aircraft, Lilith knew who was piloting the plane.

After giving a delighted whoop, Nakotah glanced at Lilith and tried valiantly to keep a straight face.

The Swallow lifted up, passing over the Cedar House, settling slowly over the crowd. Women steadily backed up, clearing a space on the grass. They were laughing, applauding, as the tiny craft dropped lower, at last settling gently before the building. Slowly, the tilt-rotor blades began to decelerate, whirling to a standstill. The cockpit door flew open.

As Whit jumped out, the crowd noise rumbled into a deafening cheer. With a sheepish grin, she waved back, then turned and jogged toward the Cedar House door. A multitude of hands reached out to her as she passed, ruffling her glossy, shoulder-length dark hair, thumping the back of her burgundy warrior's jacket. Children, teenagers, and matrons alike, were all obviously delighted.

Rubbing her forehead, Lilith murmured to herself, "And she says she hates politics."

☾2

Whit strode into the Artemis Council Room, glancing around appreciatively. Cathedral-like, cedar beams supported the high, vaulted ceiling. Mahogany paneling and polished slabs of pink quartz made up the surrounding walls. Square, creamy white tiles covered the floor. Colorful banners hung on the walls and the Delphi emblem—a purple, six-pointed star with a dolphin leaping through the center—hung behind the Leader's chair. The circular, richly polished pine table was nearly invisible behind the Council members who stood talking earnestly, gesturing emphatically.

With a husky laugh, Whit tucked her thumbs in her black leather gun belt and realized how much she had missed this.

Before her were all manner of women, most of them dressed in what looked like their working clothes. Business executives in trimly-tailored suits were clustered together, while the grain traders were huddled further away, dressed in their more casual attire of khaki and leather. Several white-coated Healers talked somberly with denim-clad fisherwomen. Right beside them, two grayheaded clothing merchants in long, pastel robes were loudly gossiping about "the elegant Cimbri Braun."

Suddenly, spying Whit hesitating near the entrance, Marpe and Samsi rushed over to greet her. "What's this all about, Tomyris?" Marpe exclaimed. Samsi chimed in, "Surely, *you* know!"

Whit spent the next few minutes opening and closing her mouth, a feeble facial reaction to a fusillade of questions. Though Whit made not one verbal reply, it didn't appear to matter; both Marpe and Samsi seemed delighted just to have her trapped between them.

Then, all at once, most of the Council members were shifting back toward the table, hurrying to sit down. With excited good-byes,

Marpe and Samsi bustled away. Across the hall, Whit saw her friend Nakotah, head and shoulders above the crowd, escort Lilith to her position before the Delphi emblem.

Pausing before the ornate chair, Lilith announced, "Council is called to order."

The room fell silent and Whit was left standing alone, wondering where she was supposed to be. She had just noticed the small group of women standing near the Delphi emblem, when Nakotah came around to Whit's side of the circle and subtly motioned for her to join them. Nakotah gave a nod at the automatic camera mounted high on the wall near Whit, and with a groan, Whit belatedly realized that this Council Meeting was being telecast on the comline.

Lilith's resonant voice filled the hall. "Tomorrow, May 1, 2094, is Beltane, our national holiday. On this day of beginnings, we have much that will be undertaken."

Striding quietly over to the women waiting beneath the purple emblem, Whit spotted Cimbri smiling at her from their ranks. She grinned back, then nodded politely to the other women. There were others in the back she couldn't quite see, but Lilith was talking and Whit was intent on blending into the group. Taking a place next to a redheaded teenager, Whit returned her attention to Lilith.

"...one of the reasons for this meeting, is that I am formally announcing my retirement...."

A loud chorus of protestation rang out, and Lilith put her hand up. The scattering of voices fell away.

"Come now," Lilith laughingly reproved. "You've all expected it for months. I have enjoyed serving as your Leader these past fifteen years, but I wish to join my partner Styx in her work as Colony Herstorian. Although we have survived both the AGH plague and a civil war in this century, a Second Dark Ages has engulfed the world around us. All knowledge is priceless. In particular, collecting, preserving and cataloging whatever printed-paper books remain is of the utmost importance. It is to this endeavor that I wish to devote my energies now."

Searching the round table Council members, Whit found Styx in her habitual seat. Rich brown skin and a braid of heavy, gray hair threaded with black clearly marked Styx's ancient-Mayan heritage. Even from this distance, those large, dark eyes seemed to glow with a guileless intuition. Her well-worn khaki shirt and trousers looked dusty, and a streak of dirt accented the edge of her jaw. Whit knew, then, that Styx had been busily at work in her warehouse of antiquities while the welcoming procession had paraded through the streets of Artemis. Like Whit, Styx had little time for ceremony.

Lilith continued, "Last week, I asked the citizens of Artemis to nominate three candidates for Leader. Here are the women you have nominated for the position." Turning gracefully toward the group beneath the Delphi emblem, Lilith stated, "As your name is called, please come forward."

The women near Whit stirred eagerly.

How does this concern me? Whit wondered. *I don't even live here anymore.*

"Nominated for Leader of Artemis are," Lilith paused for dramatic effect, then stated, "Lieutenant Griffin Bowdash, Captain Nakotah Berry, and Healer Cimbri Braun."

The three nominees stepped up beside Lilith and were showered with excited applause. Whit watched Cimbri reach out, grabbing Nakotah's hand. After a few moments, Lilith waved for silence and the room gradually quieted again.

"We will hold the elections in early August, just before the Lammas festival." Lilith thanked the three women and they moved to the side of the Leader's chair.

After seeming to still herself for a moment, Lilith began again. "And now for the news that has caused this Council Meeting to be telecast via comline, throughout Freeland."

Someone touched Whit's shoulder and she glanced instinctively behind her.

A pair of raven-black, almond-shaped eyes smiled into her own. Whit blinked, puzzled, and then the recognition slammed home.

Loy! Whit's jaw dropped, her heart lurched into an erratic rhythm. Fifteen years disappeared in the space of a breath. Torn between great conflicting waves of nostalgia and misgiving, Whit stood there, staring, unable to utter a word.

"...and since January, when Tomyris Whitaker and Kali Tyler returned as private citizens to Isis," Lilith was saying, "events there have been accelerating with the speed of an avalanche."

Dark eyes skewered Whit, reading her helplessness. The side of Loy's mouth curled up in a familiar, distinctive smile. There was more triumph than humor in the chilling grin. "Better pay attention to this part," Loy whispered.

Whit turned around, completely confounded. *Loy is Deputy Leader of Boudicca! What's she doing here?*

Lilith's voice intruded, "...the Seven Leaders Council has decreed a transitional stewardship for Isis..."

Whit's head snapped up. *A stewardship?*

"...to ensure an organized and secure re-creation of the city-colony." The rich fabric of Lilith's long, royal blue jacket rippled in the light as she turned. Her startlingly blue eyes seemed to hold the face of each woman in the room in her gaze.

Mother, she's good at this! Whit realized.

"There is much to be done," Lilith stated quietly. "The ruins left from the Elysian raid, ten years ago, must be cleared aside. Utilities must be installed, houses built, businesses established. Due to the often precarious conditions present when founding a city-colony, we can accept no settler under the age of seventeen. Reconstruction will be arduous and must be accomplished before the autumn snows arrive in the Cascades. "

Turning again, speaking directly to the camera mounted on the wall, Lilith addressed those who watched on the comline. "Once a stable, healthy economy and tax base are in place, a free election will ensue. A Leader and Deputy Leader will be voted into standard five-year terms of office, and children will be welcomed."

Lilith stopped and looked around at the women seated before her. Beaming, she stretched out her arms. "In other words, Isis has been granted a national loan and is officially re-opening for settlement."

There was a brief second of silence, and then the room seemed to vibrate with the exalted cheers of triumph that poured from every throat. Women jumped to their feet. Some punched the air in victory, others grabbed for their neighbors, exchanging fierce, exuberant hugs. For the next few minutes, total bedlam reigned.

Isis lives again, Whit thought, her throat tight. She was seized first by Nakotah and danced in a merry circle, then ended up in Cimbri's teary embrace. Once released, Whit dashed away a few tears herself, feeling oddly dazed. She had expected it for some time, now, but actually hearing those words—"re-opening for settlement"—well, it was overwhelming. *I wish Kali were here.*

Lilith raised her hand, waiting for the Council to notice her and come to order. Slowly, the noise level dropped and women returned to their seats.

Interlacing her slender fingers, Lilith continued, "As you may recall, I mentioned that the Seven Leaders Council has established a transitional stewardship to oversee Isis."

The Council stilled, their faces expectant.

"That stewardship consists of three women." Turning once more to the group below the Delphi emblem, Lilith remarked, "Please come forward as your name is called."

Three women? Inwardly, Whit groaned. *Oh, no. Not government by committee.*

"Arinna Sojourner," Lilith called.

A stunningly attractive woman glided by Whit, her wavy, long hair and pale-green dress drifting behind her as she moved to Lilith's side.

"In her home colony of Tubman," Lilith resumed, "Arinna is a gifted computer-scientist. She has created numerous system designs, enabling efficient communication and record-keeping for the population of Tubman. We have thus chosen her to provide Isis with a similar technology. Arinna Sojourner has been named Systems Director."

The Council members applauded enthusiastically, and Lilith waited for the noise to subside before going on.

"Loy Yin Chen," Lilith announced, "has taken a sabbatical from her duties as Deputy Leader of Boudicca."

With a suave, self-assured smile, Loy moved past Whit and joined Arinna and Lilith before the attentive assembly.

"An expert financier," Lilith stated, "Loy will be in charge of developing a sound and viable economic policy for Isis. Loy Yin Chen has been named Fiscal Director."

Spirited applause pervaded the chamber.

Glancing about, Whit noticed that the remainder of the women who had been standing with her were quickly moving away.

Whit was left beneath the Delphi emblem, curiously eyeing the girl beside her. Red-gold hair curled over the collar of her white, Buccaneer-style shirt, and the crisply-pressed brown trousers accentuated her slim hips and long legs. Studiously avoiding Whit's gaze, the girl kept her eyes fastened on her boots.

Whit frowned in puzzlement. *Who, on Gaea's sweet earth, is this?*

"The third member of the stewardship is another young woman from Boudicca," Lilith asserted. "Her architectural designs were submitted, along with the work of numerous others, to the Seven Leaders Council. Following careful, impartial review, Danu Sullivan has been named Architectural Director."

The redheaded teenager walked toward Lilith, head down, her shoulders hunched.

That kid is an architect?! Whit thought, amazed.

Again, Lilith waited for the polite applause to conclude.

Projecting her voice, Lilith now declared, "Due to the need for solid organization, swift progress, and a specific chain of command, Isis will begin as nearly every Freeland colony began: under martial law."

A murmuring filled the hall as women turned to one another, commenting among themselves on this bit of news.

Whit glanced down at the smart uniform she wore and felt the hair rise on the back of her neck. *Martial law—as in a military presence.* When she looked up again, it seemed all the eyes in the hall were on her.

"Major Tomyris Whitaker is hereby ordered recalled from reserve duty to active duty status," Lilith intoned, her voice ringing across the hall, "and given the assignment of Military Governor of Isis."

For a moment, Whit couldn't breathe.

"Major Whitaker is formally in charge of the Fiscal, Systems, and Architectural Directors..."

By the expressions on their faces, it was suddenly very apparent to Whit that both Arinna and Loy were as surprised as she was, and not entirely pleased.

"...in charge of the four hundred warriors being dispatched to Isis for construction duty..."

Four hundred!

"...who will report directly to Major Whitaker and carry out her orders as they would my own. Major Whitaker will name a second in command and a staff of chiefs to assist her in her duties. Council of Artemis and people of Freeland, I present to you, Major Tomyris Whitaker."

Aghast, Whit stood there, listening to the shouts of approval. Women were leaping to their feet, again, their enthusiasm obvious.

For several minutes they cheered her. Incredulous, Whit looked around at the gleeful faces, speculating that they were probably cheering the idea of a new Isis as much as they were cheering her. Yet, all the same, as the applause rolled over her, buffeting her ears, Whit solemnly resolved that she would do everything in her power to justify their faith in her.

☾ ☾ ☾

A short time later, the ceremony and comline telecast concluded, and Lilith guided the new group of Isis dignitaries to a small, mahogany-paneled conference room nearby. Primarily furnished with a rectangular, madrone table and five chairs, the room was purposefully Spartan.

After announcing that in the capacity of advisor she would be attending this first planning session, Lilith took a chair at the far end of the table. Loy and Arinna sat opposite each other. As the others settled into seats, Loy's and Arinna's aides hovered in the background, two lines of five young women along opposing walls. Whit dropped into a chair beside Loy and across from Danu.

"Whit," Arinna began, already poised with a pen and paper pad before her, "we'll need a full report on the current state of things in Isis." In a friendly, persuasive voice, Arinna cajoled, "I want detailed information. You know, head count, available housing, status of utilities, fresh water, sanitation, airfield readiness...."

Loy interrupted, "Actually, what we *really* need to know is the amount of the national loan. I've got to plan a budget, appraise building supplies, purchase provisions for the civilians. After that comline telecast, settlers are going to be pouring in."

With a mischievous grin, Whit turned to Danu Sullivan. "And what do *you* want?"

Sky blue eyes fell away from Whit's and the redhead blushed deeply. A freckled hand extended a data chip box to Whit. Danu murmured, "The approved city plan, complete with detailed blueprints of various government buildings and proposed residential housing."

Whit nodded, registering the girl's reticence. Deftly, Whit slipped the chip box into the waist pouch on her belt.

Arinna's lovely face creased with mild frustration. "Perhaps we *all* should evaluate the city plans," she proposed.

"They've already *been* evaluated and approved, as is," Whit assured her, then added graciously, "Once I get a look at what we're dealing with, I'll be glad to share them. Now, let me update you on the information you requested."

Pulling out a pad of paper, Loy leaned across the table, addressing Lilith. "What about the national loan? How much is it?"

In response, Lilith only raised her eyebrows.

Loy's dark-eyed gaze slid back to Whit, reluctantly acknowledging that all monetary figures were going to have to come from the Military Governor.

Even Danu forgot her timidity, and along with everyone else, watched the long, measuring look Loy and Whit exchanged. It was a carefully expressionless look, while at the same time, it was a look rich with unresolved passions and unforgiven offenses.

Knowing she had to settle this now or be doomed to endure Loy's shrewdly subtle defiance for months to come, Whit's husky voice dropped lower and firmer. "We'll get to the loan in a few minutes, Loy."

Stiffly, mildly indignant, Loy stood and jerked her knee-length black jacket off her shoulders, revealing the clothing underneath. Svelte and athletic, Loy was encased in a skin-tight, orange bodysuit.

Uh-oh, Lilith thought, as Whit's gray eyes widened.

Meanwhile, Arinna and Danu were staring, too.

Catching their gazes, Loy turned and directed a searing look at each of the three women, one right after the other.

Whit broke the gaze, reddening slightly.

Danu went scarlet and became fascinated with the table.

Annoyed, Arinna's long lashes lowered demurely. "I'm listening, Tomyris."

Tossing the outer garment to an aide behind her, Loy sat down.

Whit loosened her western string tie and pulled uncomfortably at the collar of her starched, white uniform shirt before she began reeling off data. "Located ninety miles southeast of Artemis, twenty miles from

Mount Tahoma, Isis currently consists of two hundred and thirty-seven women, most of whom are camping in the meadow by the Isis Cedar House. We have a meal hall and a nearly completed hostel, which will facilitate the quartering of possibly three hundred women."

"We can squeeze in more," Loy pronounced. "Bunk beds, eating in shifts, and so on."

"These are women you're speaking of, not worker bees," Danu stated softly.

Looking nonplussed, Loy stared at the girl. After a moment, Loy conceded, "Alright, most women I know would rather endure a tent than face life in a sardine can. We'll enlarge this...hostel, first. Maybe create some sort of command center there."

Without actually looking at Whit, Danu observed, "There's a design for that on the chip I gave you."

"Thanks," Whit returned, studying Danu.

"What about utilities?" Arinna pressed Whit.

Frowning, Whit related, "First, I'll give you some idea where we stand. I've been alternately driving a motorcycle or hiking all over the mountain valley, inspecting and cataloging what remains. There's extensive damage. After the devastating Elysian attack on Isis in 2083, the colony was abandoned for ten years. What little survived the bombs and fire has deteriorated beneath heavy annual snowfalls."

The determined faces around the table remained undaunted.

Seeming satisfied by their response, Whit concluded, "Luckily, the hydroelectric plant by the Nisqually River is nearly intact. The generators will only need a mild overhaul. I have a team of Engineers working on it." Whit leaned back in her chair and flicked her gaze from Arinna, to Loy, and then to Danu. "In the deep forest, the sewage-fertilization processors need a system-clean and the re-introduction of bacterial enzymes. Both utilities were far enough from the city center to have escaped notice during the Elysian raid. That was a piece of good luck."

"And..." Loy prompted.

Quietly, Whit admitted, "Not much else survived the attack. For example, the miles of underground electrical wiring and sewage tubing throughout the colony are going to have to be replaced."

Regarding Whit with a steady gaze, Arinna asked, "How are you managing fresh water?"

"We're pumping spring water right now," Whit replied, raking a hand through her hair, "but population growth will mandate something more advanced."

"And the roads?" Loy demanded, her dark eyes snapping with alarm as she realized how primitive things really were.

With a sigh, Whit stated, "Weed-grown, weather-eroded. I'm using a big, re-tooled cycle to get around, but even a motorcycle has trouble with the craters all over the city center. The four-wheel drive construction trucks seem to blow a lot of tires."

There was a heavy silence. For a moment, everyone seemed to be thinking of the bombing, envisioning the Elysian heli-jets swooping low over the fair city Isis had once been.

"The airfield," Whit finished, "was repaired years ago, when Isis was designated a war memorial."

Stroking her chin thoughtfully, Loy mused, "We're starting from scratch, aren't we?"

"But with a substantial loan," Whit replied, and then stated the exact amount Lilith had whispered in her ear earlier, during a congratulatory hug in the Council Room.

Imperiously, Loy held up her hand. An aide stepped forward, placed a small computer in Loy's palm, and then retreated. Loy bent over the unit, intent on coordinating estimated costs.

Arinna twisted a strand of curly hair around her finger and peered at Whit. "How will the colony ever pay back such an amount?"

"As I'm sure you know," Whit returned, "Isis once led all of Freeland in computer-sciences. Thanks to Maat Tyler, the first Leader of Isis, an incredibly profitable industry developed. I think we could repeat their success."

"Yes, yes, I've read about that," Arinna stated dismissively. "Salvage ships flying all over Freeland, gathering up machines left over from the twentieth century. Sounds rather like a glorified rubbish-collection."

Unable to keep still after such a remark, Lilith interjected. "Not rubbish—jets, trucks, cranes, bulldozers, looms, surgers, even saw-mills. They reconditioned all kinds of machines, computerized their basic functions, then created manufacturing programs, so that the implanted computers could run the machines." Settling her keen blue gaze on Arinna, in particular, Lilith went on, "Isis was the first colony where valuable personnel were freed from the more mundane tasks of daily life. Their efforts to secure food, warmth, and clothing were assisted by super-intelligent systems adapted for an inconceivably diverse array of needs."

"So they were able to produce far more than they could consume," Loy commented, her voice grave with the respect she felt for profit.

Lilith chuckled as she thought of her former lover, "And Maat's computerized hydroponic techniques are still in use, right here in Artemis."

Brushing her dark, silky hair back from her face with her hand, Arinna's light green eyes moved to Whit. "I've heard that there were also computer programs which targeted medical issues, but there doesn't seem to be any documentation of them. The analysis and treatment of viruses, the production of medications?"

Whit became distinctly agitated under that penetrating look. "I'd rather not get into that," she muttered, shifting uneasily in her chair.

"Why?" Loy asked. "If it turns a profit...."

"Much of that knowledge died with Maat," Lilith interjected. "She destroyed her records, I think because she distrusted our supposedly advanced nature."

"I don't understand," Arinna murmured, fixing her gaze on Lilith.

Rubbing her forehead, Lilith explained, "During the first incarnation of Isis, most of the lethal bacterial diseases in Freeland—smallpox, polio, measles, typhus—were being controlled with childhood vaccinations. And after Maat mass-produced a vaccination that defeated the AGH virus, curtailing other viruses became a series of relatively uncomplicated procedures.

"After a while, only the grim possibility of bio-warfare seemed to justify the continued computerized research that was going on. Rumor had it that Maat was nervous about just where all this experimenting was taking us."

"What do you mean?" Loy asked Lilith. "You make it sound so sinister. How can health care be sinister?"

"Not health care," Whit responded. "R and D—research and development. Maat was running R and D programs, scores of them." Nervously, Whit leaned forward, checking their faces as she spoke.

"DNA manipulation, cloning. The deliberate development of new and more virulent strains of viruses. The distillation and refinement of obscure, dangerous drugs. Maat finally shut the whole thing down the year before Isis was attacked."

"Hmm," Arinna remarked, surveying Whit.

"Oh, how absurd," Loy observed under her breath, then asserted, "That's progress. Why not take advantage of a successful market?"

Cutting a look at Loy, Arinna seemed intrigued with that thought.

Noting Arinna's attention on her, Loy briefly locked eyes with the new Systems Director, then abruptly turned on Whit. "So, what's the plan, Whitaker? Where do we go from here?"

Ignoring the flat disrespect in Loy's voice, Whit began, "Tomorrow is Beltane, but in Isis, we're foregoing the festivities and treating it like a normal work day."

Mockingly, Loy commented, "Gaea, you're really pushing those women—no wonder you've been appointed Military Governor."

Whit enunciated each word. "We had a vote. This is what they *chose* to do."

"Oh," Loy returned, her voice still mildly castigating.

As if intent on changing the mood, Arinna proposed, "Why don't we visit Isis tomorrow? Just an informal tour, no fuss. I want to look the place over."

Whit replied, "As you wish. The day after tomorrow, we'll begin operating as a full-fledged city-colony. I plan to call a meeting of the settlers in the Isis Cedar House, where we'll distribute parcels of land and issue building permits."

"That's the day I'll move in, then," Arinna laughed.

"Me, too," Loy agreed. " I can't decide which is worse, living in a tent or living in a barracks."

With a sinking feeling, Whit watched Loy look from Arinna to Danu, recognizing the almost feral expression. *Still the sexual tiger, still wanting only the ones that are hard to catch.*

"Are we done, Whitaker?" Loy asked, her tone clearly indicating that she thought they were.

Whit asked the others, "Anything more?"

No one spoke.

Simultaneously, they all stood up.

Danu headed directly for the door.

Arinna and Loy strolled out of the room, discussing lunch at a renowned Artemis restaurant, which was located down by the Sound. They moved off, down the hallway, each surrounded by her personal entourage. It was very obvious that neither of them would invite Whit to join them.

Wearily pushing a hand through her hair, Whit turned toward Lilith, frowning.

Dryly, Lilith stated, "Welcome to the game."

Whit grumbled, "What?"

Chuckling, Lilith clarified, "The game of power."

☾3

*T*he next day, May 1st, 2094, all of Artemis resounded
with Beltane festivities. By nine in the morning, throngs
of women again gathered before the Cedar House, but this time they
were clad in rain slickers and warm sweaters. A cold, wet fog hung over
the city-colony, yet the weather did nothing to dampen their spirits.

From the balcony, Lilith gave a short speech commemorating
the Mothers of Freeland. As Lilith spoke, reminding them all of their
herstory and sisterhood, a seventeen-year-old redhead stood alone
among strangers. Danu was shivering, chilled despite her cotton
turtleneck and green, wool shirt. She knew Loy and Arinna were
somewhere in this assembly. Though they had started out with Danu in
the walk from the Leader's House, where they were all Lilith's guests,
Danu had lost sight of them once they had entered the crowd. She
suspected that she had been shed like a tag-along little sister.

When the speech ended, Styx appeared by Danu's side. Hands
in her trouser pockets, her big-boned frame seemingly made larger by
a bright red sweater, Styx asked, "Hungry?" At Danu's eager nod, Styx
stated, "Me too. I know just the place."

By the time Lilith joined them, the crowd on the broad, grassy
expanse had dispersed into numerous sidestreets. It seemed that everyone else was intent on getting breakfast, too.

Danu found herself escorted up the hill, walking between Styx
and Lilith. A strong, slender woman, Lilith appeared reedlike next to
Styx's robust size. Danu noticed that the two older women were dressed
very dissimilarly. Next to Styx's casual attire, Lilith looked almost
royal in her long, robe-like navy blue coat; intricate, multi-colored
embroidery graced the sleeves and lapels. There was a knife-like press
to her pleated pants and her shirt collar was closed with a large, golden
labrys pin.

They walked past a stylish restaurant and Danu glanced through the window. In that quick look, Danu saw Loy and Arinna sitting at a table, surrounded by several beautiful young women. A feast of delectable foods covered the table, and Loy was bending near Arinna, laughing. Pulling her gaze away, feeling very young and unwanted, Danu kept pace with Lilith and Styx, giving brief answers to their stream of polite questions.

"How is it you're an architect at seventeen years of age?" Lilith asked.

"Apprentice architect," Danu corrected. "Accelerated university work. Next year I'll get my degree."

"Even so," Lilith persisted, "you're years ahead, and I know you're unusually gifted. The city plans you submitted for Isis are extraordinarily complex and highly functional."

Realizing that she was being prodded for the truth, Danu gave it. "I'm a Think Tank Baby," she said shortly, and then stiffened, waiting for them to withdraw from her, to make some excuse and cancel the invitation to breakfast. She was not just the product of a parthenogenic procedure, as most of the women in Freeland were; she was an "innovation," a human altered to have "talents."

"So am I," Styx replied simply.

Startled, Danu stared up at her. *But she can't be! She must be in her fifties, at least, and they weren't even doing DNA manipulation in those days.*

Seeming to read her confusion, Styx explained, "I was in the first test group. There was a problem with cystic fibrosis in my family, and my birth mother and her partner wanted to weigh the odds in my favor—protect me from the bad gene."

Styx squared her shoulders, her voice dropping. "So, the Healer did the standard parthenogenic procedure to create me, and then used an early genetic adaptation program to make a biochemical map. The Healer pinpointed the location of the defective gene, targeted it for replacement. Using a gene from my birth mother's partner, my unhealthy inheritance was engineered right out of me before my first double helix ever unzipped."

"It must have worked," Danu observed, her eyes taking in Styx's hearty build.

"Yeah, it worked," Styx grumbled. "They got rid of the cystic fibrosis. But then the Healer went a step further: during mitosis, she basted my little embryonic self with a nourishing gravy of enzymes to enhance my latent abilities."

Danu thought bitterly, *The Think Tank! That's exactly how I feel about it—like someone cooked me up!* Styx's soft, compelling dark eyes held her, as Danu asked, "So they made you a genius?"

Lilith laughed. "Styx is many things—but she's no genius!"

"Then, what..." They had stopped before a small, corner shop. Delicious smells were wafting through the air, diverting Danu's attention. A sign, which read, "Pele's Paradise," hung above the large window.

"Here we are." Styx strode through the narrow doorway.

As Lilith and Danu followed, a stocky woman came hurrying out from behind the wooden counter. Rubbing her floury hands on her big, white apron, she informed them, "Cinnamon rolls, just out of the oven! Blueberry pancakes and omelets with fresh salmon! Grilled mountain trout! And of course, hot brew!"

Danu gaped at her, mouth watering.

"Hi Pele," Lilith laughed.

"I'll have the usual," Styx announced, then gave Danu a gentle push, steering her into a booth by the window. Lilith slid in on the opposite side, while Styx plunked down beside Danu. Flipping a thumb in Danu's direction, Styx told the plump chef, "She'll have the usual, too."

Smiling at Styx, Lilith ordered a cheese omelet.

The shopkeeper set utensils and napkins before them, and then hustled back behind the counter, through a door to the rear.

Danu noticed that the room was packed with women, sitting around tables or lounging in the wooden booths that lined the walls. It seemed every eye in the place was on Lilith, Styx and her. Overwhelmed, Danu's shoulders hunched, her gaze dropped.

Observing Danu's shyness, Styx quipped, "They're just checking to see if you're trying to take Lilith away from me."

Stunned, Danu shot a look at Lilith and found her trying to repress a laugh. *Are they making fun of me?* she worried.

"It's called teasing," Styx murmured, "and you're supposed to laugh. Okay?"

Eager to please, Danu nodded. Meanwhile, restless curiosity made her braver and her eyes roamed around Pele's Paradise, taking in everything. Scarred, hardwood floorboards ran the length of the room. Decorative woven-grass baskets and original oil paintings seemed to cover every space that was not taken by a long, narrow window. The room was packed with women, and all of them seemed to be talking at once.

The delectable aromas of things baking, frying, and grilling swirled from the back of the shop, overpowering her senses. Gathering all her courage, Danu finally looked at Styx and asked, "What's 'the usual?'" She had to know. She was starving.

With an innocent look, Styx replied, "A cup of hot brew."

Danu swallowed, horribly disappointed, then realized that Lilith was sending Styx a mock-threatening glare.

Styx sighed, then disclosed, "It's a huge plate with portions of everything Pele serves here."

Relieved and ecstatic, Danu grinned.

Appraising her, Styx commented, "How is it your mother is letting you wander around like this?"

With a shrug, Danu said, "Loy is with me."

"That's what I mean," Styx muttered, and then jumped. If she hadn't known better, Danu could have sworn that Lilith had kicked her under the table.

Just then, Pele returned with an armload of plates, each of them heaped with steaming food, and Danu was aware of little else for the next half hour. As she savored every mouthful, she kept a careful vigil at the window, and watched Artemis slowly emerging from the fog.

I can't wait to get to Isis, she thought.

Soon, she would be overseeing the construction of her designs, working at the side of the Military Governor of Isis. This entire experience was going to be the culmination of so many dreams. And at this point, Danu really could not say where her love of her vocation left off and her instantaneous infatuation with Tomyris Whitaker began.

☾ ☾ ☾

A short time later, Danu, Lilith and Styx walked across the tarmac of the Artemis airfield. The sun broke through the fog as Nakotah and Cimbri appeared, and then as Loy and Arinna joined them, they all boarded the jetcraft for the trip to Isis.

While Lilith piloted the plane and the other women made polite conversation, Danu sat beside Styx looking out the window. Thoughtfully, she watched the sweep of land below them: earth-brown, newly-planted grain fields, rich with the silt of the Snoqualmie River, gave way to dark green fir forest, then swelled into timbered foothills and finally mountains. Here and there ribbons of blue-green glacial streams cut through the valleys, becoming racing whitewater torrents where the bedrock kept their passage narrow. Slowly, the huge presence of Mount Tahoma loomed closer, the dramatic white cone overshadowing the crests of the great Cascade Range. And then Danu saw a charred, grey smear on the earth. *Isis*, she thought, feeling a surge of reverence. From the air, only the landing strip and the Cedar House seemed to be still in one piece, visibly undamaged. The craft dipped lower and Danu turned from the window, sighing heavily. She looked up and found Styx watching her.

"I guess I'm kind of wondering if I'm up to such a task—rebuilding a whole city," Danu offered.

Styx gave her a reassuring smile. "Lilith says you're a very good architect."

"But I'm still..." Danu was going to say *so young* but thought better of it. "...a student." She was not going to buy into that nonsense about how young she was. Loy and Arinna had just spent much of last night remarking on her age to anyone in Artemis who would listen. She was seventeen—well beyond her first blood and so undeniably a woman. And it was *her* package of plans, of the many submitted, that the Seven Leaders had selected for the city of Isis.

The jetcraft settled into a delicate landing, and the hum of engines moaned lower as Lilith shut them down.

Styx commented, "Another student, Kali Tyler, will be working with you...."

Kali—the P.O.W., the lone survivor of the Fall of Isis, Whit's partner. Danu was torn between her innate sharp curiosity and the assumption that she would definitely not like this half-foreigner who had entrenched herself in Tomyris Whitaker's life.

Black eyes fastened on her and Styx cocked her head as if she registered that last thought. Danu flushed, suddenly remembering that Styx was reputed to be a telepath. Styx continued, "You'll also have Artemis's Chief Builder, Lupa Tagliaro, overseeing your work."

At the mention of Lupa's name, Danu reacted, grimacing before she could stop herself. Styx caught it, and leaned closer to her whispering, "Heard of old 'Harrowing Hecate,' have you?" Danu felt the embarrassed heat in her face steadily increase, and Styx burst into a hearty laugh.

"I like you, Danu," Styx pronounced. She narrowed the black eyes, as if swept with a sudden, new, sobering emotion. She regarded Danu for what seemed like a long time, then stated, "With effort, you may develop the ability to see beyond surface appearances. Remember, despite her manner, Lupa is a good friend."

Danu looked back at her, vaguely alarmed. *That was a warning.* "I will remember, Styx. Thank you," she said softly. Then she returned her attention to the window, trying to recover her enthusiasm for what was to come.

It was just past noon when the group disembarked onto the tarmac and followed the weed-grown road to the city. Without intent, they began to move along two by two; Lilith and Styx in the front, Cimbri and Nakotah next, and then Loy and Arinna hanging back, deep in whispered discussion.

Behind them all came Danu, her inquisitive eyes noticing everything. There was a new stiffness in Styx's shoulders and a weariness in Lilith's walk. Cimbri suddenly reached out and took Nakotah's hand, like a child looking for comfort. Nakotah herself was saying something—no, she was chanting a prayer for the dead, soft and low. It made Danu's hair stand on end.

In the distance, Danu could hear the grinding gears and throbbing engine noises of bulldozers at work. Beneath the scrubby tufts of grass, she could see small boulders and stones, the glacial scraps of the Ice Age, now scorched black by a firestorm that would continue to stamp this land as an old battlefield for centuries more. The stale smell of an old fire still hung in the air, a faint, acrid sharpness beneath the fresh wind.

After a half mile, they walked over a slight ridge and the view below made them all stop. Awestruck by the scene before them, Arinna and Loy became silent.

In the bright spring sunshine, the remnants of catastrophe were being stripped away. Charred, crumbling stone house shells, twisted steel beams, blackened, splintered two-by-fours—were being plowed down, shoveled up and tossed into dump trucks. Seven huge bulldozers were spaced apart, simultaneously moving in parallel lines, dislodging the clutter of junk before them. In the scraped clean areas, backhoes were digging up and wresting out shredded electrical lines, broken water and sewage tubing. Other backhoes were filling in large craters with earth.

There were a few warriors, young women in gray jumpsuits, but they were mainly operating the machines. The vast majority of laborers were middle-aged women, civilians. Behind the bulldozers and dump trucks, away from the backhoes, these women were working in small groups. Some were measuring off squares of land with computerized surveying units, then tapping small sticks into the ground and running string around the plot. Others were unrolling huge coils of wire, or unloading pvc piping from truck beds, intent on replacing the utility hardware that had just been torn out of one of the narrow, continuous trenches left by the backhoes.

The scene was punctuated with a series of shattering, crashing noises as some of the more stubborn ruins reluctantly gave way. And although the machine noise from the bulldozers was thunderous, the women who were laboring made no perceptible noise at all. They were silent, their faces smeared with dirt and their grim eyes fixed on their task.

On this Beltane day, their work was as much an ending as a beginning. There were salvageable remnants, human belongings, lying in small piles in front of this or that ruin, evoking memories. Broken pots, soot-stained tools, the blackened frame of a child's bike. Danu knew, then, that the women working below her were sifting through tragedy, immersed in horror. Happiness and laughter would come later—when the past was buried and the future was more tangible in their working hands. For now, the reminders of calamity were everywhere.

As they descended the hill, the somber group began walking along the scarred remains of a road that led around the ruins of the city.

Suddenly Danu wanted to be by herself. This was a graveyard, consecrated by the women who had died here. She needed to make an offering to the Goddess before she could plunge into the rough work of re-birth with good conscience. Abruptly, she called to the others, "Okay if I meet up with you later? I want to...make some notes on the surveying underway."

Cimbri and Nakotah nodded sadly and kept walking. Lilith wiped her eyes and leaned against Styx, who studied Danu with those dark, Mayan eyes and said quietly, "Make an offering for all of us." Then the group began moving off along the trail.

Unseen by the others, Loy and Arinna paused. Studying Danu, Arinna asked solicitously, "Are you sure you'll be alright by yourself?"

Certain she was being patronized, Danu's frustration with these two finally surfaced. "What do you think I'm going to do—get lost?"

Arinna gave a startled laugh.

Grinning, Loy observed, "So, the little pup has a bite, after all." The piercing dark eyes swept over Danu, as if Loy were seeing her for the first time. She kept that nonchalant, yet unsettling gaze on Danu as she proposed, "Arinna, maybe we should all split up. You take the north side and I'll take the south. If you find Whit, give a yell—that goes for you, too, Sullivan."

The two politicians set off in separate directions, picking their way around the rubble, following what appeared to be the old outline of streets between mounds of burned houses.

Once they were far enough away, Danu knelt in stony debris and grasped the green stalk of a plant that not only dared to grow, but seemed to thrive in the midst of this desolation. Danu could see the same type of plant poking through the scorched remnants of masonry all around her. Holding the new spring life between her fingers, she made a heartfelt prayer to the Goddess.

Gaea, may we all strive to equal the strength and love of those who began this colony. May we nourish the land and each other.

Then all at once, she was engulfed in a cloud of billowing dust. She turned to find a bulldozer advancing on her and scrambled to get out of its path. She was still clambering through the rubble, several streets over when she noticed the small wooden sign someone had hammered into the ground.

She was on Cammermeyer Street, and across the road from her, a blonde woman in a blue jacket-vest and a faded denim jumpsuit was working alone, operating a jack-hammer. Her slender frame leaned into the tool. Loose yellow hair fell over her shoulders, riffling in the breeze.

Danu watched her abruptly lay the jack-hammer aside, and then begin picking up rocks and tossing them aside. There was a sort of frantic exhaustion to her efforts that made Danu pause, and then quietly go closer. The woman's back was turned, and so she was unaware that she was being observed as she suddenly staggered and crumpled down, her breath escaping in ragged sobs.

The despair in that sound. Moved beyond conscious thought, Danu went closer, hesitated, then in a burst of compassion extended a comforting hand to the woman's shoulder. With a cry of sheer terror, the woman dodged clear of her. Before Danu could say a word, the blonde snapped off a kick that thumped into Danu's chest and launched her backwards. She heard her head crack as she landed, and then there was nothing.

When Danu opened her eyes again, there was blue sky above her and her head was pounding. She dimly heard a voice asking, "You're alright, aren't you? Please say something."

Danu tried to sit up, then groaned and immediately lay back down. Her head hurt more than she'd ever known it could hurt. The soft voice was making an apology, but Danu couldn't make much sense of what else was being said. Then she heard the assurance that Whit was coming, and with a determined effort, Danu pushed off the restraining hands and struggled into a sitting position.

The small two-way radio on the blonde woman's belt broadcasted a clear message. "I'm getting help, Kal. Keep her still." Then the blonde woman took a deep breath and seemed to collect herself. She softly entreated, "Your head is bleeding. You're making it worse—please lie down."

Wishing fervently that the world would stop floating in a slow spin around her, Danu stubbornly stayed upright. "You kicked me!" she croaked.

"I thought you were...." The woman stopped.

"Who? Who on earth do you go around kicking?" Now that the initial agonizing pain was subsiding into a stabbing ache, Danu felt a defensive burst of temper. She pushed away the hands on her arms, scrambling to get to her feet. If Governor Whitaker was coming, she certainly didn't want to present herself as a mewling baby, injured the first day she reported for work.

Halfway up, her knees gave out and the woman who had attacked her was catching her. Danu struggled against the black dots swarming before her, the roar rushing in her ears, but it was of little use. She slid into total unconsciousness.

❨ ❨ ❨

Kali lowered the girl to the ground and quickly shrugged her way out of her blue, down vest. Hands trembling, she folded the soft material and then tucked it beneath the crisp red hair.

Taking another deep breath, Kali straightened. The girl lying unconscious at her feet had come upon her so quickly that she had panicked, lost her head, and now—*Oh, Mother, please don't be badly hurt, whoever you are!*

This morning she had assured Whit that she could handle this, that she could confront the ruins on Cammermeyer Street, the ruins of the Leader's House, where she had once lived with her mother and Branwen. Kali had accepted this assignment without fuss, anxious to contribute something while Whit oversaw the town clean-up.

However, Kali had spent the morning driving the jackhammer into her past, crying incessantly as she broke up the remnants of the foundation. Among piles of broken stones and fractured wooden beams, she had been unable to avoid the bitter grief and the avalanche of memories. The sudden appearance of the girl had taken her by surprise. Kali had been sent reeling back into a past where surprises could be lethal. Her reaction had been stupid and childish and bewildering...beyond her control.

Straightening up, Kali noticed someone else making her way across the clutter of stones and twisted steel. Seeing her, Kali ceased her self-recriminations. This was another stranger, moving athletically, her eyes taking in the still form of the girl at Kali's feet, and then Kali herself.

Against her will, Kali was riveted; the woman was bewitching—with fine features and a slim, strong build encased in a green bodysuit. She had never noticed much about other women. She was Whit's partner from their first days together—enthralled by Whit's body, by Whit's grace of movement. But already, she sensed that this stranger could appeal to her.

The woman's dark eyes probed her confidently as she marched closer. Under the singular, piercing gaze, Kali felt her face grow hot. She looked down suddenly, for the oddest reason lapsing into Elysian female behavior.

A melodic voice, full of amusement said, "You *are* her, aren't you? Kali Tyler?"

Kali pulled her gaze up, annoyed with herself for becoming so confused. Of course, someone else must have described her. This was just another traveler, another visitor curious to actually meet "Maat's daughter." She thought somewhat bitterly that she had become a local oddity, "the warrior who spent ten years in Elysium and lived to tell about it."

And then, the smiling woman was full of concern as she strode over to the still form of the girl. Kali stepped back, but the woman captured her with a gentle hand on the shoulder. She pulled Kali close, held her, and whispered in her ear. "Beltane blessings. I'm Deputy Leader Loy Yin Chen, of Boudicca. Now, *how* on earth did Danu do this to herself?"

Kali swallowed hard, unable to speak for the rush of reaction she was registering from all over her body. The woman released her, commenting, "Hmmm. You're shy, aren't you?" Her cheeks on fire, Kali bent her head, completely at a loss, now. The soft, suggestive voice finished, "Shy as a little rabbit."

Kali gestured at the girl on the ground, whose eyes were open again, watching them. "She—I—"

Trying for a smile, Danu lied, "I tripped and fell."

"No, she didn't," Kali told Loy.

"Yes, I did," Danu told Kali, her voice firmer.

Kali knelt down. "Sorry," she breathed.

Loy squatted on her haunches, narrowing her eyes at the blood steadily trickling down the back of Danu's neck. The pale green collar of her cotton turtleneck was already stained. "So, have you two been formally introduced?" Loy asked.

"Danu Sullivan," the redhead mumbled.

"Kali Tyler." The words had barely left her mouth when the red-headed girl began scowling at her.

Holding two fingers before Danu's pale, freckled face, Loy asked, "How many?" Loy grinned as Danu grunted the correct answer, as if this young one entertained her. Kali noted it, and found herself listening, glimpsing the deepest part of Loy's inner thoughts.

She's attracted to this girl—she finds her body nubile, her innocence irresistible—like a clear computer screen waiting to be written upon. Shocked at herself for invading Loy's privacy, and then shocked even more by this startling ability to do so, Kali yanked her awareness back.

How is this happening? Kali frowned, frightened and yet marveling at the strange sensation buzzing through her. So far she had told no one about this incredible link with others' minds—thoughts appearing in her head, speaking to her—thoughts that were not her own. So far it had only occurred with Whit, usually as Whit sat nearby, silently brooding. Lately though, she sometimes heard Whit when they were miles away from one another. The whole thing seemed too bizarre to reveal comfortably to anyone, even Whit.

Abruptly, Danu announced, "I've got work to do. Help me up, Loy." The last part came out faintly, as Danu started pushing herself upright.

"Oh, please—stay down," Kali implored.

Loy didn't even bother trying to dissuade the stubborn young-ster. Instead, she gently touched her fingers to the back of Danu's head and with a small cry, Danu lurched away from her. She showed Danu the sticky red substance she brought away, then produced a clean bandanna from her pocket. Deftly, she unclipped the canteen from her belt, poured some water over the cloth and held it against the wound in the red-gold curls. Danu took a sharp breath and leaned forward, placing her head on her drawn up knees.

Flashing a smile at Kali, Loy continued to solicitously press the wet cloth against Danu's head. "I'm the new Fiscal Director and she's..." Loy indicated Danu with a nod, "...the architectural genius who's supposed to shower Isis with all manner of wonderful urban buildings. We'll both be spending the coming months in Isis, helping in the reconstruction project." Glancing around with consternation, Loy ended, "Arinna Sojourner—the new Systems Director—is *somewhere* around here."

With relief, Kali caught sight of Whit approaching with a group of settlers. As she neared, the gray eyes shifted to Loy. To Kali's keen eyes, Whit's distraction was obvious. After a moment, Loy slowly rose.

The group of ten or so women who had come with Whit, were all watching Loy. A few of them shook their heads, though some grinned at each other. Then, all at once, everyone seemed to be shooting Kali surreptitious glances.

Whit muttered, "Loy, this is Kali, my partner." She nervously raked a hand through her unruly, dark hair.

"We've met," Loy said simply, her manner again taking on that slow, suggestive sexuality. Kali found herself receiving a frank assessment. Loy pronounced, "Very sweet, Whit."

Then Whit and Loy were staring at each other. Kali wasn't exactly sure what was going on, but had no doubt that this woman, at some time, had been involved with Whit.

Someone jogged Whit's elbow, bringing her back to the moment. "We don't have a clinic or a Healer. What should we do with the girl?"

Whit looked down. Danu mumbled, "I'm okay, really," and then in a quick, unsteady move got to her feet. She swayed and Kali ducked under her arm, supporting her.

"So this is my architect?" Stout, gray-haired Lupa Tagliaro pushed through the crowd of women and gave Danu a withering appraisal. "What's the matter, girl? Can't keep your footing in the rubble?" she barked.

"I kicked her," Kali confessed.

Everyone stared at Kali, astounded.

"My fault. I kind of grabbed her," Danu clarified.

Mutually embarrassed and strangely united by it, a perplexed look passed between Kali and Danu. Kali tightened the arm she had wrapped around the girl's waist.

Loy cleared her throat meaningfully. "Sounds like an interesting interlude, Whit," she said, an irreverent grin twitching up one side
of her mouth.

The group broke into tittering laughs. Whit, Danu, and Kali all
stayed straight-faced, examining each other expectantly.

What is it I'm sensing? Kali wondered. *The three of us
meeting—it's something significant, something...something what?*

And then Cimbri and Nakotah were suddenly among them.
Already fishing in her med-pak pouch for a somascanometer, Cimbri
approached Danu. "We heard Kali on Lilith's radio," Nakotah explained, then asked, "What's so funny?"

"Barracks humor," Whit said lightly, and the laughter abruptly
stopped.

During the silence of the next few minutes, Cimbri made a
quick evaluation. Weakening, in spite of her resolve, Danu's head
sagged forward and she leaned a little more on Kali's shoulders. Cimbri
pronounced, "Looks like a cut and a good lump. Whit, I want to take her
to the Cedar House. I need to clean this and get some ice on it."

Nodding, Whit asked for two volunteers to help Cimbri take
Danu to the Cedar House. Two large warriors waved their arms, then
moved toward the girl Kali still held.

"Good," Loy pronounced. "That settles that. On to business."
She narrowed her eyes at Whit. "Why don't you apprise me of what's
going on here, Governor?"

Despite Danu's protests, the two warriors plucked her uncer-
emoniously from Kali. They draped her between their shoulders and set
off with Danu's feet barely touching the ground.

Kali cast a single, troubled glance at Whit, who was already
involved in a discussion with Loy. Frowning, Kali fell in step behind
Danu and her Amazonian escorts.

(((

The sky had become overcast, so it was hard to tell that it was
almost two o'clock in the afternoon. As Whit and Loy made a walking
tour of an area already cleared, they were flanked by a small crowd of
future citizens. Loy noted that the dirt and grime that covered Whit,

covered these women as well. They were all as old or older than she and Whit, and looked tired and disconsolate, but they seemed determined to participate in Whit's meeting with the Fiscal Director.

Pulling a rolled-up set of blueprints from her backpack, Whit delineated the utility overlay grids with a sweep of her finger. Then she turned and pointed out to Loy the trenches nearby where new wiring and tubing already rested in place.

Loy studied the grids, then asserted, "But this is ludicrous! All this tearing up of the old utilities is a needless expense. Why didn't you just dig new trenches, run new links beside the old ones?"

Several of the Isis settlers walking with them turned to stare at Loy, as if incredulous that she dared to challenge a decision Whit had made.

Whit strove to hide how stung she was by the bluntness of Loy's criticism, though she was sure her wince had betrayed her. Loy was starting the battle already—baiting her, looking for chinks in Whit's armor. *I feel like I'm sixteen again and doomed to endure her or drop out of flight school.* Studying Loy, Whit replied, "Because that would not be environmentally sound. Plastic doesn't break down, and our society, unlike Old America, does not leave its trash for another age to dispose of properly."

Loy made a face, as if that were a lame reason. She reached over and took the blueprints from Whit's hands, turning the pages to view other plans. She came to the blow-up prints Whit had made of Danu's designs, the sketches of what the new Isis would be. "I see we are basically following Maat's city plan. Danu leaned too heavily on it, I think. I would have thought you'd both want to try for some originality."

Trying to give herself time to count to ten, Whit carefully delayed answering. She stood brushing dust from her gray warrior uniform, paying particular attention to her leather flight jacket. "Maat's original plan was excellent. Danu has only improved upon it," Whit stated, struggling to keep her voice even. "And many of us who lived here *want* to recreate what was lost, at least to some degree."

Glancing at the other hostile faces around her, Loy obviously registered the emotional importance of Maat's design and abruptly changed her tactics. "Yes, there is something comforting about familiarity."

Taking back her roll of blueprints, which suddenly seemed to have become some queenly scepter denoting rank, Whit finished, "It is more than familiarity, Loy. Our city was destroyed. But it will be rebuilt, almost exactly as it once was. It is our act of faith in each other, our act of defiance to those who would destroy us again, if they could."

Once more, Loy checked all the faces to see how this was being received by the other women present. They were listening, some with a hand reflexively resting on the sedation pistol that each of them wore. Their eyes were haunted, their shoulders slumped with what each of them had endured today.

Whit surveyed the women, too. She quickly stooped and plucked a spire from a bushy plant growing in the crevice of the road curb, then held it out toward them. "We are all like this fireweed."

The settlers stirred, looking to her for hope.

Gesturing at the flattened city block around them, Whit's voice grew passionate, her face flushed with feeling. "The mountain heather that once grew here was fragile, unable to recover from the visit the Regs paid us. Now, the heather is gone. But the fireweed grows, a hardier plant. Lush and strong, it covers this whole area, thriving despite the disaster that preceded it. Next month, in June, we'll see the fireweeds' dark, pink flowers sprouting everywhere. And Isis will be rising."

There was a long silence. One of the settlers reached out and embraced Whit, murmuring thanks. The rest followed, each one stopping to touch Whit, some of them wiping tears from their eyes, before the whole group drifted away. Then Whit was left alone with Loy, the subject of intense scrutiny.

Loy spoke quietly, using the clear, caressing voice that had once charmed Whit into bed. "I did not expect such unaffected eloquence from you. The brash, rangy-limbed teenager has vanished and in her place I find this disciplined, competent," Loy reached out and stroked Whit's cheek, "ravishing warrior."

Sensing that Loy was about to propose something that Whit really did not want to hear, Whit began walking away.

Trailing after her, laughing softly, Loy asked, "Are you running away from me?"

Undaunted, Whit threw over her shoulder, "You once knew me better than that."

With a quick step, Loy caught up with her, seized Whit's arm and pulled her around. Dark, provocative eyes searched Whit's face as Loy demanded, "Have you forgotten what we were like together, Tomyris?"

Firmly, Whit extricated her elbow from Loy's hard grasp and stepped back. "I have forgotten nothing. Not the way you pursued me, caught me, or the way you tossed me aside. Nor have I forgotten how skillfully you lied and cheated your way through warrior training and flight school."

Calmly, Loy narrowed her eyes at Whit. "And at thirty-one, you're still as envious of my achievements as you were at sixteen."

"From what I've read of the Boudiccan Council," Whit continued, her hands on her hips, "your political career has been much the same. As Deputy Leader, you've taken credit for ideas and projects that your overworked staff was actually responsible for delivering. *You*, on the other hand, spent much of your time deceiving your constituents and filling your own pocket." Flushed with irritation, Whit leaned closer. "And there is a persistent rumor about the fate of a certain young woman, a rival during your first campaign for a Council seat...."

"It was an accident," Loy hissed. "She was a fisherwoman who made her living on the sea. The boat sank—it happens."

"On calm seas, for no known reason, her boat blew up," Whit snapped harshly. "The official report quotes another fisherwoman in the fleet as saying 'it was like a bomb went off.'"

"Are you daring to accuse me of *murder*, Major?" Loy snarled.

Whit met her icy gaze without flinching.

"*Well*?" Loy prodded. "*Are* you?" When Whit didn't answer, Loy warned, "Because if you're making an accusation, you'd better have some proof!"

Fearlessly, Whit stared her down.

And then, in a shockingly swift move, Loy grasped Whit's collar with one hand and yanked her to her. Whit found herself being kissed with a sureness and fire born of long experience.

Shoving Loy aside, Whit gasped, "Damn you!"

In answer, Loy gave a low, mean chuckle. "I have many, many lovers, Whit," Loy crooned. "Don't fight me—we were so good together."

"Sweet Mother!" Whit retorted, exasperated. "You just met Kali—I told you that we're partners!"

"Whatever we do together has nothing to do with your shy little rabbit."

Whit burst into an incredulous laugh. "Loy, I *love* her. Everything I do has to do with Kali."

Loy's eyes changed. She held Whit's gaze for a moment, obviously not used to being refused. "Then I will come to the point. Make me your second in command, and I promise I will leave you in peace and carry out your orders with devotion."

Suddenly it all made sense to Whit. Loy was not pursuing her so much as she was pursuing the power that Whit was in position to bestow. *Nothing has changed with this woman*, she thought, repulsed. Looking away, Whit breathed, "You're unbelievable."

"Appoint me your second or prepare for the fight of your life, Major," Loy whispered. "I will make your life a living hell." And with that, she quickly set off in the opposite direction, walking south.

❨ ❨ ❨

Later in the afternoon, after the party of visiting officials had collected Danu and flown back to Artemis, Whit returned to the Cedar House. She passed through the Council Room to the lab, to the small, Spartan bedroom she and Kali had rigged up there. Whit found Kali sitting on the floor, finishing a meditation session.

"Lilith wants us to come to Artemis tonight," Whit began. "She says that Beltane is for laughing and dancing. And she thinks that, after today's work, we need to do some of both."

"Okay," Kali replied quietly.

Whit waited for the questions about Loy, but none came. Kali just watched her a little more closely than usual, the brown eyes following Whit as she peeled off clothes and headed for the shower. When Whit emerged from the warm spray, feeling refreshed and more settled, she found Kali sitting on the side of the bed, the blonde head bent. Deep in thought, she had started to undress and stopped. She now sat twisting a sock in her hand, staring at the floor.

Naked, wet-haired, Whit toweled off and padded back into the room. Kali looked up at her, a mixture of concern and wariness in her glance.

"Sorry, Kal," Whit said softly. "I should have told you about Loy yesterday."

Kali ventured, "She was your first, wasn't she?"

"During flight school. We were both sixteen, unbearably cocky. This insane rivalry developed between us and we drove ourselves and everyone else around us crazy...."

Tugging the sock free, Whit tossed it aside, then leaned over Kali. She unsnapped the denim jumpsuit, sent her hands across Kali's breasts in an almost possessive reaffirmation.

"Whit, it's after four o'clock. We'll miss the shuttle."

Gently, Whit pressed on, peeling the worn denim down, exposing the fruit she was after. She bent down, tasting the salt along the length of Kali's neck. Brushing her hands over downy arms, answering in a murmur against skin, Whit said, "It's long over. Does it bother you?"

Her breath quickening, Kali whispered, "A little."

Firmly, Whit pushed Kali's shoulders down on the mattress, planted an arm on either side of her. "I'm so in love with you."

The brown eyes stayed fixed a moment on Whit's, worried. Then the eyes drifted down Whit's exposed flesh. By the expression on her face, Whit could tell Kali was almost unconsciously responding to the physical presence above her, while her mind continued to whirl. Whit watched the brown eyes change. Anxiety was quickly being replaced by undisguised desire. As Whit leaned lower to kiss her, Kali unexpectedly sat up and pushed by her, saying, "Oh, no you don't. We'll be late."

Single-minded, Whit grasped Kali's slim arm as she left the bed, staying her. "You're mad at me."

"I'm not. But the shuttle...we'll miss it if you...get me started." Kali swallowed, and the heat in her glance reassured Whit.

And with that, Kali tugged free of Whit's hand. Quickly, she shucked off the jumpsuit and underwear, then stepped into the shower. Whit flopped onto her back, watching that lithe body move behind the plexiglass shower door. "Later," she murmured, making a promise to herself. "And it will be a perfect way to anoint our new house."

(4

*T*hat evening, despite the exhausting, distressing work of the day, many Isis settlers joined Whit and Kali in catching the evening run of the twice daily jet transport to Artemis. When the enterprising young warrior piloting the cold fusion craft caught sight of Whit coming aboard, she ushered her to the navigator's chair. Whit, dismayed at the status the Military Governorship seemed to have brought, politely insisted on sitting with everyone else in the passenger section. As Whit flopped into a seat beside Kali, rolling her eyes in mock exasperation, Kali burst into quiet laughter.

"You may as well get used to it, Whit. You're the closest thing to Lilith we've got here in Isis," Kali observed.

Whit spent the rest of the ninety-mile, twelve-minute flight, pondering that remark. She was not Lilith's equal, of that much she was sure. Lilith had spent years refining her firmly gentle style of governing. And yet, as Whit thought about it more, what better person to model herself after than the well-respected Leader of Artemis?

And what would that involve? Whit considered carefully the traits that made Lilith so admirable. She remembered the advice Lilith had given her, once, years earlier, when Whit had earned her Lieutenant's bars: "Leading doesn't mean *ordering* women to follow you, it means *inspiring* them, so that they *want* to follow you." *And that's what I've tried to do. Now if I can just keep my temper when Loy tries to bait me....*

By the time the Isis contingent arrived, Beltane Night was in full swing. On the grassy lawns of the Agro-Center campus, the musicians were playing, the dancers were swirling, and flirtatious conversations were flowing as steadily as the wine. Beltane was building to its usual rowdy conclusion.

In ancient times, in an attempt to encourage the fertility of the land, Beltane often ended in a night of multiple-partnered delights in the wood. For modern Freeland, Beltane had become a night to celebrate the overthrow of puritanical patriarchy. While there were, as yet, few multiple-partnered delights in the wood, the wild, erotic nature of Beltane seemed to increase with each successive spring. It was only the most resolutely chaste who ended up in bed by themselves.

Styx was whispering love-speak in Lilith's ear, making her weak as they danced together, when a cheer went up farther away. Curious, Lilith lifted her head and searched for the source of the voice she now heard, a voice pitched like one addressing a crowd.

Near the huge, oaken wine casks, in the colorful glow of the Japanese lanterns strung above them, Lilith saw hundreds of women gathering. Loy Yin Chen stood on a tree stump, outlining her vision of the future Isis, obviously making a campaign speech.

Lilith grabbed Styx by the hand and led them closer.

With her straight, dark hair slicked back and her eyes flashing, Loy was an alluring sight. Her short-waisted, red jacket and black bodysuit seemed to magnify the image of power and competence. Around her, trusting and engrossed, were the faces of hundreds of current and potential Isis citizens.

Oh no, Lilith groaned inwardly. *I had not thought she would be so damned beguiling.* She glanced around as Styx dropped her hand and hurried away, then fell into a critical evaluation of what Loy was proposing.

Gesturing grandly, Loy stated, "We can solve the energy needs of Isis very easily. Not by making methanol from grain, like you do here in Artemis. I've been down to Morgan and I've witnessed the effectiveness of solar power. We can do the same...."

The crowd responded with an excited murmur. Lilith knew it was not only because this woman was a new and pleasing face, but also because she appeared to have a vision. Isis was rapidly becoming a marvelous dream—but a dream without shape. The women here were ready to listen to anyone who had ideas on how to make that dream a reality.

Where is Whit? she thought.

Encouraged by the attentive audience, Loy continued energetically, "As you know, Morgan is almost desert terrain. With their ocean desalinization plants and miles of solar panels, they've made technology work for them! And if they can live comfortably in a desert, surely we can succeed easily in the mountains!"

A strong voice cut off the beginnings of applause. "This is not sunny Morgan we are planning." Lilith recognized Whit's husky voice, spotted Styx pushing her forward, through the listeners. "This is Isis," Whit went on. "We are much farther north. Up in the mountains we have to deal with months of snow and rain. Frequently there are overcast skies throughout the entire winter. How can solar power be the main source of energy?"

Inquisitive faces all swung back to Loy, waiting for a response. Temporarily thrown, Loy stared down at Whit. Then she demanded, "Would you have the mountain valleys planted, then? Have Isis compete with Artemis as the breadbasket of Freeland?"

"No," Whit called. "The topsoil is far too shallow. We would produce little and ruin the ecological balance."

"Well, Isis is not on the mighty Sacajawea River, like Boudicca," Loy challenged. "You cannot harness the current of water with hydroelectric plants! So what do you propose?"

Whit was right beside Loy. Styx set down the wooden vegetable crate she had grabbed and half-shoved Whit up onto it. Dressed in a loose white shirt, an open, colorfully embroidered vest and tight black trousers, Whit caused a murmur of appreciation as she came into view. Dark hair gleaming in the soft lantern light, she glanced about, gray eyes dubious, as if she wasn't exactly sure how she had ended up addressing this mob.

Someone called, "Tell us, Major!"

Another voice responded, "It's Governor, now," and a scattered chorus of enthusiastic warrior yells went up.

Embarrassed, Whit gave a resigned little shrug. "We may not be on the 'mighty Sacajawea,'" the husky voice stated, a touch of humor in the tone, "but we have waters of our own to harness." The crowd laughed appreciatively, obviously glad Whit had taken a poke at Loy's smug reference to her home colony of Boudicca.

Whit offered, "We have what was used originally in Isis, the Nisqually River and countless streams that carry glacial runoff. But we also have high mountain passes where the wind is a constant force. Our greatest source of energy may be in constructing windmills, as Maat Tyler once proposed, years and years ago."

At this point, the elders in the crowd bellowed their approval, enthusiastic that at least *someone* had been researching what had worked for Isis, what had been deliberated for projected energy goals during the first settlement. To the elders, the majority of those expressing interest in the ruined colony were not only very young, they seemed incredibly unprepared and cavalier. The young women of Artemis were all ablaze with pioneer fever, openly espousing the merits of unproven experiments and gimmicky, trendy technology. Many in Artemis feared that without a strong, knowledgeable leader, the resettlement effort would end in failure, or worse, catastrophe.

Whit waved the crowd quiet and finished, "And once the colony is established, we ought to consider building a cold fusion electric plant. Once overhauled, the hydroelectric facility from Maat's time can get us started, but the future will demand a modern energy plan."

Again, the women shouted their agreement.

Loy folded her arms across her chest. "This sounds like a campaign speech. Are you offering yourself for Leader of Isis?"

An expectant hush fell over the gathering.

Whit sent Loy a sideways, speculative gaze. "Excuse me—perhaps I've misunderstood. Isn't that what *you're* doing?"

A ripple of quiet mirth moved among the women, swelling into outright laughter.

As Whit and Loy exchanged ornery grins, a third person elevated herself beside them. Arinna Sojourner stood on another crate, her green eyes reflecting the deep emerald of her long, clinging gown.

"What these two haven't mentioned," Arinna began in a warm, vibrant voice, "is how much Isis needs *you*. Currently, there are only two hundred and thirty-seven brave souls out there, striving to build their dreams together. A city-colony is being born again to Freeland, but where are her future citizens?"

Immediately riveted, like the rest of the crowd, Whit and Loy managed to pull their gazes away and glance at each other in surprise.

Standing in the midst of the listening crowd, Lilith, too, felt the shift of interest. Arinna's golden-brown face glowed with her obviously fervid commitment. Long, wavy hair cascaded over her shoulders as

Arinna stretched out her arms and demanded, "Where are the citizens of Isis?"

All around Lilith, young women, old women, some lovers with their arms circling each other's waists, all began to stir.

Near the front, Lilith saw Marpe, one of the most successful clothing merchants in Artemis, raise her hand. "I will be a citizen of Isis!" Marpe declared. Right beside Marpe, Samsi shouted, "Yes, we go tomorrow!"

In an uneven pattern, voices began calling to Arinna, "I'll come," "I'll be there." Then, women were turning to each other, everyone talking at once, making decisions and planning.

The roar of discussion drowned out Loy's attempt to renew the debate. Bemused, Whit sent a hand through her thick, dark hair, and then hopped off the vegetable crate. She weaved swiftly through the crowd and disappeared into the banquet area farther away.

Lilith watched Arinna descend from her box and trail purposefully after Whit. Loy, noting Arinna's direction, followed right behind them.

They are equally matched contenders, Lilith mused. *And now the jockeying for position begins in earnest.*

☾ ☾ ☾

About a hundred yards away, at the edge of the dancing field, Kali was trying to guard Whit's plate from Nakotah's nimble-fingered raids, when Whit finally came back.

As she retrieved her dish from Kali, Whit demanded, "Hey, what happened to all my hummus and bread?"

Nakotah wiggled her dark eyebrows. "You're lucky I didn't steal your woman, too, O Mighty Governor. The hummus was tempting and Kali is even more so."

Laughing, Whit leaned into Kali, nuzzling her neck in that way that made Kali instantly defenseless. "You *do* look good, Kal."

Heat rose in Kali's face. Self-consciously, she glanced down at her outfit: a russet-brown tunic fell midway to her knees, with a long, tan sash tied gallantly across her middle. But it was the snug, tan-colored tights beneath that bothered her; they seemed so revealing. "I feel half-dressed," she confessed.

Moving back, raising a soft taco toward her mouth, Whit pronounced, "Honey, in Elysium you had to hide those legs, but not here."

Kali thought, *In Elysium, not even an AGH tattoo would have stopped the Regs if they'd caught me in something like this. But here....* Kali looked up and found a beautiful woman in a long, form-fitting, emerald dress standing before her. The woman's green eyes were just leaving Kali's tan leggings.

"With thighs like that," the woman murmured, almost apologetically, "you have to be a warrior."

Whit gulped down a mouthful of food and flipped a brusque hand between them. "Arinna—Kali. Kali—Arinna."

Bending toward Arinna, Nakotah interjected, "Kali's Warrior Reserve, or I'd have her on patrol duty with me tonight. We'd be inspecting those dark, secluded woods over there while her partner played politics."

"Ha!" Whit returned. "Big talk when Cimbri's not around."

Kali smiled. This was a game they had all fallen into months ago. Almost to dispel the knowledge that Whit and Cimbri had once been deeply involved, Nakotah paid Kali courtly compliments and pretended to rival Whit.

Nakotah reached over to Whit's plate and plucked up several fat, green beans.

"Come on, if you're so hungry, 'Kotah," Whit invited, moving toward the large tables of food in the distance. "I want seconds, and you can get your own plate."

"I'm on duty," Nakotah reminded Whit, and tapped the holstered sedation gun on her belt.

"Then pick out what you want to steal from me and I'll get enough for both of us."

Nakotah hesitated, and Whit linked elbows with her, tugging her along. As the two tall women moved off together, Arinna faced Kali. "If you're not a warrior, then what are you?" she asked pleasantly.

Yes, what am I? Kali wondered. "A student, I guess," she offered lamely. "I'm working on a construction crew by day, studying secondary school courses by night."

"Secondary school?" Arinna frowned, perplexed. Then enlightenment burst over her expressive face, "That's right. You're Maat's daughter—the prisoner of war. You and Whit started this return to Isis by having a house built on Whit's family property."

Nodding, Kali clarified, "It's just about done."

The green eyes again swept over Kali's legs.

"I run—in the morning," Kali explained, feeling as if she had to justify her apparent fitness. She certainly had not been this sturdy picture of health when she had first arrived in Freeland, five months ago. "I kind of...crave...physical exertion. I was a peasant farmer for so long...."

Arinna nodded. "I understand. I know all about physical cravings," and then with a slight smile, she gazed into the crowd before them. The women were all turned away from them, facing the dancing field and watching a swirling reel.

All at once, Loy emerged from the crowd, saw them, and beamed a captivating smile. As Loy approached, her dark eyes moved over both Kali and Arinna, considering them.

"There are some handsome women here tonight," Loy stated, "but you two have to be among the finest."

Dipping a small curtsey, Arinna's smile deepened.

Kali nodded coolly. *I don't like the way she looks at me.*

"Who wants to dance?" Loy asked, her eyes almost caressing Kali's tan tights.

"Why don't you go, Kali?" Arinna proposed graciously.

Looking off in the direction of the banquet tables, Kali hesitated. Arinna seemed to read her hesitation, remarking, "I'll tell Whit where you've gone."

Loy held out a hand to Kali. "Please. If you don't dance with me, I'll have to try something far more fresh."

At that moment, Whit abruptly shouldered her way between the two women near Kali's elbow, almost spilling the contents of her plate on them. "*I'll* dance with you, Kal," the husky voice almost snarled.

Startled, Kali stared at her lover. Whit clearly felt that, while risque banter from Nakotah was one thing, it was altogether different when it came from Loy. *Why? Does Whit really think I wouldn't be able to handle this flirt?*

Narrowing her eyes, Loy let her hand hang there, palm down, extended out to Kali.

Kali suddenly became aware of the crowd. Many women near them were surreptitiously watching. The moment was rapidly becoming fraught with political implications.

Loy and Whit were both government appointees, both aspiring to eventually become Leader of Isis. If Kali turned down Loy, after Whit's obvious resentment, it would become the gossip of the night before the refusal fully left her mouth. And yet, Kali knew that if she *didn't* turn down Loy, Whit would be vexed. Kali had already decided how she wanted to end this night, and it did not involve a fight with Whit.

All at once, Arinna stepped forward and slipped her hand into Loy's palm, firmly grasping it. "You should have asked me, anyway," Arinna told Loy, with an endearingly congenial smile.

Recovering from her amazement at this development, Loy threw a smug, prideful look at Whit, then led Arinna away. Whit stood beside Kali, glaring.

Taking Whit by the elbow, Kali propelled her in the opposite direction. "Why did you do that?" Kali asked, keeping her voice low.

Whit gazed at her, still upset. "She's...an enticing, seductive woman, Kal. You haven't been exposed to a woman like that. You don't know...."

"Oh? Remember Branwen?" Kali gave a soft curse. "Whit, I was broken in by a woman like that. Do you honestly think I'd be tempted by that sort of nonsense, now?"

Sighing, Whit handed her plate of food to a lanky, young warrior they passed. The young woman laughed her thanks and Whit pulled Kali into a gentle embrace.

"Dance with *me*, Kal," Whit whispered in her ear. "This is Beltane, and we belong together."

❨ ❨ ❨

Arriving late, well past ten in the evening, Cimbri spent twenty minutes searching through the Beltane celebrants before she finally found her friends. Beneath the shadowy glare of the electro-torches that were staked in a large ring around the grassy campus lawn, Whit and Kali could be seen dancing with hundreds of other women. The great concentric circles of women were passing in opposite directions, the dancers weaving in and out of one another's arms. Wild, joyous, pulse-quickening music pounded into the moonlit night.

Nearby, having fulfilled their security duties, Nakotah and her patrol of ten were being relieved by a new detail of warriors. Upon seeing Cimbri, Nakotah came over and gave her a kiss, just as Whit and Kali left the dancers and joined them.

Glancing at Cimbri's white Healer's's coat, Whit asked, "What happened?"

"There was an accident out at Isis," Cimbri began, then seeing Whit's alarm, quickly related, "It's alright—very minor—I've got the patients in my clinic. They're sleeping."

"What happened?" Kali asked, her steadying hand on Whit's shoulder. Cimbri noted it and wondered at how effortlessly Kali read Whit's needs. Though Whit usually appeared stalwart and impossibly capable, Cimbri knew from experience that Whit was not as tough as she seemed.

"At the hostel construction site," Cimbri began, "one of the external scaffolding platforms collapsed. A warrior patrol was making their rounds and they were hit by falling boards and paint cans."

Nakotah said, close to Whit's ear, "I got the report on the radio, earlier. Sergeant Iphito says she's cordoned off the area until daylight, in order to make a safety check. I didn't tell you sooner because I wanted to get Cimbri's report first."

Whit's gray eyes widened. "How many warriors were hurt?"

"Only two," Cimbri answered. "Both women suffered painful contusions on shoulders and arms, but that's all. The rest of the patrol managed to dodge clear."

"We'd better go home, then," Kali observed.

Whit nodded.

"We'll see you off," Cimbri proposed.

Nakotah, Cimbri, Whit, and Kali walked across the Agro-Center campus, all of them suddenly anxious and quiet. As they reached the street, it was very clear that the carefree holiday was over for all of them.

Weary from her unexpected duties at the clinic, Cimbri gratefully lowered herself onto the bench beneath an old maple tree, her eyes searching the road ahead for the shuttle bus. On one side of her, Nakotah and Whit plunked down and began discussing the details of the accident: the exact actions of the passing patrol before the scaffolding came down, the type of materials used and how well-built the structure really was. On the other side of Cimbri, Kali paced, moving with that oddly sinuous grace that, for Cimbri, often brought to mind a cougar.

Whit folded her long legs, her face somber. Efficiently, Nakotah relayed Sergeant Iphito's report that no one had been working at the hostel during the last twenty-four hours. At sunset last night, the last construction crew had departed. Subsequently, all colonists had spent Beltane cleaning up the last of the old Isis ruins. There was no known reason for the scaffold to collapse after a day without use.

Kali murmured, "Maybe it wasn't an accident."

Cimbri peered at her, completely taken aback by the comment.

Whit and Nakotah exchanged an inscrutable look.

"Beltane blessings," a young voice called. "Am I interrupting?"

They all turned. Through the shadowy moonlight, Danu Sullivan shyly approached them. Dressed in a billowy, pale yellow shirt and black jeans, she was trailed by another young woman.

"This is Alborak. She'll be running one of the utility crews out at Isis," Danu explained.

The squarely built Alborak smiled and gave a confident nod of her head, then signed a general hello to them all as Danu made introductions.

Nakotah complimented Alborak on her long, shining brown hair, and, unbidden, Danu fell to signing for her as Nakotah spoke to Alborak orally. Alborak smiled her thanks.

With a rather sheepish grin, Danu said to Kali, "I heard you were asking around about me. I thought I'd better come and show you I'm alright."

Kali grinned back. "I'm glad you did. I heard you got a few stitches. Does it hurt?"

Meanwhile, Cimbri was noticing how Alborak watched Danu's hands move, as if she were reading more than casual expression in Danu's graceful strokes through the air.

The redhead shrugged. "It's just a lump and a little cut. I can't believe it bled that much."

Blushing, Kali confessed, "I can't believe I kicked you."

Whit stated matter-of-factly, "The first time I met Kal, she hit me, too."

Kali shook her head. "Apparently, not hard enough. You're still spinning tall tales...."

"You *did* hit me! You shoved me into that muddy bank!" A teasing light flickered in the gray eyes.

"I forced you off—you were crushing me!" Kali spun around to the rest of them, making her case. "I was hiding in an irrigation ditch and she jumped right on top of me!"

"Watch out for that Tyler temper," Whit told Danu, who couldn't quite look Whit in the eye. Not seeming to notice Danu's reticence, Whit stood, stepped toward her and ruffled the short curls on the healthy side of the red head. "Glad you're okay, Danu. After the voter registration tomorrow, we'll be issuing land parcels and building permits. Seems like a good time to show your architectural designs on the Council Room monitor—let everyone else see what's coming."

Head down, her face darkening with color in the surreal light of the moon, Danu only seemed able to nod assent. Breaking into a baffled, but indulgent smile, Whit signed to Alborak, *Is she always like this?* Her long, light brown hair gleamed as she shrugged, and her eyes were playful, as Alborak signed back, *I just met her. So far, I only know I like the way she dances.* When Whit laughed, Danu's head popped up again, her pale blue eyes wondering. Alborak took her hand and patted it reassuringly.

With its steel-plated underside following an invisible, electro-magnetic rail buried in the concrete of the roadway, the driverless shuttle bus came gliding out of the night. Danu and Alborak wished everyone a good rest, at which Nakotah laughed outright, then the two youngsters moved off into the moonlight together.

As Whit and Kali climbed aboard the bus, Nakotah grasped Cimbri's hand and tugged her along. "Let's ride out to the airfield with them and then catch another bus home."

Whit slipped enough coins into the fare box for all of them, even as Cimbri complained, "It's early. I don't want to go home, yet."

"You're tired and my watch is over. Besides," Nakotah crooned suggestively, "there's fun at home, too."

Cimbri smiled. "This will be the first Beltane Night I've spent in my own bed, I think."

As she moved down the aisle of seats, Whit teased, "Then Nakotah has caught you, for sure."

Smoothing a hand over Cimbri's buttocks, Nakotah remarked, "Nah. I'm the one with a hook in my mouth."

"Is that a compliment?" Cimbri asked Kali. "I think it is, but I can never really be sure."

Kali merely laughed in reply.

❰ ❰ ❰

Around eleven o'clock, just after the shuttle transport jet returned to Isis, Whit lingered at the airfield and spent a few minutes interviewing Sergeant Iphito. Unable to gain any new information about the scaffolding collapse, Whit arranged to meet the Sergeant at first light and tour the scene.

Disturbed, Whit crossed the tarmac to her motorcycle. Kali was already sitting astride the back of the long saddle, waiting patiently, watching her closely.

"Sorry," Whit stated, slinging a long leg over the bike.

From behind, Kali's arms slipped around her and a low voice whispered a delicious invitation in Whit's ear. Her mood abruptly changing, Whit turned in the saddle.

Blushing, brown eyes bright with both exhaustion and excitement, Kali looked incredibly eager. Whit laughed and returned, "And I know just the place to do it. Do you mind going on another little trip tonight?"

Kali smiled enthusiastically.

Whit revved the near-silent motor and sent the motorcycle tearing along the trail to the Cedar House, where they disembarked and quickly walked to their quarters in the lab. Hurriedly, they packed a jumble of supplies and sleeping bags, then climbed aboard Whit's motorcycle and rode into the moonlit night.

In mystical illumination, they followed the trail through the meadow, over the timbered ridge, down across the grassy valley. They parked the cycle before a large house that seemed to stand expectantly in ghostly white light. Each woman shouldered a knapsack and a sleeping bag and they walked arm and arm across the muddy yard, feasting their eyes on the frame of a solid, granite building where they hoped to spend a lifetime together. On this day of grinding physical exertion, relentless emotional turmoil, and then abandoned celebration, they both finally experienced the sweet comfort of coming home. It had been a long time in coming.

They climbed the wooden porch steps, boots clomping softly as they moved across the boards. At the entrance, Whit paused and raised her hand to the Sheila-na-gig mounted next to the stone threshold. Whit caressed the small stone sculpture of a squatting female with her yoni exposed, a fixture from the days of ancient matriarchies. This was a protective spirit, a symbol of the power of women. Whit dipped her fingers into the little well of water at the vulva, then touched her fingers to her lips. Kali repeated the gesture. Thus blessed by the Goddess, they stepped through the door and into the darkness.

There was no electricity yet in Isis, save at the Cedar House, where Whit had hooked up a methanol-powered generator. Yet Whit knew the design of the house well enough to find her way. Leading Kali by the hand, she took them up the broad madrone staircase, the smell of freshly cut wood all around them. On the upper story, occasionally bumping into things—a sawhorse first and then a pyramid of paint cans—they made their way to the end of a long corridor. An arched doorway revealed a rectangular room, with a large, four-poster bed at its center. Above the bed, built into the high, cathedral ceiling, was a skylight through which poured a magical flood of moonglow.

Standing beside Whit, Kali gave a small gasp of delight.

After shutting the bedroom door, Whit dropped her pack. She strode across the room, untied her sleeping bag and with a single, authoritative shake, spread it out across the vast bed.

Whit noticed Kali opening the bedroom door again, trying to accomplish the feat as inconspicuously as possible. With a worried frown, Whit reflected that her time in prison had left Kali with a permanent anxiety about closed doors, and apparently these ensuing months of freedom had done nothing to alleviate that apprehension.

Kali was moving behind her, confessing softly, "It's my first real Beltane, Whit. I was so young the last time...." There was a slight pause, then, "Okay?"

Is she as tired as I am? Whit mused, hardly trying to make sense of that last statement. She took Kali's sleeping bag from her and joined it with her own, making a large, long blanket to wrap around them.

Moving closer, Kali whispered, "All night long I've been watching you dance. Gaea, I want you."

Whit felt a prolonged, powerful shot of adrenaline hit her; those words had effectively chased away most of her fatigue. Inflamed, she put a hand to Kali's shirt buttons but Kali impatiently pushed it away. "No, Whit—tonight I'm the initiator." Another pause, then, "Okay?"

Whit replied, warily, "Okay."

In the large, silent room, in the shaft of moonlight that sliced down through the skylight, Whit stood before Kali, allowing herself to be slowly undressed. As each garment left her, she was lovingly caressed and given satiny kisses in a random, ardent pattern. Her reward for enduring this slow, delicious torture was seeing Kali's eyes change, become steadily more and more intense.

When her clothes were all off, Whit climbed into their sleeping bags and watched Kali strip. The blonde hair shimmered with moonshine. Kali's breathing was different now, quick and shallow, evident in small, white puffs in the chill air of the house. Though Whit whispered, "Take your time," Kali did not. Shortly, her wiry body slipped beneath the warm fabric and Whit was covered with soft, warm skin. At once, Kali was moving expertly against her, writhing beneath Whit's roaming hands.

She's on fire, Whit thought, trying to hang onto some semblance of lucid thought before the storm of lust fully hit.

It never failed to amaze her—Kali's sweetness, that quiet, good-natured exterior, hid the aggressive tease that Whit met in bed. She had a knack of breaking off a kiss before Whit was quite ready, causing Whit's whole body to ignite with the desire for more. Sometimes, Whit felt like she was actually trying to catch the lithe form moving over her, trying to gather Kali close before her busy bee mouth moved on to another flower, another highly charged erotic zone on Whit's responsive body. Steadily, each teasing kiss grew deeper and hotter, each ear was tongued and coaxed to shivering awareness, each breast was suckled to blazing life. And Kali's hands were just everywhere, except where Whit more and more needed them to be. Soon, the swirling, skimming ecstasy was coaxing tiny, helpless noises from Whit's throat. Whit could feel her heart thumping, her back arching, her entire body becoming Kali's to do with as she pleased.

Kali knew how to drive her, how to surprise her into sensations beyond anything Whit had ever experienced. Even now, Kali was alternately lapping at and ravening a nipple. The electric shocks of passion were maddeningly exciting. Whit felt herself gasping, heard herself pleading for those gentle, skimming fingers to land between her legs. She started thrashing helplessly, as Kali circled, then began zeroing in on the target, closer, closer.

Yes! Sweet Mother, please! There! "There! Ounh..."

Launched over the edge, Whit heard herself yelling. In a swift move, Kali was straddling her leg, gliding her own moist center of joy back and forth along Whit's thigh. Whit curled toward Kali. She was still coming in widening, ascending waves when she felt Kali stiffen and jerk with her first orgasm. They each shook with release, clutching each other, grinding together in sweat and yoni juices, and Whit was barely aware of where she ended and Kali began. Whit came again and then again in quick succession. Then the rush of molten, erotic ecstasy began to slow, pooling into a mellow warmth. Finally, Whit stretched, sluggish with afterglow.

"One more," Kali whispered. There was no mistaking that she was giving a command.

"I can't...too tired," Whit groaned. She wanted to save *some* strength, or she'd never be able to finish Kali properly.

Kali seemed to still herself, her intent, pleased eyes moving over Whit as if she were in the midst of some project. Whit lay on her back, drowsy, yet determinedly sliding her hand up Kali's thigh.

Kali pulled away, opened the sleeping bags, and Whit thought for a moment that she was leaving. Instead, Kali shifted positions, slid down as she swung her hips over Whit, whispering "Beltane blessings."

And then the mouth was on her, licking, inflaming, catching Whit wide open and powerless. Grasping the thick cotton of the sleeping bag beneath her, Whit went rigid. She felt several fingers reach inside of her, searching for that hidden quarter inch of bliss. "Is this it?" Kali murmured.

Whit's body answered for her. Spread-eagled, arms flung wide, she convulsed, her voice a full-throated wail. Chuckling softly, Kali began to work the site, licking Whit's clitoris all the while. Whit felt as if her entire body, her very soul, were melting, being stroked into liquid oblivion.

Sensation displaced everything. The moon above seemed to drop through the skylight, burning, gushing into her, fusing with her in a hot, mercurial mix. For an immeasurable time, Whit lost herself completely.

Then the silence of the room registered, a silence that seemed to ring with the quiet vibration of a noise abruptly ended. Kali withdrew her fingers and Whit incoherently said something—even she did not know what. She gave up trying to talk, too dazed to do more than breathe, "Oh, Kal."

Pulling the sleeping bag back over them, Kali snuggled close and sighed deeply, happily. Whit lay there in the moonlight, damp with sweat and honey. She felt as if all the tension and anxiety of the last week had been emptied from her, and her soul filled up instead with silvery, ethereal moonbeams. She was limp, drifting, devising endless ways to return the pleasure, but somehow, she couldn't seem to muster the energy to move.

Then came the soft buzzing she knew so well; Kali was asleep.

$$\mathbb{C}\,5$$

*T*he day after Beltane, as the sun still hovered behind the eastern slopes of the Cascade Range, Whit and Kali drove across the meadow on Whit's motorcycle. As they approached the hostel construction site, they could see young Sergeant Iphito waiting patiently beside the twisted, metal frame of an external scaffolding structure. A bright orange rope surrounded the scene, restricting trespassers.

The large pine clapboard structure, with its steep, cedar-shingled roof, looked massive in the morning light. Constructed in the shape of an E, two of its wings were complete and painted white. The third wing of the E was still a raw lumber surface.

The hostel was being built as a temporary dormitory for the first settlers arriving in the city-colony. Once private homes were built, and the city was underway, the hostel would serve as a residence for business travelers and tourists from other colonies.

For the next half hour, while Kali's stomach grumbled for breakfast, Whit and the Sergeant poked around the unfinished wing of the building. Carefully shifting aside the random pattern of planks and metal, Whit and the patrol leader examined the stony ground. When they finished, Whit asked the Sergeant numerous questions in a low voice, then had the Sergeant remove the orange cord.

As Whit mounted the bike and readied the motor, she swung around to Kali and asked urgently, "Why did you say that last night, about this maybe not being an accident?"

Taking a deep breath, Kali shrugged. "Just a feeling."

Whit held her eyes, considering that answer.

Kali looked away. "Why?"

"Nothing certain," Whit responded, slipping her fingers through her hair. "Just no real reason for the scaffolding to fall. One of the warriors brushed against it, and it came down on them." Pausing, Whit contemplated Kali. "Two days ago, that thing was sturdy enough to hold four painters, yet last night it couldn't withstand a bump."

Whit seemed to wait for her to speak, but Kali really didn't know what to say. *What do I tell her? That I unintentionally hear her thoughts? That I just know things sometimes, without any idea how or why....* She couldn't tell Whit; it would sound crazy. *Am I going crazy?*

Noisily, Kali's stomach gurgled, and Whit chuckled.

"No wonder you're hungry," Whit pronounced, stroking Kali's cheek and grinning provocatively. "You worked hard this morning."

With relief, Kali grinned back, parts of her still tingling with body memory of how Whit had awakened her.

Frustrated, Whit decided to renew her investigation later. Turning around and scanning the trail ahead, she said, "The meal hall is probably open, by now. Let's get some food into you."

Whit revved the quiet engine into a low rumbling hum, and then they were jouncing along the trail to the meal hall for breakfast.

(((

Four hours later, around ten o'clock in the morning, a huge silver transport ship dropped out of the slate-gray cloud cover over Isis. Circling and then hovering above the vast forests surrounding her, the ship emitted a deep, droning purr. Its cold fusion jet engines were muffled by the decibel-altering devices mounted within the twin power cavities. Upon hearing the sound, Whit and Kali joined the crowd assembling at the edge of the airfield, waiting for the ship to land.

Whit was in full dress uniform: wine red warrior's jacket, sleek black pants, calf-high black boots. As the only official currently stationed in Isis, she had a duty to discharge—greeting the three Directors who would be re-locating to Isis today.

Standing beside her lover, Kali felt almost grubby in her work overalls, boots, and Whit's old blue flannel shirt. But as she glanced around her, Kali was reassured that almost everyone else looked as bad.

She was merely one of hundreds who had stopped work to come and be part of the welcoming. After all, this was herstory. Before the day was over, voters would be registered, land parcels and building permits would be issued. And today, transitional or not, the first government in ten years would be set in motion again in the Isis Cedar House.

While Whit's attention was on the craft above them, Kali inspected her carefully. Last night's pleasuring was still glowing in Whit's cheeks and eyes, and the grim lines that had settled about her mouth for days had disappeared. She was standing tall and straight, yet the shoulders within that splendid, burgundy warrior's jacket were relaxed. Satisfied, Kali nodded inwardly.

She saw the robust construction boss, Lupa Tagliaro, swaggering up to stand on the other side of Whit. The stern, dark eyes lingered on Whit, then widened with a sudden perception and darted to Kali. Lupa's brash conclusions blared through Kali's head: *Harrowing Hecate—only one thing works out the kinks that good!*

Under Lupa's knowing, approving stare, Kali ducked her head. Despite her best efforts, she couldn't help laughing.

Whit glanced at her, curious about the joke. Then the transport was lowering and smoothly settling, distracting her attention. Swiftly, the engine purr shifted into a shut-down whine. The murmuring crowd that had been milling and waiting all around the airstrip, gathered together nearer the ship.

The slight, spring breeze blew stronger, carrying the scent of rain. Kali's gaze roamed the cloud cover above, then slowly drifted to the women all around her.

Like herself, most were dressed in rugged work clothing, although many of them were wearing gray warrior uniforms with reserve unit badges proudly displayed. Ranging in age from thirty to sixty, they had all left comfortable homes and careers in other colonies and come to Isis to start over again. Already, these women had accomplished so much here in the ruins, just making the land ready for this new beginning. In another few weeks, most of the utility lines would be operational and entire neighborhoods would be under construction. This contingent of several hundred women would be the heart of the colony, the Founding Mothers of their day.

There was a shushing noise from the ship as a ramp peeled away from the shiny steel side and stretched to the tarmac. Everyone's attention went to the craft's door. The portal slid open and Lilith appeared, with Loy beside her and Arinna following close behind.

Whit called out, "The citizens of Isis welcome you," and the crowd cheered loudly.

At last, Lilith raised a hand and the warrior yells and cheering fell away. "As the local representative of the Seven Leader's Council," Lilith announced, "I have been appointed to initiate the first step in establishing democratic government. Voter registration will now commence at the Isis Cedar House!"

The crowd roared again, then began moving toward the newly repaired road that led to the Cedar House. Meanwhile, Lilith, Loy and Arinna moved down the ramp, followed by a virtual parade of very young women, many of them teenagers.

Greeting Lilith with a hug, Whit nodded at Loy and Arinna. As Lilith left Whit's arms and moved into Kali's, Whit watched the young, excited company of women pouring out of the ship. They were carrying tent kits and packs, yet many were dressed in town clothes hardly suitable for arduous labor or outdoor living. Giving Loy a contemplative look, Whit asked, "What's going on? Are these tourists or colonists?"

Loy merely smiled, then turned and told the youngsters to follow the older women to the Cedar House.

Poised and affable, Arinna answered, "These are colonists, Whit. Loy made a speech in the Artemis marketplace this morning." She waved her hand gracefully at the steady stream of young women disembarking from the transport. "You can see what an inspiration it was. We must have signed up four hundred new voters. There will be at least three more shiploads landing later."

Nearby, burly Lupa Tagliaro gave a snort and scratched her gray head. "And half of them will be gone in a month—once they realize colony-building is raw blisters on your hands and sleeping in a cold tent. *Work*, not heroic adventure," she muttered.

"With respect, Chief Builder," Whit said mildly, eyes still on Loy, "may you be proven wrong. Isis needs the energy and spirit of these young women, as much as it needs the counsel and sagacity of mothers and crones."

Lupa only gave another distrustful snort.

Then, as Whit made introductions all around, Danu Sullivan came down the ramp, the straps of three duffel bags precariously balanced across her shoulders. As she reached their group, Danu began stumbling. Lupa grunted with disgust and walked away. Kali moved quickly, freeing two of the bags from Danu, checking the owner tags on each, and summarily passing duffel bags to Loy and Arinna.

Loy grinned at Kali, obviously amused by the silent reproof in Kali's gesture. Arinna accepted her luggage with a show of good grace, then stepped back and unobserved by the others, scrutinized Kali thoroughly. Sighing her thanks, Danu bent over and became absorbed in searching the contents of her bag. Lilith and Whit turned toward each other, deep in discussion of city design plans.

Temporarily ignored by the others, Kali found herself being openly examined by both Loy and Arinna. With a start of discomfort, Kali realized she was registering Loy's thoughts.

Loy's sexual preoccupation fairly shouted in Kali's mind as the almond shaped eyes slithered over her. This brazen woman was actually creating mental pictures of lovemaking, of what she would do to her if she got the opportunity. A flash of answering body reaction burst through Kali, and she automatically slipped into Elysian female behavior, looking down in confusion. She gave her head a mild shake, exasperated at herself. With annoyance, she focused on banishing Loy's images and found it surprisingly easy to do.

Rallying, further asserting her will, Kali looked into Arinna's eyes. Oddly, the messages of those thoughts were mere wisps—like tendrils of smoke—hinting of something slowly smoldering, that is, as yet, hidden from discovery.

Kali broke her gaze with Arinna, admonishing, *I shouldn't be going around listening in on people like this. I ought to just tell Styx about it and ask her how she controls it.* With a glance at the emptying transport ramp, Kali asked, "Lil, didn't Styx come?"

Lilith heard the disappointment in Kali's voice. She came over and with a motherly stroke through Kali's hair, responded, "As Herstorian, she's updating the Artemis census and voter registration files. We have an election coming up soon ourselves, and a great many young women relocated today."

Shifting her duffel bag to her back, Loy declared, "Let's move along to the Cedar House, then, shall we? There are decisions to make and it's time we got started."

Raising an eyebrow, Lilith remarked, "Loy, you realize, of course, that the Directors are only an advisory group and that your role is to develop policy for the Military Governor to enact."

Loy shot a tense look at Arinna, then replied, "I understood that my role was to assist in directing the rebuilding of Isis."

A hand gently rubbing her own forehead, Lilith clarified, "Martial law is in effect here. The chain of command is specific. Whit is Military Governor, the ranking officer. She will be supervising the warriors stationed here for service on the construction teams, and she will be the ruling authority over all civilians as well.

"You are the fiscal and economic expert who will act as a liaison between the Governor and the community. You and your staff may make recommendations, develop concepts, submit designs and attempt to *influence* decisions." Lilith paused and her dignified demeanor became stern. When she spoke again, her voice was quieter, firmer. "But you are not in authority here. I hope I will not need to remind you again of the chain of command."

"I understand," Loy answered simply, her eyes meeting Lilith's with a cool serenity.

Involuntarily, Kali heard the true reply, which involved a string of furious insults to both Whit and Lilith. With a chill, Kali realized that although Loy knew the chain of command as well as everyone else, she had no intention of adhering to it.

Smoothly, Arinna stepped forward and addressed Lilith, "Loy is bringing her experience as a Boudicca Deputy to this task. Naturally, she will be perceived as a gifted organizer and leader. However, I'm sure Loy is aware of the hierarchy of command here, and will give Governor Whitaker her complete cooperation."

Skeptical, Kali studied Arinna. *Is she just being nice or is she aligning herself with Loy?*

"Thank you, Arinna," Loy murmured. "I could not have put it better." But there was no mistaking, now, by the icy ferocity in her eyes, that Loy was deeply offended.

Lilith gave an accepting nod and then turned to Whit. With a slight, disconcerted bow, Whit extended her arm to Lilith and began the walk to the Cedar house. Lilith knew trouble was afoot.

With Isis as both the stage and the prize, the roles had just been cast. Whether or not everyone played their part, by the rules, remained to be seen.

Lilith quickly grasped Loy's plan. She had arrived in Isis with a constituency, albeit a young one. But most of her followers would be eighteen by the end of the summer and so would be eligible to cast a vote for the Leader of Isis. Once all of Loy's recruits arrived, roughly four hundred voters would be listening to *her* recommendations. Whit, aside from the warriors who were here on assignment and would not be voting, could really only count on the two hundred or so women who had been camping out in Isis, preparing for re-settlement, for over a month now. Whit might be the ranking command, but the majority was already listening to somebody else.

And where does Arinna stand in all this? Lilith wondered. So far, the beautiful Systems Director seemed generous and competent, but had she left Tubman and come all this way solely to help build a new colony?

Behind the rest, Kali fell in step with Danu Sullivan. The redhead clutched a memory chip case awkwardly to her chest as she tried to manage the heavy duffel bag. Reaching for the bag, Kali asked softly, "Need some help?" After a moment's hesitation, Danu handed Kali the bag. By the time Kali grasped it, she had heard a rush of thoughts, the prominent worries of an intense, unsure young architect.

Hoping to avert "hearing" any more of Danu's thoughts, Kali blurted, "Your work—the designs that caused you to be sent here, Whit has shown them to me. They're very good."

Pale blue eyes met Kali's gaze, and Danu nodded gratefully.

Kali stopped walking and Danu paused beside her, feeling the pull on her mind. The blue eyes blinked slowly, losing focus, becoming half-lidded. Then, helplessly, Kali felt herself merging with Danu, sliding into some sort of strange trance.

Gazing at Danu, falling into a blurring, visual sweep, Kali absorbed information—exact measurements, precise calculations, an amazing network of structural stress and support reckonings. These were the dreams of a master architect. Then, all at once Kali found the well-concealed adoration Danu cherished for Whit, and Kali gasped aloud, delighted by pure, idyllic romanticism—the worship of a girl for a mentor.

Danu put a hand out, making a sluggish effort at resisting whatever it was she felt enmeshing her.

Abruptly, Kali stepped away, removing her mind's grip from Danu's, softly apologizing.

Danu's eyes widened with awareness.

"Sorry," Kali mumbled again, anguished by her inability to stop this compulsive rifling through the thoughts of others.

Danu gave a bewildered shake of her head, then they both began walking, hurrying to catch up with the others farther down the road. Yet the glance Danu sent Kali from the corner of her eye was rich with distrust and alarm. And Kali's heart sank, as she realized that this young woman was someone she really liked—and so far she had only succeeded in assaulting her—first physically and now, mentally.

What am I doing? Kali worried frantically. *What on Gaea's sweet earth is happening to me?*

☽ ☽ ☽

The Cedar House came into view, first the white belltower against the darkening sky, then the tumultuous mob of women gathering before the entrance. As Whit walked across the meadow, she swallowed hard, for the scene before her was clearly a disaster. With an apology, Whit disengaged herself from Lilith and set off at a run.

The Cedar House had been chosen as the voter registration site when the population turnout was estimated to be several hundred women. The unexpected arrival of Loy's recruits had already effectively doubled the numbers and what few warriors Whit had appointed to manage crowd control had been overwhelmed. Women were crowding into the Cedar House in a chaotic horde, completely overwhelming the careful preparations Whit had made earlier.

By the time she jogged to a halt, Whit was seething with anger. The throngs of youngsters jostling for position barely noticed her as she passed. They were too busy bellowing for entry at the Cedar House door. There were simply too many of them, and they were not bothering to form a civilized queue in order to register and subsequently receive their land grants and building permits. Instead, these new arrivals were belligerently trying to push ahead of their elders, shouting something about being promised first service, about tents to set up before the rain that was threatening actually began.

Looking behind her, spotting Loy dashing up and entering the chaotic throng, Whit demanded, "What's this about 'first service?' What did you promise them?"

Appearing startled, Loy justified, "They have no shelter yet, Whit, and your people do. And I thought you'd have it set up better than this. I mean...this is awful!"

"You never told me you were bringing colonists with you!" Whit snapped back. "Why didn't you at least use the comline?"

Abruptly, Whit broke off, unwilling to indulge in a blame-fest with Loy. Enraged, she strode into the commotion, elbowing her way into the Cedar House. Within, the furor was, if possible, even worse. Loud and tempestuous women were pressed together in the hallway, pushing toward the Council Room, which couldn't possibly contain all the women attempting to gain entry. Invoking her full status, Whit barked orders, charging the warriors present to evict everybody.

With disappointed, petulant groans and objections, the crowd began to disperse, pushed back outside by the warriors. Whit pushed ahead, into the Council Room, repeating her command, stubbornly, aggressively directing the more quarrelsome settlers toward the main door. Checking the halls and chambers that bordered the Council Room, she found these were also packed with an overflow of women. Whit marched along, shouting "Everyone out!" The warriors came after her, making sure her orders were followed.

And then, Whit came across a youthful group lounging about in Maat's lab, where Whit and Kali had their temporary residence. Youngsters were raiding Kali's knapsack, helping themselves to the fruit Kali customarily kept stashed there. Others were trying to turn on the computer, some of them aimlessly scanning Whit's paperwork, there on the desk. Still others were trading jokes, walking around, and generally complaining about how badly organized this voter registration was turning out to be.

"Out!!" Whit bellowed, infuriated by this invasion, lunging for the closest girl.

The youngsters all began to scramble at once, dodging Whit as she grabbed for them. Lupa Tagliaro, who had followed on Whit's heels, burst into an uncharacteristic fit of laughter, completely overcome by the sight of Whit trying to catch girls who had never moved faster in their lives.

When the last woman was out of the Cedar House, Whit marched to the meadow outside and confronted the entire assembly of over three hundred new settlers. The loud bickering that had been ongoing among the women escalated, even as Whit, gray eyes blazing, slammed the door shut behind her.

"What a *miserable* beginning for a Freeland Colony!" Whit roared.

The tumult quickly subsided into silence.

For an instant, seeing how red-faced angry Whit was, Lilith was tense with apprehension. Kali moved closer to her and they grasped each other's hand, both realizing this was a turning point.

"We are a *community!*" Whit exhorted. "We are dependent upon each other for our welfare, our livelihood, our survival!"

The women all stared back at Whit, most of them still defiantly angry. Some of the faces, however, were becoming sheepish, and some looked slightly mortified.

Standing by herself, off to the side, Loy Yin Chen had removed herself from things and was prudently allowing "the chain of command" to operate. At the front of the crowd, Arinna Sojourner turned and softly reproached someone who was griping under her breath.

Drawing a deep, steadying breath, Whit seemed to struggle to get a grip on her own emotions. Pitching her voice softer, she continued, "We are in the shadow of thousands who died here ten years ago, fighting for liberty, fighting for their very lives."

The women looked around themselves, studying the spring meadow, the fir forest in the distance. They were remembering. The hush became thick with a dawning respect.

And then, making a sincere, inclusive entreaty, Whit asked of them, "Can we not do better than this?"

"We can," a bold youngster called back.

"Sorry, Gov," a woman shouted.

"We won't let you down, again, Whit," rang out from someone in the back of the crowd.

Whit surveyed them all, the gray eyes lingering on individuals, meeting the many pairs of eyes focused on her. Satisfied that she had turned the tide, Whit ordered, "Registrars, please resume your posts!"

A group of twenty older women quickly filed back into the building, obviously pleased to get back to their computer lists and make ready for a more orderly process.

"I ask your patience," Whit requested of the others, "while I give some preliminary directions."

Shifting quietly, the crowd seemed ready, even anxious to comply.

Projecting her voice, Whit announced, "There will be twenty places to register once you are inside the Council Room. We will use a two by two line, which is merely a way to get you beyond the narrow doorways and halls. After you register to vote, you will receive a building permit and choose a lot of land on the colony map, one lot per woman. Remember, some lots have already been designated as communal and will belong to everyone."

The women murmured with excitement.

"Any questions?" Whit asked.

No one responded.

"Then, I'd like to introduce my second in command," Whit announced, "who will be inside the Cedar House, available to address any problems that may arise, later. A reserve warrior and a woman of solid experience, she has offered to return to active duty service for the duration of this reconstruction project. I am pleased to accept her offer."

Loy strode forward, straightening the western string tie that closed the collar of her neat, white shirt, flexing her shoulders against the tight, black leather jacket which accentuated her shoulders. As she passed through the crowd, a wave of whispering began. Loy's expression was, at once, both sardonic and expectant.

Whit glanced at Loy, then returned her attention to the women before her. "My second in command," she repeated, her voice acquiring a steadfast significance, "Captain Lupa Tagliaro."

Loy's sauntering approach to the front of the crowd ended in a surprised stumble. Those near her, who had read her assumption, broke into laughter until Loy whirled on them, glaring.

Waving in response to the applause, Lupa Tagliaro elbowed her way past a group of youngsters and grimly passed through the door of the Cedar House.

The first cold smattering of rain began to fall and women groaned, dropping their packs, hastily digging for slickers and parkas.

Then, her voice softening, Whit concluded, "I would take it as a personal favor if settlers who are already situated helped the newcomers make camp."

"Right, Gov," a voice laughed. "Does that include sharing our blankets?"

The responding laughter seemed to counter the increasingly, large drops of rain. Friends huddled together, sharing soft remarks about who looked interesting in this multitude of roving eyes.

"Okay," Whit grinned. "Now I need a two by two line."

With elaborate calm and courtesy, the women began to assemble in twosomes, gradually forming a line which snaked across the meadow. There was congenial chatter and laughing, now. The rain came down harder, but no one seemed to mind much, for the line moved along steadily. And as each couple passed through the door, Whit greeted them with a handshake and welcomed them to Isis.

Lilith stood with Kali, sheltering beneath the eaves of the Cedar House. "She handled that well," Lilith commented.

Kali nodded. She was hearing unspoken words, knowing somehow that Lilith was anxious, that Lilith knew both Loy and Arinna were going to be not only talented Directors, but accomplished adversaries.

As if on cue, Loy and Arinna walked over to join Lilith and Kali beneath the eaves.

"Lilith, I know the arrangement is temporary," Loy began, "but it really smacks of elitism." She smoothed a hand over her dark, wet hair and glanced at Arinna for support.

Looking distinctly uncomfortable, Arinna turned and studied some women struggling with a tent pack that had fallen open.

Sighing, Loy stubbornly renewed her plea. "Whit and Kali are taking up space in the Cedar House, the only government building in the colony. I've talked to some others about it and the general consensus seems to be that...."

Before Loy could get any further, Kali frowned and interrupted, "We're moving out. We'll be able to manage in the new house, now. There's still some work to be done, but...."

Surprised, Lilith counseled, "That's not necessary."

"We can manage," Kali assured Lilith, who still looked unconvinced.

Relieved, Loy said to Lilith, "Then you won't mind if Arinna and I make use of the quarters Whit and Kali set up in the lab?"

"*I* mind," Kali answered, her voice rising.

Arinna's detachment vanished. She turned to gaze at Kali, her delicate eyebrows arched with surprise.

Confused, Loy sputtered, "You have no authority over who uses that lab."

Lilith opened her mouth to reply, but Kali snapped, "It's my *mother's* lab! *Her* equipment, *her* computer system...."

Loy countered, "The Cedar House super-computer was your mother's?"

"The one in the Council Room is a separate system," Kali asserted. "My mother designed and assembled the computer in the lab. She used it to store her private research."

"Actually, Loy," Lilith explained, "the lab itself is a private workspace that came to be housed in a government facility. Maat never charged Freeland for the magnificent results of her research. Freeland repaid her by providing Maat with ample supplies and the latest in scientific equipment."

With a slight laugh, Loy persisted, "Well, with Maat dead, what harm can come of Arinna and I using the lab?"

"You're not getting in there!" Kali burst out.

Lilith dropped a gentle, cautioning hand on Kali's arm, and Kali took several quick breaths in an effort to control her temper.

Intrigued, Loy regarded Kali. "What a transformation. Little rabbit to big, bad wolf."

"Loy, We have already arranged quarters for you and Arinna." Lilith interjected firmly. "With all these new hands, the hostel will be completed by nightfall. And there are ground floor rooms reserved for each Director. Your room will be small, furnished with a cot, a footlocker, some shelves, and a desk. Meager quarters, but probably more comfortable than what Whit and Kali have made do with throughout the winter."

In a soft, interested voice, Arinna asked, "Is your mother's computer still functional, Kali?"

"It is, and I'm using it to access school courses on the comline," Kali replied, her eyes still on Loy.

Loy gave Kali a sincerely apologetic look. "Well, then, we'll have to ask the Seven Leader's Council to decide who the lab and the computer system belong to...."

Kali had to clench her teeth together to keep from telling this arrogant woman what she thought of her.

As if seeking to relieve the rapidly escalating tension, Arinna asked, "Kali, would you mind showing me your mother's lab? I'm very interested in that sort of thing, you know."

With a tight nod, Kali instantly strode away, and Arinna had to hurry to keep pace with her.

Loy watched them depart, venturing, "Care to gossip a little, Lilith?"

"What do you wish to know?" Lilith answered.

Brushing her short hair back, squeezing rainwater out with her long, thin fingers, Loy asked, "What's this I hear about an accident at the hostel last night?"

Lilith watched Kali pause and talk to Whit at the Cedar House door, before following Arinna over the threshold, out of the rain. With a slight smile, Lilith responded, "You'll have to ask Whit, won't you?"

Glancing away, Loy muttered, "If people are injured during her watch, she's responsible. That's the way of martial law, isn't it?"

Lilith didn't reply.

☾ ☾ ☾

By sunset, the hostel was finished. Settlers had worked in teams throughout the day, completing the third wing and then helping everyone secure some sort of shelter. Those women who had been working at Isis during the past month were assigned a bunk in a two-bunk bedroom. The later arrivals had all set up mountain tents, deciding to stay and camp until more housing could be built.

They ate in shifts, a dinner of whole grain bread and stew in the large meal hall. At approximately nine o'clock, with the long, Pacific Northwest twilight still glowing in the west, the weary settlers came walking across the green meadow to the Isis Cedar House. Whit had called an all-citizens meeting for tonight, but no one had any idea why.

In the meadow before the Cedar House, Danu stood beside Whit, watching warriors manage the orderly seating of hundreds of women. She knew that they were congregating outside the building rather than in it, because there were already too many of them to ever fit within those walls. Nearby, huge, temporary screens had been assembled for this occasion, ready to illustrate whatever technical information Whit wanted to impart during her briefing. Like the others, Danu was gazing at the two large screens, wondering what to expect.

Since Isis had already been attacked and destroyed once before, and since the Elysians responsible for that horror still lurked a half a continent away beneath their electromagnetic shield, Danu speculated that this evening's meeting would probably be a review of strategic self-defense measures.

Whatever the meeting was about, Danu hoped it would begin and conclude quickly. She was having trouble standing straight, and her eyes blinked with weariness. Having lent her skills with a power-hammer to the construction project, Danu was sore and thoroughly exhausted.

After studying her carefully for a moment, Whit commented, "Hope you didn't wear yourself out trying to impress Lupa Tagliaro...."

Danu bent her head. That was exactly what she had been trying to do all afternoon—show the old construction crew forewoman that she knew how to build as well as draw. Unfortunately, Lupa had only glared at her every time their paths crossed.

Ignoring Danu's chagrin, Whit went on. "...because tonight is *your* night. *You'll* have to deal with this mob, not me."

Alarmed, Danu's head snapped up fast. "But—isn't this a battle readiness review?"

"That's tomorrow night. They'll need to see Isis before we ask them to build it—let alone fight for it. And right now, Isis only exists in your designs."

Lupa Tagliaro strode over to them, fuming. "I won't serve as Chief Builder under this infant," she announced, glowering at Danu.

"She has a duty to discharge, same as you and I," Whit returned, meeting the hard stare as it flicked over to her.

"A duty?!" Lupa snapped at Whit. "This infant?!"

"Hey—you haven't even seen the plans," Danu protested, her Irish rising at being so obviously singled out for harassment.

"Well, it doesn't matter what I think, does it? I'm *stuck* with you. You're my *architect*," Lupa retorted, making a pretentious sing-song out of the last word. "I've been building for thirty years without the need of an architect!"

Whit draped an arm around Lupa's broad shoulders and remarked, "Never built a city, I'll bet. Want to see her designs?"

"I don't need to..." Lupa began, but Whit laughed in response and pulled the small super-computer remote from her waist pouch.

Whit called to the crowd, "Want to see why I called this meeting?"

In the waning light, the noisy crowd quickly began to quiet, though Lupa continued a loud commentary on her vast range of experience.

"Want to see what Lupa's raising a fuss about?" Whit fingered the remote, keying in commands to the super-computer located within the Cedar House. On either side of Whit, the two enormous screens began displaying what Danu had spent most of the past winter creating, and Lupa's tirade about impudent university students ended in mid-sentence.

Suddenly self-conscious and terrified, Danu stared down at her boots, wishing she could disappear. She was still not convinced the citizens of Isis, or Whit herself, would like her ideas.

She had spent most of the winter on this work. As soon as she had heard the news that Tomyris Whitaker and Kali Tyler were going to build a house in Isis, her imagination had fired. The colony was opening for settlement—the need for a city would not be far behind. From the start, she had known the importance of keeping the aspect of the new buildings within the comfortable framework of what had once existed in Isis. The city would be as much a living monument as a newly recreated, functioning urban area.

Feverishly, Danu had consulted Maat's old computer documents, working within the parameters of those original city designs. She had based her concepts on the ones that had succeeded for Maat and the first city planners. Yet Danu had also taken chances, created new designs for her additions to the scheme. And the results had been functionally impressive, aesthetically beautiful.

The women in the meadow sat fascinated, thrilled, exclaiming with delighted approval when they saw various buildings in the proposed merchant district that would encircle the marketplace. Undertones of appreciation greeted the extensive layouts of the medical clinic, where the Delphi unit—their means of parthenogenic reproduction—would be entrusted. A few women cheered when they saw the graphic rendition of the many small schools that would be located along a circular stretch of parkland which ringed the inner city. Youngsters and elders alike applauded the newly conceived community theater and sports hall. But the most profound reaction of all greeted the computer graphics illustrating the design of the Leader's House.

The original structure, like much of the city, had been a simple edifice, constructed of pine and granite, only recognizable as a place of significance by the Delphi emblem—a purple six-pointed star with a leaping dolphin in the center. By tradition, this was mounted above the main door. Danu had taken that archetype and embellished it with grandeur. The scale was larger, the cedar shake roof steeply sloped to survive winter snow accumulations. In the government sections of the building, windows spanned entire walls. The eaves of the roof and the large pillars of the porch were adorned with carvings—painted in intricate patterns—ancient symbols of womanhood and matriarchy.

Then came the internal layouts. The women oohed over the wide madrone staircase, elegantly flowing without visible support to the next floor. The muted color tones of the painted walls complemented the hardwood floors and the paneled hallways. There were a succession of office areas—computers fitted flush into desk tops, chairs with keyboard armrests, wallscreens placed for comfortable and private viewing. The crowd's approval grew appreciatively upon the demonstration of wall shelves that rotated into the wall for storage, and were capable of locking away—secure and discreet—all sorts of material. The upstairs living area was spacious, comfortable, yet Spartan and efficient. Freelanders didn't want their rulers living an opulent life of privilege or exorbitant wealth. The quarters struck the desired balance of need, application, and aesthetics.

As the memory chip display concluded and the screens went blank, the crowd began standing up, applauding heartily, and wouldn't stop. Even Lupa gave Danu a grudging grin. As Danu tried to escape, thoroughly embarrassed, Whit intercepted her with an arm about the shoulders and made her stay. A cavalcade of women suddenly had to talk to Danu and Whit, asking questions, delivering advice, and generally pestering the life out of them both.

At one point, as two rather opinionated elders lectured Danu simultaneously, Whit leaned down and whispered in Danu's ear, "Thank the Mother, I think you're the one thing everyone has managed to agree on." The breath in her ear shot a sensation through Danu that left her electrified. Danu closed her eyes, internally reeling.

Then Whit was asking if anyone still needed help with a tent or a campsite. And as Whit moved away, smoothly organizing again, Danu's enamored gaze trailed helplessly after her.

And far at the back of the jabbering women, Loy stood alone, an eyebrow raised, watching.

☾6

*C*hilled and tired, Danu dug a hand in her jeans pocket and wished she had thought to pull a jacket over her blue cotton sweater before leaving the hostel less than an hour ago. She was discovering that, even in summer, it got cold in the mountains when the sun went down. Squinting as she leaned over the papers on her desk, she readjusted the synfuel lamp, but it didn't help much; the finely crafted lines of the blueprint were still hard to read.

It was now mid-June. A month-and-a-half had passed since Beltane and they were nearing the summer solstice. It had been a month-and-a-half of long hours, grueling physical labor, and exhausting mental gymnastics.

Danu was trying to work at her desk in the Command Center, the third building in Isis to be completed after the second hostel for settlers. A small, rough-hewn, pine building situated in the heart of the planned city, the Center provided the Military Governor and her Directors with office space and a conference area. Like Loy, Arinna, and Whit, Danu had her own cubicle, which featured a large desk and a powerful computer. Best of all, each cubicle was private.

For Danu, by nature a solitary soul, six weeks of living in a noisy hostel, enduring gang showers and throngs of women in the meal hall, had made privacy a thing to be cherished.

Hearing the door open, Danu leaned back in her chair and peeked around the corner of the cubicle.

It was about 9:30, but the lasting, rose-gold light of a Northwest summer night highlighted the new arrivals in the doorway. Dressed in the short-waisted gray jacket and loose trousers of a warrior's uniform, Whit carefully lit the synfuel lamp which hung on the wall, then strode into the open area they used as a conference room. Arinna, in a forest-green jumpsuit, and then Loy, in a dark purple pullover and tight black pants, came through the door after her.

Danu was about to call hello and announce her presence, when Whit turned on Loy angrily. "I don't get it." Stabbing a finger toward the blueprints on the table near her, Whit's rich voice went lower as she fought for self-control. "This design has been approved, as is, for weeks. We are scheduled to begin work on the Leader's House tomorrow. Why did you wait until now to make these suggestions?"

Loy began a cool, murmuring reply as she, Whit, and Arinna gathered around the table of blueprints, on the far side of the Command Center.

Slowly, Arinna half-turned, spotting Danu.

Disturbed by Arinna's shrewd scrutiny, Danu leaned over her papers again, pretending she was absorbed in her own work. More than anything else, Danu did not want to be sent away.

The buildings were slowly but surely going up, metamorphosing from dreams and computer graphics into actual structures. And Whit was slowly being transformed in Danu's awestruck perception, too. The image of the mythic Amazon was gradually giving way to a vision of who Whit actually was: a dynamic and strong yet gentle woman who often displayed flashes of the sage stateswoman she might eventually become. Danu found the reality even more attractive than she had found the illusion.

Cautiously, Danu sneaked another glance at the three women. Loy and Whit were bordering on another quarrel and Arinna looked impatient with their increasing inability to get along. Danu noted the flush on Whit's face. In spite of her natural intellect and gift for leadership, Whit was obviously struggling with how to handle a strong-willed adversary, while also rebuilding an entire colony.

Loy finished her quiet reply, shifted her weight from one foot to another.

Whit placed her fists on her hips. "This isn't about the Leader's House, is it, Loy?"

"I'm entitled to voice an opinion," Loy countered, her voice growing hard.

Sighing irritably, Whit shook her head. "I'm a Military Governor, and that does not involve ruling by consensus."

Firmly, Arinna asked, "You're upset with us, Whit. Why?"

Whit faced her. "While both you and Loy are producing quality work—developing future economic prospects and targeting the specific systems needs—you are also consistently stretching your roles, your realms of influence."

Loy interrupted, "I cut costs with those foraging operations and you know it. By utilizing serviceable leftovers from the 20th century—nails, pvc pipe, bags of cement and mortar mix, cinder block, brick, even cans of paint—we saved a fortune in supplies."

In a low voice, Whit returned, "Lupa Tagliaro was supposed to supervise the transport and storage of various materials found in abandoned Seattle and Tacoma warehouses. The foraging operation was already in the works when you rounded up a crew of workers assigned to another detail, and just took off."

"Well how was I to know that?" Loy snapped. "You never tell us anything."

Whit glanced at Arinna, as if asking if she agreed with that remark. Arinna shrugged. Then Whit caught sight of Danu, furtively watching them, and gave a slight nod of greeting.

Loy was renewing her accusations. "Look how you handled that performance review process I tried to institute. I spent all that time, observing the different work crew teams, writing up the groups which were less productive—but you refused to even consider initiating some sort of motivational program!"

Arinna spoke up, "Oh, Loy, for Gaea's sake. I agree with Whit on that one. You *were* operating outside of your province. And a reward and censure procedure? It's archaic. Many of the older women are already over-extending their strength with these long hours and the physical demands of construction work."

Loy sneered, "Whit is just coddling her friends. Most of her supporters are in the older age groups, in case you haven't noticed, Arinna. They've already nominated her for the Leader election."

Grimacing, Whit responded, "The election is months off and completely irrelevant! We have a group of construction frameworks, but no colony." Blowing out a breath of air, exasperated, Whit began to turn away from Loy, but then reconsidered. "While we're on the topic of possible backers," Whit stated, "what's this I hear about you 'helping' some young women, fresh out of Boudicca, to bypass the hostel waiting list? There was a storm of protest from those poor devils still camping in the meadow, because a group of new arrivals moved into our newly completed, second hostel."

Dark eyes narrowed, Loy hissed, "You *didn't* kick my friends out?!"

"I most certainly did. You know the rules—we all secure shelter in order of arrival. At least until the essential business and merchant buildings are finished and we can release some crews for private residence work."

Furious, Loy pulled herself to her full height. "This was a special case! One of those young Boudiccans is an apprentice Healer!"

"Why all the subterfuge over an apprentice?" Arinna asked, looking very perplexed.

"There are nearly seven hundred settlers here and we have only two Healers! That's not nearly enough. Neith's an intern, at the top of her class," Loy spoke vigorously. "Though she *is* very young."

Danu thoughtfully sat back a moment, reflecting. *Over this last month, Loy has fashioned herself as a champion of youth.*

And Danu was beginning to understand the rationale behind this strategy. Pioneering a colony seemed to be particularly attractive to the younger population of Freeland, for the influx of youngsters from every colony in the nation was steadily increasing. And being in such a clear minority, the wise counsel and pertinent experiences of age were being brushed aside, considered unimportant.

Young though she was, Danu couldn't believe some of the infantile concepts her peers in the hostel were considering. Ideas like private cars being the primary mode of transportation, rather than using an electromagnetic rail for public shuttle buses, as in Artemis and Boudica. Ideas like repealing the mandatory reseeding-harvesting ratios Whit had imposed on the Isis Lumber Cooperative. Anyone with a knowledge of herstory knew what environmental horrors grew out of not maintaining an ecological balance. The devastated environment which was their legacy from 20th century America spoke clearly to her. The air and the land were just now beginning to recover from those irreverent ways. And in Elysium, where she heard the practices continued—the sky was yellow with pollution and trees were sparse, except on Reg protected estates.

Danu had begun to fear what might happen if Loy continued to gain popularity among the young settlers and eventually, by the sheer majority of youth, became Leader of Isis.

Undaunted by Loy's diatribe, Whit pressed on, "One last thing. It has come to my attention that you have taken to reviewing Danu's architectural designs for each building, comparing them to Maat's original work and then discussing with Danu 'possible improvements' to her conception."

Arinna glanced over at Danu, and Loy followed her gaze, discovering their audience for the first time.

Whit paused a moment and asserted, "This will stop. The plans have been approved and do not require your improvements."

With relief, Danu listened closely. So far, she had nervously endured Loy's ingratiatingly polite criticism, but she had inwardly chafed against the sessions. Loy insisted on standing so close, on leaning a hand on her shoulder; it rattled her, though she had no clear idea why.

Loy responded to Whit with a dismissive laugh. "Which brings us back to the original topic of this exercise in military dictatorship, doesn't it?" And then Loy began to point at the blueprint of the Leader's House on the table before them, as she targeted what she considered to be flaws.

One by one, Loy made determined appeals for altering this part or that part of the design, and Whit met each one with succinct, clear-headed refusals.

By now, Danu knew well the cadences of Whit's voice, and it seemed of late that the Military Governor was often resorting to this carefully controlled, dispassionate tone with Loy. After six weeks of contention over the entire city plan, Whit seemed entrenched in a detached, stubborn perseverance.

And why not? Danu told herself. Every zoning coordinate, every lot size, every building plan had turned into a frustrating question-and-answer period with Loy. While Loy rarely offered approval, or better yet, alternative suggestions of her own, she daily challenged the work going on in Isis, questioning Whit's decisions before Whit's face and behind Whit's back.

Loy had not finished with her yet. She declared stubbornly, "The Leader's House should be grander, proclaiming the exalted position of the occupant to anyone who visits Isis. We need a palace," Loy smirked at Whit, then let the sarcasm loose. "You are giving us a hut."

Whit glowered at the planning board, then her gray gaze seemed to sear through the blueprints. She opened her mouth, then snapped it shut and said nothing.

Tell her off, Whit! Danu fumed inwardly.

Then Whit lifted her eyes. "Do you have an alternate blueprint?"

Taken aback by the reasonable tone, Loy said nothing.

"Any designs?" Whit prodded expectantly.

Loy retorted, "A design—no, I thought—"

Whit interrupted resignedly, "Then we proceed with what is already on paper. We begin building The Leader's House *tomorrow*, Loy." And with that, Whit rolled up the plans on the table. "Now, if you'll excuse me, I need to get some sleep. We'll have a construction crew and two cranes waiting for us on Cammermeyer Street, just after 6:00 a.m.."

While Loy was still protesting, Whit strode through the door.

Arinna lingered in the room, idly lifting aside several other blueprints on the table.

Shoving her hands in the pockets of her snug, black pants, Loy swung around to gaze at Danu. Instinctively, Danu returned all her attention to the papers on her desk. A moment later, she heard a shuffling step and looked up to find Loy hovering over her.

"I need some blueprints drawn up," Loy stated, her eyes bright, her smile charming.

Unnerved by how close Loy stood to her, Danu merely swallowed.

Amused, Loy studied the sleeping bag rolled up by Danu's desk. "I had heard that you sleep here sometimes. Your dedication is...."

Interrupting, Danu mumbled, "Uh...someone needed my room."

Mildly puzzled for a moment, Loy seemed to give up the effort at conversation. Instead, her eyes moved slowly over Danu.

Behind Loy, Danu heard Arinna's silvery voice explain, "She's the only young one with her own private room. Every Saturday night she gives it up to the more amorous types. You know—lets them have a little rendezvous."

"Oh," Loy replied, then turned and surveyed Arinna.

As Loy turned, Danu could also see the alluring figure bathed in the soft, yellow light of the synfuel lamp by the table. Arinna's hair was shining, her jumpsuit clung to her rounded hips and chest. Standing very still, looking very disapproving, the green eyes met Loy's steady gaze.

"Danu looks exhausted, Loy," Arinna objected, her tone leaving no room for argument. "Have her work on the blueprints you want some other time."

Undecided, Loy stared back down at Danu.

Arinna moved to the door and opened it, then stood there, obviously waiting for Loy to leave with her.

Loy's face half-turned, her cunning eyes never quite reaching to where Arinna stood, slowly moved back to Danu. Bewildered, Danu felt Loy's incredibly focused, expressionless scrutiny.

What is going on? Danu wondered. *Is Loy trying to intimidate me because I've been siding with Whit?* Determinedly, she raised her chin and returned Loy's stare.

And as she looked fully into Loy's eyes, she felt something, almost like a flame flitting across her lower abdomen, except it was at once deep and electric and internal.

Very irritated, Arinna cleared her throat.

With a slight raise of the eyebrow, Loy stepped back, then turned and sauntered to the door. As she passed by Arinna, a low, pleased chuckle floated back to Danu. And then the door closed behind the two older women and Danu was left alone in the Command Center.

Danu sat there, her heart racing. Loy's attention had shaken some sensitive, inner part of her. She suddenly had a vague, though very uncertain suspicion that Loy had planned on getting more from her than blueprints.

€ € €

Two days later, on Monday, Kali stood on the second-story frame of a three-story building, dressed in her worn, khaki pants and a white T-shirt. Below her, illuminated in the glaring June afternoon sunshine, was the merchants' district. The square that would be the marketplace was filled with supplies and women bustling about. Trucks were parked, off-loading boards, bricks, pre-fab concrete-vinyl posts. All around her, work crews were crawling over multiple construction sites, slowly assembling buildings to stand alongside those already nearly finished.

Taking another sip of honey-water from her canteen, Kali noticed Alborak, below. The youthful, sewage utility forewoman, was pointing at her and with a mocking severity, signing, *Get to work!*

Laughing, Kali finished her break and turned back to her assigned task. She loved to work, and Albie knew it.

Sometime during the past two months, she had grown used to this regime of self-discipline. Her life had a pattern: a morning run, eight hours of grueling, voluntary labor in the streets of Isis, followed by a quick dinner with Whit in the meal hall, and then four hours of school sessions on the computer in her mother's lab. Lately, Arinna had taken to stopping by the lab while Kali was accessing her courses on the comline. With Arinna as her personal tutor, Kali found she could concentrate on the material even when she was bleary-eyed with fatigue.

Each day, Kali assembled the pipes and enzyme units that were built into each structure for sewage disposal. Gradually, Kali's work had become quick and efficient, and though the work was exhausting, she relished the constant physical demands of the job.

Following Albie's advice, she leaned the thick section of three-inch plastic pipe on her shoulder. She began lifting the weight slowly with the power of her leg muscles. Carefully she edged it forward, positioning it against the waiting edge of the pipe below. With her hands she began pushing up the heavy tube, wincing at the protesting dull pain from the scar tissue that ran across her shoulder—the result of a sword wound. In a moment she had the pipe in place, fitted into the pipe jutting through the floor. Quickly, she curled the attaching support around the plastic width. She fastened the support band into the wall and stood back, examining the juncture of the pipes.

Unconsciously, her hand went to her sore shoulder, rubbing, as she checked the seal. Satisfied that it was tight, she hooked up the tubing for the remainder of the enzyme unit that would empty into this pipe.

When fully operational, raw sewage would be held in the containment chamber and treated by timed secretions of enzymes, until the batch reached a two-gallon proportion. When the weight of the batch triggered download, waste would be released and pumped by underground pipe to the final treatment facility, deep in the fir forest.

Eventually, Kali knew the processed eco-fertilizer would be used as a nutrient to help re-seed vast, eroded gaps in the mountain forests. "Clear-cutting," that was what 20th century lumbermen had termed their practice of cutting down every single tree and shrub, and then leaving miles of exposed soil to blow or wash away. Succeeding generations of Freelanders called the practice sheer lunacy, and tried to do all they could to repair the damage.

As Kali finished connecting her last unit, above the general din of construction machinery, she heard her name being called. She wiped her hands on her khakis, stepped closer to the open edge of the frame and searched the street two stories below.

Seeing she had Kali's attention, Lupa pointed at Whit, who was already climbing the ladder, obviously on her way up to see her. Standing near Lupa, Danu was trying to concentrate on her clipboard, while Loy hovered at Danu's elbow, making remarks. Danu looked confused; she kept glancing at Loy and edging subtly away. And each time Danu moved away, Loy closed the space, smiling and still talking.

Just like Branwen used to do with me, Kali thought, recognizing the elaborately innocent tease. She felt a sudden, fierce need to shield Danu from Loy.

Then, farther away, Kali noticed Arinna Sojourner. The beautiful Systems Director was talking with a group of women, helping them unload lengths of sewage pipe from a truck. With admiration, Kali watched Arinna and a well-muscled partner smoothly lift the pipe from the flatbed truck, balance it, lower it, then deposit the heavy pipe on the ground. Arinna was obviously much stronger than she looked. Beside them, another woman rolled the pipe onto a steel tray. Using a cable, a crane would eventually carry the tray and a load of pipe to the next floor of this building, for Kali to assemble.

Kali retreated from the edge as Whit stepped off the ladder and advanced towards her, looking incredibly fit in her gray uniform shirt, with rolled up sleeves, and loose, gray trousers. Glancing around, Whit demanded, "We alone up here?" She didn't wait for an answer before catching Kali up in a gently seductive hug and kiss.

Laughing through the kiss, Kali pushed her back. "Would it matter? Mother, the longer and harder you work, the sexier you get. Governing agrees with you!"

Whit almost frowned, distracted momentarily, wondering if loving to be in charge of things was as dangerous as it sounded, but then Kali had a hand in her hair, pulling her head down, kissing her. Lost in the compounding passion of that kiss, Whit's fingers spread over Kali's slim buttocks, pulling her in tighter. In a calculated move, Whit pressed her thigh between Kali's legs. The slight moan Kali gave told Whit that the lead in this had shifted.

"Rated X I think it used to be called," a voice from behind them rang out.

Startled, Kali jolted out of Whit's grasp.

Whit gave a soft curse and swung around just as Loy stepped away from the ladder.

"Not much work getting done up here, I see," Loy continued, as she placed her hands on her hips.

"I'm finished," Kali defended, somewhat breathlessly.

Loy laughed sardonically, "I'll bet you are," then appraised Whit. "Is this what you meant by 'getting a closer look' at the structure?" A smile accompanied the words, yet there was more malice than humor in her cold, dark eyes.

"I'm saying hello to my partner," Whit returned, a stubborn steely glint leaping into her eyes. "I'm sorry if that turns you into a jealous fool."

Coolly, Loy came toward them, "Jealous? And just who am I supposed to be jealous of?"

Whit countered sharply, "You tell me! The way you leer at both Kali and myself, it's really rather hard to tell!"

With a harsh, derisive laugh, Loy sent her eyes around the bare wooden frame that surrounded them. "Yes, I do have a habit of leering. But don't worry, I'm harmless."

Thoroughly irritated, Whit took Kali's hand and pulled her toward the ladder. Loy ambled around the bare second story, making a show of checking the sewage piping Kali had just assembled.

Whit whispered in Kali's ear, "She's brought construction to a halt at the Leader's House. She's produced documents showing old methane lines under that area, lines we never knew were there. They're on no plans from Maat's time that I've ever seen, but, according to Loy, we're in danger of tapping into an old pocket of gas and causing an explosion." Giving a soft, disgruntled sigh, Whit shook her head.

Kali knew by the edge in the husky tone that Whit was much more upset about this delay than she was saying.

"So, now," Whit continued, "Loy has ordered Danu to draw up a new set of blueprints." Whit sent a hand through her hair. "It's all politics, of course! I've just about had it with her!"

Across the floor, Loy was examining Kali's work. "Not bad, considering you're barely literate."

Blushing, humbled, Kali turned away from her.

Loy chuckled, "But then, you're still just a good-looking Elysian peasant, aren't you?"

Furious, Whit took a threatening step toward Kali's tormentor. Quickly stopping her, Kali glanced back at Loy, then whispered, "She's not worth it. Just watch out for Danu, Whit."

"Danu?" Whit looked blank.

Kali finished with, "She has no defenses for a heartbreaking bitch like Loy."

A platform-tray of sewage piping came dangling into sight as it cleared the second floor. The crane was bringing in supplies for the next floor and Kali clambered onto the ladder, scrambling to the third story to maneuver the load to a landing platform there. Leaving Loy alone on the second floor, Whit followed, then assisted her, pulling the tray in and unfastening the cables. When they were finished, Kali leaned out over the edge of the building, signalling the crane operator below. The cable began cranking back, leaving them with the tray of pipe.

Kali was already pulling lengths of pipe from the load, wearing that preoccupied look. Giving her a quick kiss on the cheek, Whit climbed back on the ladder. "See you tonight," Whit called, then softly teased, "What will it take to convince you to take a break from your studies and spend the evening with me rather than the computer?"

Kali sent her a sheepish grin, going scarlet again. "Not much."

Whit descended the ladder, thoroughly dazzled by the love in Kali's eyes. By the time she reached the bottom and hopped off, Whit had decided for the millionth time that Lilith had been brilliant when she had conspired to leave Whit alone with Kali in a fragrant autumn meadow, last year.

As soon as Whit joined them, Lupa Tagliaro got her involved in a dispute with Danu over the external designs on the building across the street. Behind Lupa's back, Danu rolled her eyes at Whit, then quickly ran a single finger across her throat and stuck her tongue out. Whit burst into laughter and Lupa stared at her, puzzled, then whirled on Danu. The redhead gave Lupa an innocent look and began leading the way across the congested square.

About a half hour later, Loy had still not shown up and Whit was standing with Arinna, listening to Lupa's demands for efficiency of design. Arinna was checking the blueprint Lupa held, her green eyes darting probingly over the sheet.

"We need speed," Lupa insisted, "or early autumn snows may catch us before the really necessary parts of town are constructed. Frills can wait for later years, when there is time for attention to details." Annoyed, Danu interrupted, pointing out that the "frill" was fundamental to the design—actually determining how the outside walls intersected.

Suddenly, there was a thunderous blast, the detonation more of a blow to their ears than a sound, and then the noise of wood bending, groaning, cracking. Women's voices raised in screams as the building across the square—the building where Whit had just left Kali—came shuddering down in a surging swirl of dust.

For an instant, Whit stood there, disbelieving. And then with a feeble cry, she was dashing across the square. Nearly blinded by the thick wave of billowing dust, she pushed her way through coughing women, her single thought a frenzied repetition. *Find her! Find her!*

Frantically, she was scrambling into the debris, climbing over boards still rocking with the momentum of the building's collapse. Wiping her eyes, impatient with her tears, she shouted Kali's name over and over. As she was digging, tossing planks aside, she was dimly aware that Danu was a short distance away, wide-eyed and searching the broken remains with a crazed panic.

"Here!" Danu shrieked, trying to lift a broad section of pine, part of the back wall.

Sprawled below a tilted segment of pipe, Whit spotted Kali's still figure. With all her might, Whit took hold of the wall and helped Danu shove its heavy weight from the length of plastic pipe. Luckily, it had protected Kali from the worst of the falling foundation. Then Whit was diving below the angled pipe, heedless of Danu's plea to be careful. She climbed into the shallow pit in the rubble, calling Kali's name.

There was no response.

Whit made herself ignore her rising dread, the tightness clenching down on her throat. Quickly, she did a vital signs check. *A pulse—she's alive!* Then Whit fought to calm her trembling hands, exploring the lithe body gently, feeling for fractures. As Whit came over the ribs, a fragment of pipe about the size of a palm computer dislodged from Kali's shirt. Whit narrowed her eyes at the fine, dark powder on the outside of the plastic. Quickly she pulled a bandanna from her back pocket, dropped the pipe into the cloth, wrapped and then pocketed it for later examination.

With a groan, Kali's brown eyes fluttered open.

"Danu! Get a Healer!" Whit ordered.

There was a scattering of boards as Danu clambered off on the mission. Whit leaned closer to Kali, wiping the dust from her pale face, murmuring comforting words, though she scarcely knew what she said. Kali stared uncomprehendingly at her, then looked around herself with solemn puzzlement.

Somewhere in the distance, Whit heard Lupa demanding, "What the hell happened?! Harrowing Hecate, how many were in there?"

"It was lunch. We were all by the meal wagon," a youngish voice returned. "But I think Kali and Loy were...."

Another voice interrupted, shouting, "Here's Loy, under the ladder. We need help! Hurry!"

With a rush of curiosity, Kali attempted to sit up. "Don't move," Whit urged, just as Kali clamped a hand across her middle and gasped. Sinking back, obviously in pain, Kali made a pitiful, child-like noise. "Hurts to breathe," she whispered.

"Alright, Kal," Whit said soothingly, stroking the loose, golden hair back from her perspiring face. "Lie still, now."

"What happened?" Kali moaned softly.

"I don't know," Whit admitted.

Footsteps clomped over the broken wood above her and Whit looked up expecting to see Danu and the Healer. Instead, she saw Loy, her knees displaying terrible bloody gashes through the tears in her bodysuit.

"It had to be a methane explosion," Loy stated, grim-faced.

"We'll figure that out, later, okay?" Whit answered. "I'm getting nervous. I want Kali out of here."

Danu appeared then, introducing an apprentice Healer, a young African woman named Neith. Whit climbed out and the short teenager easily maneuvered herself into the small space between Kali and the pipe, dispatching her duties with a brisk sureness. As Neith's small, dark-brown hands felt about Kali's ribs, Kali inhaled sharply and attempted to roll away. Neith pulled a somascanometer from her med-pak and then used the hand-held computer to examine Kali's entire torso.

"Her ribs took a pounding, but no breaks—thank Gaea," Neith pronounced. "She'll have plenty of bruises, though."

Relieved, Whit asked, "Can we move her?"

"I'll help you," Neith volunteered.

"No, look after Loy," Whit responded. "And thanks!"

Neith climbed out of the space and gestured to Loy to join her in the square below.

Neith slipped out and Whit scrunched her way back into the tight pocket of rubble next to Kali. Squatting, Whit gripped Kali's upper torso and proceeded to haul her out from under the pipe. Stoically enduring the jostling, Kali gritted her teeth until Whit nearly had her to the surface of the wreckage. Then, as Whit shifted her grip, a slight pressure against Kali's tender side sent her into a delirium of pain.

Kali heard herself gasping, crying, and then Neith was jabbing a needle into her arm. When the drug hit, everything, even Whit's soothing voice in her ear, faded away.

☾7

T he next day, the settlers of Isis all gathered together in the merchants' district. For late June, the weather was crisp, though the bright, early morning sunshine shone down on the agitated population as they listened to the burly Chief of Security, Captain Fea Greenberg. In charge of investigating yesterday's blast, Fea delivered her findings in a hasty monotone, tugging all the while on the sleeves of her gray warrior uniform. As she finished, she glanced at Loy, who was standing nearby, for approval.

Loy nodded, as if quietly satisfied.

Whit had listened to the report with a mute suspicion, but it was the interaction with Loy at the end that solidified her misgivings. *Is Loy tampering with this report?*

Attempting to conclude her findings with hard evidence, Captain Greenberg produced a blackened, splintered pipe, calling it "proof" of a methane leak from undiscovered sewage lines.

Lupa Tagliaro stepped forward, pointing at the pipe and objecting hotly. "That's only proof of an explosive material present in the pipe!"

Greenberg stared at the Deputy Governor, clearly not following. "Exactly," the security officer stated, her brow furrowing. "There are probably old utility tubes under this sector, long unused, yet still trapping gas. Something—maybe all the vibration—opened this particular pocket, released the gas, which must have penetrated a gap in the seal of the new pipe." Snaking a large hand through the air, Fea began to illustrate her idea. "The methane traveled up the pipe, into the construction framework, and accumulated there." As if this settled matters, she concluded, "It blew out the pipe in the floor right below where Kali was working."

Sputtering, Lupa bellowed, "Oh for.... Is that your report? That's bogus nonsense!" She whirled on the other settlers, demanding, "How did a sealed pipe get methane in it?"

The crowd of women all stirred with anxiety. Someone called, "Yes, how?" Another woman shouted, "We want facts—not conjecture!"

They seemed about to summarily reject Captain Greenberg's report when Arinna Sojourner stepped forward and seemed to smooth the more unruly ones with a wave of her hand. "Come, now," Arinna pleaded, "let's not panic or jump to conclusions."

Whit narrowed her eyes. All around her, the angry, dissatisfied women who had been muttering to themselves only a moment ago, were gentled like so many high-strung fillies under the stroke of their favorite groom. Whit, too, felt almost unable to resist the soothing persuasion of Arinna's silvery voice. For the first time, Whit realized how influential her Systems Director had become.

In a soothing voice, Arinna gravely reasoned, "Captain Greenberg is offering us a very rational explanation. Let's give the information time to sink in."

The sole exception to the effects of Arinna's mesmerizing aura of serenity seemed to be Lupa. Snarling, she grabbed the scorched pipe section out of Captain Greenberg's big hand. "Has this been chemically tested?" Lupa barked.

Loy smoothly intervened. "Just after the blast, yesterday, Captain Greenberg took the pipe fragment over to the sewage treatment facility, where the eco-systems engineers have set up a field laboratory. Tell us, Captain Greenberg—what did the testing reveal?"

Glancing nervously at Lupa, Fea replied, "Extensive testing revealed the presence of high levels of carbon—no doubt the by-product of incomplete combustion of the methane."

Clapping a hand over her eyes, Lupa growled, "Oh for the love of Hera."

"Meanwhile, Whit," Arinna said, turning toward the silent, watchful Military Governor, "perhaps we need to monitor this area for gas emissions."

"Already done," Whit answered, indicating a small box featuring gauges and a large light. "There will be methane sensors placed around every construction site. The sensor will emit a clear alarm and set the light off, giving us time to evacuate."

"Whit," Lupa yelled, "you know it wasn't any damned gas that blew that building up!"

"Then what was it?" Loy asked calmly. She walked stiffly closer to Lupa, reminding everyone of the injury she had suffered to her legs. "Arinna and I tried to warn you and Whit! We had to *beg* you to stop working over at the Leader's House site!"

"It can't be a methane leak," Lupa insisted, her stout form trembling with fury. "Whit is *obsessed* with detail. The original plans we got from the Agro-Center show Isis exactly as it was built! There are no overlooked old sewage pipes in this colony!"

Baffled, Fea stared at Lupa. She motioned at the collapsed building framework. "Then how do you explain this?"

Whit glared at Lupa and shook her head, but Lupa ignored her.

"Sabotage," the elder hissed.

And in the summer sunshine, the settlers all turned to each other, aghast. The meeting dissolved into anarchy as everyone began talking at once.

☾ ☾ ☾

That same morning, Kali was at home, relegated by Neith's medical directive to spend the entire day in bed. Feeling restless and irritable at being ordered about like a child, Kali still could not actually get out of bed by herself. She ached from head to foot and became a gasping, moaning wretch every time she tried to sit up.

And then the sun rose enough to send its summer glory through the skylight above the bed. The button controlling the skylight shield was on the wall nearby, but Kali had already tried stretching to reach it twice and had gotten nothing but a blast of excruciating pain for her efforts. Now, she was no longer sure which was worse—enduring the bright sunlight in her eyes, or struggling again to reach the shield control.

Through the open door, someone—Kali couldn't see who, for the light in her eyes—came into the room. "Need anything?"

"Yes!" Kali nearly shouted, exasperated and squinting. "Shutter this skylight!"

The woman moved closer and Kali recognized Cimbri, looking vibrant and beautiful in a pastel green T-shirt and a pair of skin tight bodyshorts. "Gaea, you're starting to sound like Whit!" Cimbri joked.

Kali laughed, somewhat abashed at herself. "Mother forbid!"

Cimbri pushed the button Kali pointed to and a dark plexiglass panel slid over the broad skylight in the vaulted ceiling. Leaning over Kali, pulling the covers back, Cimbri began unbuttoning Kali's nightshirt with a peremptory briskness.

Kali yelped. "Wait—don't!" She ended up grabbing Cimbri's hands.

"Still the modest maid!" The dark-skinned Healer laughed. "I can't believe it! And after all this time getting wild with Tomyris!"

"Neith wrapped my ribs this morning," Kali reasoned, though the defense sounded weak even to her own ears.

"Neith is a third-year apprentice," Cimbri stated, resuming her ministrations. "And I am your friend who has come all the way from Artemis to check on you. Besides, you know who sent me."

Ceasing the resistance, Kali breathed, "Lilith." Then, missing the woman who had helped raise her, Kali wondered why Lilith hadn't come herself.

Opening the nightshirt, Cimbri gently unwrapped the bandage, then began palpating Kali's aching left side. When Kali involuntarily rolled away, moaning, Cimbri fished a somascanometer from her waist pouch and examined the area thoroughly. Again, her fingers lingered on the large navy-blue bruises all along Kali's left side. Kali broke out in a fine sweat as she tried to keep still and ignore the pain. At last, Cimbri slipped the palm-held computer away and began re-wrapping the bandage.

"You're incredibly lucky," Cimbri murmured.

Kali nodded, clenching her teeth, blinking the tears back.

"Don't you cry, yet, girl?" Cimbri demanded softly. "What exactly happened in Elysium that left you unable to cry when you hurt?"

Memory flashed, then slammed through Kali's brain, displacing the bedroom, Cimbri, even the throbbing ribs.

She was fourteen, somehow back in that cold, dimly lit cell deep within the confines of the Chicago prison. Three men in Regulator uniforms surrounded her as she stood there, naked and trembling. Her own gray warrior's uniform was on the floor at her feet, shredded by the knives the men had used to rip the clothing from her slim, adolescent body moments before.

They were touching her, stroking her with incessant, insidious caresses. Simultaneously, the Regs were cursing her, calling her names, names she had never heard before, yet by their intonations she knew the names were insults.

The interrogation had gone beyond trying to make her talk. She knew they could care less, now, about how the Bordergates worked, or how the invisible electromagnetic shield over Elysium was controlled. Once they had cut away her clothes, they had lost interest in any military secrets she could ever have told them. Now, they were only interested in her submission.

She was terrified, yet, she told herself over and over that this was all they could do—touch her. The Tribune had claimed her as his virgin. In Elysium, the AIDS Genital Herpes plague still raged; her virginity made her a prize. Raping her would have meant a death penalty, and these men knew it. She told herself to endure, to stay defiantly silent, to betray no fear.

The first blow fell across her back and caught her by surprise; the second knocked her to her knees. She stayed there, frozen, grasping at her panic before it escaped.

"Freeland Dyke! A real woman cries!" one Regulator sneered.

"Maybe we'll have to teach her to cry!" another one taunted, then followed through with a savage right fist. She saw it coming and made a sloppy, last-second dodge.

Steeling her will, she tried to keep her balance against the barrage of punches, tried to regain her footing and at least get off a counterstrike. Then, suddenly, she was on the chill linoleum floor, curling into a ball, trying to go limp against the kicking. *Don't cry*, she exhorted herself. *They want you to cry—don't!* And then, before she could determine if the moisture she felt on her face was tears or blood, the black oblivion descended.

"Kali." Someone was wiping tears from her face. "It's over."

She came back with a gasp for air. Their magnificent new bedroom surrounded her, and Cimbri was beside her on the edge of the bed. A tender hand wiped the tears from Kali's face.

"Mind bond," Cimbri whispered, crying openly. "Just like last autumn, when you remembered the day Isis fell and those vivid mind-pictures invaded the senses of everyone near you."

Trying to stop the sobs, Kali bent her head, attempting to hide her fear behind a curtain of blonde hair.

"You took me with you," Cimbri told her, her voice quavering as she realized, yet again, how horrifying Kali's captivity in Elysium had been. "I don't know how, but I was there, feeling what you felt, drowning in terror and pain." She finished with a whisper. "No wonder you bury those memories."

Pulling her into a comforting hug, Cimbri simply held her until the shaking subsided. It took a while. Kali allowed herself to breathe in the cinnamon, spicy scent of Cimbri, luxuriating in the peace. Then, gradually recovering, Kali pulled back, out of Cimbri's arms.

"Does that happen often?" Cimbri inquired, pushing Kali's hair aside and hooking it behind an ear.

"No," Kali whispered.

Frowning, Cimbri prompted, "It's a psychic episode, you know. You ought to discuss this with Styx."

"She's hard to get a hold of these days," Kali grumbled, knowing she was the one evading contact.

"Lilith says you asked after Styx on Beltane Day, and since then you've only left messages on their comline recorder."

"They seem so busy," Kali responded lamely. "I...guess I didn't want to be a bother."

"The Artemis elections are six weeks away," Cimbri reminded her firmly. "Styx has been helping Lilith get organized. Remember, Lilith is retiring next month—she has major projects to tie up, or at least document for the next Leader. And she's lived in that house on the hill for fifteen years. Packing up and moving her things to Styx's warehouse is turning their lives upside down. Even so, Styx would make time for you."

Trying to restrain her anguish, Kali sighed. She began wiping her face on the sleeve of her nightshirt.

You're not telling me something, Cimbri accused silently.

"There's nothing to tell," Kali answered, too upset to realize that Cimbri's lips never moved.

Sweet Gaea! A telepath, too!

Jerking her head up, Kali found Cimbri staring at her, astounded.

❲ ❲ ❲

By noon, Whit was in Artemis, disembarking from the shuttle and borrowing a bicycle for a fast ride through the city to the Leader's House. When she dismounted and leaned the bike against the old granite house, she had to weave her way around the movers to get into the house. Strong young women were carrying crates and boxes to a truck parked nearby, and for the first time, Whit realized how close to ending Lilith's reign had come.

Once inside, Whit sat down at the kitchen table, less interested in the lunch Lilith set before her than in Lilith's reaction to the report Whit had filed last night. The slender, silver-haired elder stalked about the kitchen, tense and anxious. Whit restlessly pushed the salad around on the glass plate.

"You're sure Kali's alright?" Lilith persisted. Her lovely face was flushed with emotion. She repeatedly smoothed the front of her turquoise suit jacket. "Sometimes after a general body trauma, there's a shaky period for roughly twenty-four hours, where the body doesn't adjust, goes into delayed shock...."

"Neith is young but she's very good, Lilith," Whit said, defending the apprentice who had spent last night sleepless, in a chair by the bed, monitoring Kali. Whit, in another chair nearby, had started off the evening wide awake and anxious, but after accepting a cup of brew from Neith just after ten o'clock, she had fallen into a deep and dreamless sleep. Whit half-suspected that Neith had sedated her.

Drawing herself up to her full height, Lilith seemed to be striving to appear dignified. "I'm not fussing, Whit. She's...you're *both* like daughters to me, and I worry. I gave orders for Cimbri to be flown out to Isis in the Swallow—just to put my mind at rest."

Spearing a large, hydroponically grown piece of broccoli with her fork, Whit returned, dryly, "What? You let someone else fly your tilt-rotor?"

Lilith grinned at the tease. "Though your dramatic arrival for the Council Session last month is quickly becoming the stuff of legend, many of the more conservative types in town have still not recovered from your appropriation of the Swallow for a 'non-medical' emergency." Lilith fixed Whit with a steady look. "You will not have the loan of my Swallow again," she paused, then stated, "However, you *have* greatly enhanced your reputation as an impetuous Amazon warrior."

Whit laughed.

Watching Whit eat, Lilith remarked, "I have enjoyed the privilege of having my own aircraft. It will be hard to give up, like this house."

"Will you miss being Leader?"

"Not like I would have missed Kali," Lilith confessed. "After she came back from Elysium and I finally understood who she was...." Lilith stopped and swallowed hard, unable to go on for a few minutes. "I'd go mad if anything happened to her, Whit." Dabbing at tears with a napkin, she went on, "Kali was conceived out of love. Maat and I *wanted* this child—*loved* this child."

Understanding completely, Whit stated, "I'm surprised you didn't drop everything and fly out there yourself."

"I would have, but...once I confirmed the research you asked me to compile last week, I thought it was essential to meet where there's no chance we'll be overheard, electronically or otherwise. I had this room checked moments before you arrived. It's safe to talk here."

"So," Whit sighed, not at all happy with Lilith's implications. "I was right."

"Yes," Lilith came and sat opposite Whit, folding her graceful hands together. "Someone accessed the original plans Maat stored in the Agro-Center Archives years ago, and altered the utility data. The specific material altered has to do with the sewage tubing beneath the merchants' sector and the Leader's House. The DNA trace revealed nothing, since the unit utilized was a library computer, able to be used without keying in a DNA lock. Anyone could have made the changes involved."

"But it wasn't just anyone," Whit commented. "It was someone who had something to gain from creating misleading evidence. What about the scrap of pipe I sent in with Alborak on last night's shuttle?"

"I tested it myself," Lilith replied, her voice cautiously low. "You were right. The pipe absorbed a fine residue of chemical waste upon detonation. In my judgement, a plastic explosive was used. The blast had nothing to do with methane gas and it seems to be no accident."

Seething, shoving the plate away from her, Whit balled her hands into fists. She sat there trembling for several seconds, then snapped, "Kali could have died! For what? For an election?!"

"Are you making an accusation Whit?" Lilith asked, her piercing blue eyes holding Whit's, unrelenting.

There was a long silence as Whit hesitated. "No," Whit finally retorted. "Lupa lost her temper at the town meeting this morning and called the blast 'sabotage.' As apt as the name may be, we still have no clear motive, no actual witnesses. I have only suspicions—horrible suspicions." Raking her hair with a trembling hand, Whit muttered a curse, totally frustrated.

Lilith leaned forward and placed a comforting hand on her shoulder. "Can you get Kali out of there? She seems to have become a target."

With a humorless laugh, Whit countered, "Do you honestly think I can make her go?"

Silently, Lilith conceded the point. Then she demanded, "You think it's Loy, don't you?"

Whit gave Lilith a long look and said nothing. When she finally stood up to go, she pulled Lilith into a solid, emotional hug, then stepped away, heading for the front entrance.

Lilith pursued her into the hall. "Is it a guess? Do you have circumstantial evidence or hard facts? It will have to be irrefutable evidence, you know."

As Whit went into the street, her resonant voice floated back to Lilith, as she barked, "I know. Believe me, I *know*."

☾ ☾ ☾

The late afternoon sunlight shone through the little window of the Command Center, glimmering on Danu's coppery hair. Leaning against the table, Loy watched as Danu concentrated on the wall screen. The young woman was busily entering coordinates into the computer. Dutifully, Danu was making the changes Loy had demanded of her, entering specified additions and creating an experimental graphic design of the Leader's House. But it was obvious that the girl didn't want to be here. In fact, Danu had only agreed to come and try this because Whit had flown to Isis to consult with Lilith. The girl was at loose ends without Tomyris Whitaker's heels to chase after.

As a wall on the Leader's House was re-positioned on the blueprint, expanding the upstairs living quarters, a red light began flashing on the diagram. Loy frowned at the wall-screen, perplexed. "What's that light mean?"

"Excess stress. The house would collapse," Danu replied. Her fingers were moving swiftly over the keyboards in the armrests of the compu-chair. She made some sort of adjustment, and the light went off.

"What did you do to fix it?" Loy asked softly, but she had already lost interest in the design on the wall screen. She had decided it was time to make her move.

"I increased the base dimensions. The whole building will have to be...." Danu stopped as Loy suddenly stood before her, blocking the wall-screen from view. Slowly, Loy leaned down toward her and Danu inhaled audibly.

Hovering there, pausing to give the girl time to flee if she really wanted to, Loy saw the battle in Danu's sky-blue eyes. She wanted to run, and just as badly she wanted to know what Loy intended. She was so young, so innocent, this girl. There were so many emotions on that rosy freckled face, so many responses hinting at what Loy longed to awaken in her.

After all, that was why Loy loved the girls—there was nothing like bringing a young one to orgasm and knowing you were the first to see that look of exquisite abandon on her face. It was thrilling to hold a girl's churning body, to unleash the carnal juices and plunge her into full womanhood. Being the first to take Danu, that was what Loy had been contemplating for weeks now.

At last, the nervous blue eyes ceased darting about and Danu stared into Loy's eyes, riveted. Prolonging the moment, Loy leaned closer, watching Danu's erratic breathing almost imperceptibly speed up. Softly, gently, Loy gave her a maiden aunt kiss. It was always best to let the young ones set the pace, until they were thoroughly ensnared in passion, and craved being controlled. Touching the girl's cheek, Loy continued to give her soft, harmless, reassuring little kisses. Danu seemed to relax. Her ramrod posture gradually slackened and she began following Loy's lips, moving with Loy as she shifted position.

With a smooth proficiency, Loy pulled the surprised girl from the chair, into her arms. Now, holding the slender, youthful curves tight against her, Loy really kissed her. Danu's stiff reserve faltered a little more, allowing Loy's tongue to dance in and entwine with her own. Carefully, Loy stroked Danu's sides, back, arms, until Danu was shivering, fully igniting.

Loy gave up her own control and the kiss became hard, torrid. Danu went limp, yielding with consent. Their breathing became ragged, as Loy discovered that Danu could kiss exceedingly well. Amazed, as usual, by how much these young ones empowered her, Loy's hands were moving with a terrible certainty, all over the girl. She pulled the black, cotton T-shirt from its anchor in the belted trousers, determined to get to skin.

Breathing hard, Danu jerked away, protesting, "No!"

With a knowing smile, Loy let her go. Patience, that was all that was required.

They were standing about two feet apart, still staring at each other, when the door of the Command Center opened. In the doorway, Arinna Sojourner delayed her entrance regally, her silky, dark hair lifting in the breeze. Behind her, gray-headed Lupa Tagliaro folded her arms and looked away, muttering to herself.

"I think we're finished for today, Danu," Loy said calmly.

Danu scampered for the door, tripping herself and nearly falling in her haste. Arinna stepped aside, allowing her to pass, and then Lupa Tagliaro caught Danu's arm. "Got some supply questions to discuss with you," Lupa growled, then dragged her off down the street. Arinna stepped inside and quietly closed the door.

"Tuck your shirt in," Lupa ordered. As Danu fumbled to obey her, Lupa gave her a rough shake. "What's the matter with you?! I thought you had more sense than to fall prey to that one."

Gulping, almost ready to burst into tears, Danu couldn't answer. Lupa let her go with a disgusted push. They walked along in silence for several minutes.

At last, Lupa told her, "Whit's down at the Leader's House site. She brought a well driller back from Artemis with her and she's taking core samples, looking for lost pipes or escaping gas. If the area checks out, we start building again tomorrow."

Incredulous, eyes wide, Danu stammered, "Is s-she c-crazy?! *Drilling for gas pockets?!*"

Chuckling, Lupa answered, "Crazy like a coyote, that Whitaker. By the way, she heard you were requisitioned into a private blueprint session with the esteemed Fiscal Director and promptly sent me to fetch you. The news seemed to stun her Highness's friend, the Systems Director, too, so Arinna high-tailed it on over to the Command Center with me."

Overwhelmed with embarrassment, Danu bent her head. "It won't happen again," she rasped, making the promise to both herself and Lupa.

"Oh yes, it *will* happen again," Lupa warned her. "You're on Loy's menu—you have been for some time, now. I think Loy's trying to be on her best behavior until she gets herself elected Leader, but you seem to be a pretty tempting little morsel. She's willing to risk setting off the rumor-mongers to get a taste of you."

She's talking about it like Loy was reaching for a snack! Danu thought fretfully. What had seemed so powerful, so undeniable, was being reduced to bad metaphors. She quickened her stride and purposefully wouldn't look at Lupa.

Taking her by the elbow, Lupa slowed their pace. "Loy likes the hunt. If you stopped her just now, as I think you did, then she'll want you even more. Are you prepared to be draped across a table in the Command Center?"

Fuming, Danu shook off her grip. "I'm not a child!"

"Have you ever done more than kiss a woman?" Lupa asked, her tone surprisingly gentle. At Danu's noncommittal shrug, Lupa explained, "She's a very masterful woman, Danu. I'm just thinking that maybe your first ought to be someone nearer your own age, your own level of experience."

"Like who?" Danu burst out, feeling utterly miserable. She was a Think Tank Baby—a fact which seemed to frighten people. And since her growth spurt had started earlier this year, she had felt big and clumsy and completely undesirable. Part of her couldn't believe Loy would pursue her and part of her was clinging to the possibility that such a womanizer was actually attracted to her.

"Who?" Lupa barked. "Are you so enamored with the wondrous Whitaker that you can truly see no one else?" Stuttering, Danu attempted to deny her feelings for Whit, but Lupa rushed on, paying no attention. "Harrowing Hecate, you *are* naive! Why do you think Albie's hanging around you all the time?"

"She's...just a friend," Danu retorted. Then frowned with doubt. "Isn't she? I mean—how do you tell who's what?"

"Look over your shoulder."

Danu narrowed her eyes, perplexed, then followed Lupa's aggravated nod. A short distance away, Cimbri Braun was emerging from one of the newly erected buildings in Isis, the medical clinic. Lingering before the freshly painted Victorian, Cimbri was gesturing as she talked with the small, wiry teenager at her side. Neith Murray, her fine, black hair cropped short, her wiry frame hidden in a loose, khaki jumpsuit, stood with her hands in her pockets, smiling at Danu.

Danu smiled back, and then went beet red.

Giving a snort, Lupa blustered, "That's how you tell! Neith always smiles at you like that, you lucky imp! Now see if you can talk to her and then *do* something about all that sexual energy."

Shaking her head, Danu mumbled, "I can't. I've tried."

Looking her over, Lupa pronounced, "Bashful, eh?"

Lupa appeared to ponder the problem a moment, checked to see if Neith or Cimbri were watching, then gave Danu a swift kick in the shin. Astonished, Danu cried out and hunched down, grasping her leg. From across the street, the two Healers came running.

"What happened?" Cimbri asked, pushing Danu into a sitting position.

Grimacing and holding her sore shin, Danu was speechless.

Cimbri unlaced Danu's boot, then tugged the pant leg free.

With a grave authority, Lupa said, "She slipped and fell earlier today. I guess the pain just caught up with her, now."

Looking skeptical, Cimbri remarked, "I never heard of such a thing."

"Cimbri, let Neith do this," Lupa insisted. "Whit asked me to have you come take out a bad splinter she got yesterday, during all that digging when the building collapsed."

Lupa clearly knew the mention of any injury to Whit, even an injury as minor as a splinter, would be enough to accomplish her goal. Moments later, Lupa was hurrying to keep up with Cimbri as they went down the street.

Danu was left alone in the golden, late afternoon sunshine, sitting in the street while Neith's small, dark hands coasted expertly along her lower leg. For an instant, Danu gazed at her in panic, unable to say a thing. Then Neith smiled, the teeth white and even, the eyes a soft, sweet brown beneath thick, curling lashes. A brief flicker of bravery made it seem easy to take the next step.

"Uh...dinner." So much for this being easy. She swallowed and pressed on, "Would you...if you'd rather not, it's okay...but...if you're free...." Danu lapsed into silence, confounded by her inability to make sense while Neith smiled like that.

"I'd love to have dinner," the Healer replied sincerely. "Let me help you stand." Neith took Danu's hands and tugged her upright, then put an arm around Danu's waist, as if meaning to steady her.

"I'm not really hurt." Danu felt she had to explain.

"Well, that's still quite a lump down there. Why don't we hike over to the meal hall together?"

Danu just stared down at her, entranced, noticing how lovely her brown skin looked in this rich, summer light. *Dinner with Neith? I can't believe this is happening.*

And arm in arm, they walked down the street in a haze of bashful delight.

☾ ☾ ☾

Much later, at the vacant lot that was the future site of the Leader's House, Whit and Lupa were dismantling the well drilling equipment and preparing to call it a day. Cimbri had long since removed Whit's splinter and taken Lilith's Swallow back to Artemis. Though Whit and Lupa had drilled deep and repeatedly for hours, they had found no evidence of gas.

Through the last glow of the long Pacific Northwest twilight, Loy and Arinna came strolling toward them, looking displeased and officious.

"Work has been suspended in this area," Loy announced, her manner sincere concern. "You're violating the safety code...."

Interrupting, throwing Loy a contemptuous look, Lupa snarled, "Save it, sister. There are no pipes, there is no gas, and we work again tomorrow. It's all filed right here." Lupa patted the palm-computer in her hand. "The documents you waved before us were rigged, weren't they?"

Whit interjected quietly, "Don't make accusations you can't prove, Lupa."

Lupa snorted. "What's with you?" she asked Loy. "Is discrediting Whit so important that you're willing to blow up buildings, injure innocent people, to say nothing of delaying the entire reconstruction project?"

Loy hissed, "That's slander!"

Walking closer to Lupa, Arinna replied calmly. "In ancient times the builders would consecrate a structure by burying some poor unfortunate in the foundation. Is that what you intend to do here, Chief Builder? Listen to no one, rush ahead and ultimately cause a disaster?"

"You two are the disaster!" With a grimace of disgust, Lupa turned away from them, toting the heavy drill bit toward her truck. "Damn politicians," she grumbled. Lifting her face to the rising sliver of a new moon, Lupa shouted, "Fortuna, curse them and their wicked ways!"

Darting before Lupa, completely shedding her mild, urbane manner, Arinna asserted, "Don't you dare curse me, Old Woman!"

Loy and Whit finally ceased glaring at each other and turned to watch the other two, amazed at the open hostility crackling between Arinna and Lupa.

Stepping around Arinna, nonchalant, Lupa chanted a rhyme Whit hadn't heard since childhood. "Spirit and bone, a curse upon you. Liar and sneak, I curse what you do. Your outcome sours, your plans go wrong, Wicca, Wicca..."

"Stop!" Arinna raged.

Laughing, stout Lupa finished, "Wicca, Wicca, hear my song!"

Her polished political persona was gone. Arinna's green eyes glittered and she quivered with fury. At last, she flung at Lupa, "Foolish old hag! You'll regret this!" Then she spun on her heel and stalked away from them.

"What are you going to do?" Lupa shouted after her. "Get me fired?"

"She just might," Loy warned. "You and Whitaker are out here operating unauthorized equipment, ignoring a stop-work order, probably making an unsafe job site even worse!"

"Bah!" Lupa answered, and spat on the ground. She re-adjusted the heavy weight of the drill bit on her shoulder, and resumed her clean-up activities before the daylight completely failed.

Whit set the speed wrench and let the little computer unit unpin the last supports in the drill housing. Pocketing the wrench, she disassembled the steel supports.

Loy stood by, watching her work. "How's Kali?" she asked, curtly.

"In a lot of pain," Whit answered, "but no major damage."

Nodding, Loy fell silent, but didn't leave.

As the last of the drill was laid on the ground, Whit plucked a rag from her pocket and wiped her hands. Gazing at Loy expectantly, she asked, "Why are you still here?"

Shifting her weight from one foot to the other, Loy uttered, "I just want to tell you...I'm sorry it has to be this way."

Whit shook her head. "It doesn't have to be this way, Loy. We're not kids anymore. We're supposed to be working together."

With a sneer, Loy replied, "Ever the idealist."

Whit's temper flared and she retorted, "Ever the egotist."

Shrugging, smirking cynically, Loy began to leave.

Whit stepped closer, gripped her arm and made one last comment. "Just stay away from Danu, Loy."

Loy laughed, genuinely amused. "Or what?"

Whit stared into her eyes and knew, finally, that this woman was so far from the teenaged friend Whit had once known and loved that it seemed impossible that they were one and the same. Raw feeling in her voice, Whit asked, "What's happened to you, Loy?"

The smug countenance before her was swept with emotion; Loy looked stricken. For an instant, Whit thought she saw the real Loy, the sensitive woman beyond that hard, calloused shell. And then Loy recovered herself. She gave an amused chuckle and said softly, "The irony is that the little architect's in love with you, Whit."

Whit stepped back, drawing in her breath sharply, knowing instantly the truth of it.

Softly, Loy remarked, "You see, in the games that really matter, you always win." Turning, Loy walked into the gathering darkness.

Whit shivered, feeling oddly disoriented by this encounter in the twilight. She quickly loaded the last of the drill parts into the back of the truck and waved as Lupa pulled away with the load. Exhausted, she climbed aboard her motorcycle and raced the machine all the way home, gripped by a suddenly burning desire to see and hold Kali.

8

*I*n a pair of baggy, blue shorts and one of Whit's sleeveless gray warrior T-shirts, Kali sat before the computer wallscreen in her mother's lab, trying to master the implications of an advanced mathematics lesson. Around her, the familiarity of the room gave a subtle comfort. Long, slate lab tables stood above a myriad of cupboards and drawers, but the high tech equipment that had once dominated this place had long ago been stored away. Now, the only reminder of Maat's work was the complex computer Kali was using.

A warm voice called, "Okay if your tutor comes early today?"

Looking up, Kali found Arinna Sojourner pausing in the open doorway. From behind Kali, the bright mid-July sunlight poured through the lab window, casting a golden radiance on Arinna as she approached. The Systems Director looked outstanding in her summer-weight canvas pants and a pink tanktop, her wavy hair gathered in a ponytail high on the back on her head. During the past few months of outdoor work, Arinna's skin had tanned into a deeper shade of nut-brown, and she fairly glowed with sleek good health.

Noticing Kali's discreet appraisal, Arinna smiled. She pulled up a lab stool near Kali's compu-chair.

"Godel's theorem," Kali admitted, ruefully. "I'm trying to accept the idea that computers—even the ones with a thousand MIPS—can never be as intelligent as humans."

"Ah yes," Arinna chuckled, leaning closer to Kali conspiratorially. "A disappointing discovery for most computer scientists. It's hard to concede that the computer's knowledge will always be limited by that fixed set of axioms—the truths built into the machine by those who initially designed it. As thinking, evolving intellects, however, humans are beyond limitations. We can discover truths or concepts never imagined possible." Arinna sighed thoughtfully. "Godel's theorem is a great reassurance, sometimes."

Cued by that slightly aggrieved response, Kali tucked her left arm against her sore ribs and turned to face Arinna. "Why are you so early? It's only a little after one o'clock, isn't it?"

Arinna smiled sadly. "Aren't you glad to see me?"

"Yes, but you left work at the Leader's House site. The weather is good and I know there's plenty to do. If it weren't for Neith insisting that I have to give these ribs a month to heal, I'd be there, myself. What's going on?"

Smoothing a hand over her ponytail, Arinna commented, "Loy and Whit got into another argument. I left."

Frowning, Kali sat back. "Oh, no. And Whit told me last night that she was being unfailingly diplomatic with Loy."

Arinna linked her fingers together and contemplated them. "Ever since late June, working with them has been maddening."

"Whit tries," Kali defended.

Arinna remarked, "Whit patronizes Loy and it makes Loy mad."

Struggling to remain calm, Kali reasoned, "You must admit that Loy has trouble working as part of a team."

Arinna tossed her head and the tail of hair swung over her shoulder. "Loy's a natural leader. She needs to be in charge of something, that's all."

"She's *supposed* to be in charge of developing a healthy economic base," Kali retorted softly. "Instead, she's constantly trying to undermine Whit's command."

"Not constantly," Arinna almost sniffed. "Don't exaggerate."

Raising her voice slightly, Kali reminded her, "Loy presented her own set of blueprints and lobbied that we should build her version of the Leader's House in an altogether different location. No one else in the transitional government agreed." Curtly, Kali pointed out, "You yourself voted with Danu and Lupa Tagliaro against Loy's design."

Sighing, Arinna allowed, "That was after Lupa Tagliaro spent several evenings in the Rough & Ready Saloon. You were still laid up in bed then, so perhaps you missed all that." Reading Kali's perplexed expression, Arinna revealed, "Lupa parked herself by the bar, buying drinks, regaling anyone who would listen with tales of 'the Gov' drilling every foot of the stony soil around the Leader's House site. After half the colony heard about Whit pulling up core samples from twenty feet down, without incident, Loy's warnings about mysterious methane pipes underground seemed ludicrous. Much as I wanted to support Loy, I couldn't."

Kali studied Arinna's heightened color, considered the softness in her voice when she spoke Loy's name. She focused on Arinna's eyes and was surrounded by a deep, warm, complex emotion. "You're in love with her," Kali surmised.

Slightly alarmed, Arinna's green eyes locked with Kali's; the softness disappeared and a glittering shutter slipped into place. Kali felt herself expelled from the warmth.

"Sorry," Kali breathed, looking away, squinting into the shaft of afternoon sunlight streaming through the window.

"You seem to have an amazing insight into people," Arinna stated. She leaned forward, her gaze intent.

Kali refused to make eye contact. Discomfited by this growing need to intrude on private thoughts, she tried to smooth over what had just happened. "Loy is very attractive, very desirable."

Her voice hushed, Arinna persisted, "But you knew it was love, not desire."

Kali stared at the mathematics lesson glowing on the wallscreen before her. "Lucky guess."

No one said anything for a long moment.

Kali's question popped out almost of its own volition. "You and Loy are lovers?"

Seeming to hesitate, Arinna gave a slight smile and disclosed, "I had no intention of getting involved with her—just watching her eye Danu made it very clear to me what sort of woman she is. But she would stop by my room each evening, to discuss colony affairs, she said. She was entertaining, attentive, physically appealing." Arinna sighed. "I evaded her...for a while."

Pausing, gripping her hands together tightly, Arinna dropped her gaze. When she began to speak again, her voice was sensual and sonorous.

"There was...this enigmatic tension between us. At last, I let her steal a few kisses. And then, she had me in bed, half out of my head, before I even knew what happened. I kept thinking, at first, that it would be purely a physical release, no strings, no expectations." Arinna gave her head a brief shake. "She's very dominating, very intense. I'm...not used to that. She's thrilling, captivating. I keep wanting more of her; lately, I can't seem to get enough." Blushing, Arinna fell silent.

Kali watched her, amazed at the detailed confession.

Arinna asked, "Do you know what that sort of passion is like? How overpowering, how consuming?"

A brief memory moved through Kali's mind. Branwen's hands on her that first night, years and years ago. Yet, for all the power of those sensations, Whit was the one who had taken her body and made it incandescent. Not just once, but regularly.

Then, Kali realized that Arinna was thoughtfully studying her. Arinna stated, "You know what I mean."

Solemnly, Kali nodded.

"Yes," Arinna chuckled. " As Whit's partner, I thought that you would."

Arinna let the topic go after that.

They spent the next four hours working on her last secondary school mathematics program, and Kali ended the session by successfully taking the required exam.

Around five in the afternoon, as Kali filed her test in the schooling program, Arinna asked, "How much more do you have to complete before you start the university level options."

Kali yawned, then replied, "Some 21st century herstory and a course in Freelandian computer designs."

"You're almost done, then," Arinna observed, scrutinizing Kali with a canny respect. "You're mastering this material pretty fast."

Shrugging, Kali allowed, "I'm catching up, I guess."

Maat's original main program menu flashed onscreen as the computer shifted from the comline connection with Artemis's Agro-Center to the cpu-control in Maat's lab. Arinna asked Kali to stop.

Pointing to the heading "Medical Research," Arinna asked excitedly, "These are your mother's files?"

"Yes."

"Have you ever accessed this?"

Kali shook her head.

"Let's look at it," Arinna urged.

Hesitantly, Kali accessed the program. A long list of scientific abbreviations appeared on the wallscreen.

Her voice hushed with reverence, Arinna demanded, "Do you remember what these headings mean? Are they the lost experiments?"

Kali examined the phrases, wondering. She had quit her mother's lab and enlisted as a cadet warrior just after her twelfth birthday. She and her mother had been at odds, then, in a war of wills that had begun when her mother left Lilith. It had been over thirteen years since she had seen these garbled headings.

"It's the Think Tank Project, isn't it?" Arinna asked, shifting her stool closer to Kali.

"I think so," Kali murmured, slowly remembering some of the abbreviations. "Recombinant DNA engineering. Mother was using her own group of specialized enzymes to snip a gene from one organism and splice it to another. While we lived in Artemis, she set up a computerized manufacturing program, supposedly the most advanced plasmid replication system ever developed. It was disassembled by the time I was eight."

Arinna acknowledged, "I know." Then she prompted, her face eager, "What I don't understand is *why* she ended it. In all the official reports, there's no explanation. A year before the Regs attacked Isis, the whole project was shut down by Maat herself. Why?"

Kali avoided Arinna's probing gaze. "Mother was using biotechnology to correct nature's errors—the usual stuff—Parkinson's, cystic fibrosis, heart disease, various types of cancer. But using genes with healthy information as a replacement for defective genes was not what *really* motivated my mother." Taking a deep breath, lowering her head, Kali finished, "Mother was interested in how exposure to certain enzymes affected the DNA molecule; she was trying to enhance natural intelligence—create a more advanced human being."

Arinna was staring hard at her, and Kali realized that she was blushing furiously. At last, Arinna asked, "Are you an example of your mother's work?"

Kali lifted her head, not certain she was ready to face the prejudice she was sure she would find in Arinna's eyes. She had seen how Danu was treated by some in Isis—as if she were a flesh-covered, walking computer, devoid of feelings or normal human needs.

But to Kali's relief, Arinna did not seem to be judging her; the green eyes were soft with understanding and compassion. "I know you are the parthenogenic product of both Maat and Lilith," Arinna stated. "Yet, you seem to have an extraordinary gift for learning. You're making up years of missed schooling in a matter of months. I've seen you driving Whit's motorcycle, steering those big construction trucks, operating cranes. It's quite a bit for a former peasant farmer to be mastering so easily."

Sheepishly, Kali admitted, "I can fly Lilith's Swallow, too."

"No! The tilt-rotor?" Her eyes widening, Arinna regarded Kali with a barely concealed wonder.

"Whit taught me when we had the loan of the aircraft—just in case she wasn't available and an emergency arose."

"I'm very impressed," Arinna announced, and then broke into a dazzling grin.

Kali gazed at this beautiful, self-assured woman, all at once feeling slightly befuddled.

Arinna's smile dimmed as she pondered, "With such results, why did your mother ever terminate the Think Tank Project?"

Thoughtfully, Kali massaged her tender left side. "I have dim memories of a child care hostel—lots of other children—but one little girl in particular. I must have been around three years old. Mother and the other adults couldn't understand why I wouldn't play with this child, why I consistently rebelled against any intentional pairing of us."

Tilting her head to one side, Arinna asked, "Why did you?"

"She was like me," Kali confided, "a human innovation." She stopped and tried to control the surge of panic that still accompanied these hazy recollections. "Like me, and yet not like me. Although we may have evolved from the same genetic engineering technique, spiritually, we were very different. She was...*cruel*. And she knew enough—even at that young age—to hide it."

Arinna looked intrigued. "What was her name?"

Kali shook her head, "I can't remember. She went away one day and I never saw her again." Kali sighed. "But I always suspected that Mother finally saw in that girl what I saw."

"Which was what?" Arinna sat up very straight.

"She was evil," Kali stated firmly, acknowledging with the certainty of adulthood what she had instinctively known and feared as a child. "Over a period of years, I think my mother came to the conclusion that intellect alone does not advance the species. I think she finally saw that there must be another quality, something humankind often calls 'the soul.'"

Nodding, Arinna waited for Kali to go on.

Brushing her bright blonde hair back with her hand, Kali finished, "For my mother, the paradox was too disturbing. When I was eight, Mother suddenly shut the project down, destroyed all the data."

"And the little girl?" Arinna asked.

"I don't know what happened to her."

"If the data was destroyed," Arinna asked, her eyes keen, motioning with her hand at the list of research files, "then what is this?"

Puzzled, Kali studied the wallscreen. "I saw mother burn the palm computer chips and her lab notebooks. I'm not even sure if there's information under these headings."

"Well, let's look at a few and see," Arinna pressed, her voice soft, yet insistent. "Can you pull up a file for me? Say—cloning? Or the DNA manipulations?"

Kali examined the list on the wallscreen. Representing the combined results of years of work, this was all that remained of her mother's once powerful effect on Freeland. For an instant, Kali experienced a distinct sensation of deja vu. She had spent much of her childhood being trained as a computer scientist, working beside Maat, first in Artemis, and later in Isis. Just now, she felt as if her mother were at her elbow, her hands busy with some task, asking her to pull up a file she needed.

Then a voice she remembered, a voice long past the capacity for speech, sounded in her ear. *You chose to be a warrior. Do your duty.*

Her breath coming fast, her heart pounding in her ears, Kali quickly exited the program, exited the usage menu, shut off the machine. She sat there, rigid, gripping the armrests and staring at the blank wallscreen.

"Kali?"

She sent a sideways glance at Arinna and discovered a look of true concern on her face.

"Are you alright?" Arinna asked.

Kali nodded. "You're not disappointed?"

"Certainly, I'm disappointed," Arinna said honestly, "I'm terribly interested in that work." Then Arinna smiled reassuringly. "Your mother was my childhood hero, Kali. So brilliant and forceful."

Kali gave a small grin. "Yes, I remember the forceful part."

Arinna laughed softly. "We'll look at her research some other time, then, shall we?"

"Some other time," Kali repeated, although, in the back of her mind, she had already decided that she would only access these files when she was completely alone in the lab. She could still hear her mother's voice in her ear, warning her.

(((

That same mid-July afternoon, in the center of the city, at the Leader's House site, Danu was concluding a long day of working with Alborak and Lupa, going over the floor plans, getting the building's utilities coordinated.

The rest of the women who made up the construction force working on this site were putting away their tools, emptying the last of their canteens in deep, thirsty swallows. Soon the hostel meal halls and gang showers would be crowded, and the night of quiet personal time would begin. Some would be processing dirty laundry through the hostel cleaning units. Some would be walking through the city and surveying the rapid progress now more and more apparent. And others would be lining up to make use one of the various comline units, contacting home and loved ones left behind.

Yet Danu was still at work, following Albie through a maze of construction materials, all carefully sorted into transport batches in what was called the supply depot. The skeleton framework of the Leader's House loomed in the background.

Albie had sought out Danu earlier in the day, gesturing convincingly that a problem was developing in the assembly end of providing each building with sewage fertilization units. Since Kali's injury, Albie had lost two more of her capable staff. One woman had hurt her back while unloading pipe from a truckbed. Another crew member had come down with a bad case of poison ivy after a romantic frolic in the woods. Albie had been insistent about needing to talk to someone about the production schedule, and Danu was willing to listen.

Danu followed Alborak around the tall stack of lumber, wondering where they were going. When they were thoroughly screened from the remainder of the construction crew, Alborak turned to her, motioned her closer. Wide-eyed, puzzled, Danu went over and stood beside her. Albie's eyes crinkled slightly, not really laughing so much as expressing a barely controlled delight.

"Do you want me to fill in for one of your workers until they can come back?" Danu asked, noting absent-mindedly that Albie barely watched her hands.

In reply, Albie slowly leaned closer, cupped Danu's chin and guided it very gently down. Before she could do more than blink, Danu was given a solid, convincing kiss, and then released. As Danu stood there, gaping, Albie broke into a very broad grin.

Tricked you! she signed.

"What?" Danu said stupidly, then recovered herself in a rush of annoyance. "You mean, this is what you wanted? There is no problem?"

You! Albie signed, making an impatient face. *You're the problem. I keep asking you to do things with me and you keep turning me down! I want to spend some time with you—but you're always working!*

"I have to make sure it's all coming out right—I have to catch the mistakes before they're too far gone...."

Albie moved in and her lips took possession of Danu's mouth. With a slight push, Albie induced her to step back, and Danu found herself against the stack of lumber, her shoulders and hips pressed into the rough board edges by Albie's shorter, more muscular frame. Sure of herself and intentionally presumptuous, Albie began taking full advantage of this first moment of intimacy between them.

Dazed by the fingers in her hair, the gently aggressive mouth moving over her own, Danu was rapidly being swept into Albie's heated eagerness. Then her nose registered a sharp, biting scent.

Fire! her brain trumpeted.

Jerking free of Albie, Danu pushed herself away from the lumber. Albie obviously had the scent, too. Their heads swiveled from side to side, anxiously checking for signs of smoke to track, and then spotting it rising over the lumber directly behind them.

They dashed around the boards, darted through two large, neatly squared piles of brick. And there it was, orange and hot and feeding on the five-foot-high, fifteen-foot-long recycling bin, which was filled with the rough, uneven leftovers of the building's wooden framework.

Flames leapt, curling high into the air, as Danu kicked her foot uselessly into the hard, stony soil. There was no dust here to throw on the fire. She already knew the closest water hydrant was across the street and there was no hose. As she glanced about, suddenly realizing that the five gallon cans stored nearby contained turpentine, she saw Albie struggling to lift a large, heavy paper sack from a supply pallet.

Danu ran to her, in complete accord with Albie's thinking. Together, they carried the bag closer, broke into the sack with Albie's utility knife, then reached in and began throwing handfuls of dry cement mix over the spreading blaze. Albie dashed back to the pallet of bags, grabbed a shovel, and then used that to scatter the retardant.

The dust puffed up about them, covering their sweaty arms, legs, and faces, leaving a film on their clothes. The slight wind changed and Danu caught a gulp of hot smoke; she ended up doubled over, coughing until her eyes were streaming with tears. Albie shot her a worried glance but continued to work. Finally, she had put out most of the fire by herself.

After a few minutes, she attempted to rejoin the effort, but Albie shook her head in fierce refusal and pushed away the hands Danu tried to plunge into the sack. The young architect stood aside helplessly blinking her eyes and clearing her raw throat, watching Albie toss cement mix into the recycling bin.

At last, Albie signed, *That ought to do it. Let's get you to Neith.*

"No, I'm okay. I have to report this," Danu croaked.

Brushing herself off, Albie nodded, then draped an arm about Danu's shoulders. *Guess we threw off some sparks*, she said, flashing a devilish grin.

Upset as she was over this seemingly inexplicable fire, Danu couldn't help laughing.

                    ❆ ❆ ❆

Less than half an hour later, Danu and Albie were back at the Leader's House site, inspecting the supply depot area with Lupa, Arinna, Loy, and Whit. The recycling bin had been tipped over and Whit was steadily ignoring cautionary words from the others as she kicked her boot into the dusty, charred boards and half-burned kindling scattered on the ground.

"We have to determine how this got started," Whit told them.

"What's important is that it was caught in time and it's out, now," Loy retorted.

One of Whit's kicks opened a section of burned board and produced a spray of red embers.

Concerned, Loy warned, "Whit, don't burn yourself."

"I won't," Whit assured her, her voice strong with her usual self-reliance, yet at the same time, soft with gratitude.

It was such a rare show of sentiment between them, that the rest all exchanged looks of frank amazement.

Bending down suddenly, Whit asked for a stick. Danu tossed a long surveying marker to her, and then Whit poked among several well-burned boards until she fished out what looked like a flimsy, black lace handkerchief. She held it up, narrowing her eyes at the barely compiled collection of threads, then leaned forward and sniffed.

"What is it?" Arinna asked, moving closer.

Beside her, Lupa pronounced, "Smells like turpentine."

Arson? Albie gestured to Danu.

"Who would do such a thing?" Lupa demanded angrily. "We haven't had rain in three weeks! All these building materials around—this stack of turpentine cans, the lumber that hasn't been fire-treated, yet. And the forest is getting dangerously dry! It could easily have turned into a disaster!"

Danu swore in her croaky voice, provoking a sudden, unexpected smile from them all—except Albie, who responded with a delayed grin to Lupa's frog sign.

Meanwhile, Loy stepped up next to Danu, nonchalantly pausing to ruffle the short red hair. Albie's grin shifted into a hard, contentious stare. Raising her eyebrows, Loy calmly pretended to ignore Albie, but moved away from Danu, all the same.

"What are you going to do?" Arinna asked Whit.

"What *can* I do?" Whit returned. "There's no sign of footprints—the ground's too hard. Everyone in the colony has been back here, fetching one load of supplies or another, so there will be fingerprints everywhere. All we can do is ask around, quietly. See if we can narrow down who was in the area toward the end of the day."

Arinna turned and asked Danu, "Did you two see anyone?"

Danu murmured, "No," then felt the heat rush to her face. They all watched her closely, their eyes speculative. Then slowly, one by one, they turned to study Albie, who was equally red despite her dark tan.

"What were you doing back here?" Arinna pressed.

Tell her we were counting bricks, Albie told Danu.

Lupa, who was also fluent in sign, began to chuckle, and then seeing Arinna's consternation, she laughed heartily.

Whit winked affectionately at Danu. Then, carefully carrying the stick and cloth ahead of her as she moved, Whit walked out of the burned debris and started winding her way through stacks of material, heading for the street.

The others all fell in step behind her.

"What are we going to do about this...vandal?" Loy called to Whit.

"Now that we know for sure that we have one, we'll just have to be ready for her the next time," Whit reasoned.

"Next time?" Loy asked, clearly not pleased by that answer.

"You think there will *be* a next time?" Arinna joined in.

"I *know* there will," Whit declared gloomily. "After all, this is the third bizarre accident that has plagued us since Beltane. I have no doubt that there will be more."

❨ ❨ ❨

Thirty minutes later, Kali spied Whit walking into the meal hall. From her seat at a long, crowded table near the door, Kali waved, but Whit didn't see her. A group of women trailed her lover, earnestly debating among themselves, and Kali realized that Whit was in the midst of some sort of problem. Wiping the last of the vegetable hash from her bowl with a biscuit, Kali decided to stay where she was for a moment, and just watch.

Beneath the high ceiling, surrounded by walls of sanded and stained pine board, the meal hall was packed with noisy, boisterous women. Upstairs, a second wide-open level served as another dining room, and the sounds of boots clomping back at forth above them only added to the din of plates being scraped clean and conversations shouted between tables.

Whit was flanked by her three Directors, her Chief Builder and Deputy Governor, Lupa, and Alborak, the Utility Forewoman. As Whit and her officials took a place in the food line, still trading worried glances and grave remarks, the sizable Chief of Security, Captain Fea Greenberg, marched over to them.

The women burst into a new exchange, everyone talking at once, and Loy moved to stand beside Danu. Quickly, Danu shifted away from her, edging to the periphery of the group. Loy smoothly closed the space, slipping an arm around Danu's waist and laughingly giving her a squeeze before releasing her and turning away again.

For the first time, Kali noticed that Danu and Alborak both had black smudges on their faces, hands and clothes. Her gaze traveled over the rest and discovered Whit's blackened boots and pant-legs. Slightly alarmed, Kali stood up and approached the women.

She was only a few feet away when she noticed that Danu was staring at Loy's back, her gaze half-lidded. The freckled hands were slowly unfolding a large jackknife and locking the blade in place. The women near Danu went on talking, completely focused on their discussion, while Danu cocked her arm back, the knife clenched tightly in her fist. Shocked, Kali watched the young architect take a step toward Loy.

Kali tried to call out, tried to move, but she was frozen. It was so like that dream, months ago, when she had found herself standing on a cliff in the moonlight, with the Reg flying straight at her. Time seemed to slow down to separate, and very singular seconds.

Danu's arm began moving forward, initiating what was certainly a stabbing stroke. Focusing her concentration, Kali lunged for Loy, caught the front of her black T-shirt and yanked her clear of the blade. As Loy plunged past her, falling to the floor, Kali caught Danu's wrist. Holding it, Kali rudely drove her knee into the slim arm. Still clutching the knife, Danu battled to get her arm free.

With a savage might, Danu used her free hand to strike Kali across the face. Staggering from the punch, Kali almost lost her grip. Then Whit was grabbing Danu from behind, yelling at Kali to let go and get clear of the knife. Instead, Kali stubbornly held on. Repeatedly, Danu jerked against her grip, wearing down the power in Kali's grasp. And as Kali fought to endure, she was chilled to see that the young, soot-stained face was completely devoid of emotion, the blue eyes vacant. Twice more, Kali drove her knee into the fragile bones of Danu's wrist, but Danu didn't seem to feel a thing. Meanwhile, a deep, agonizing ache was spreading across Kali's side and back, leaving her gasping.

"Drop the knife! Drop it!" Whit ordered.

Blue eyes blinked, as if registering that particular voice, though everyone was shouting. The meal hall was a swarm of motion in Kali's peripheral vision.

Fea Greenberg pointed a sedation gun at them. Danu instantly pushed Kali into the line of fire. Roaring at Fea, "No, don't shoot!" Whit at last succeeded in tripping Danu. Then Kali, Danu and Whit all fell together, hitting the polished hardwood planks with a bang.

Instantly, Danu went limp. The knife slid from her hand, clattering to the floor.

Kali pulled the young architect into her arms, weeping with relief. Above them, Loy hovered, staring at Danu. Then Fea Greenberg stepped closer, edging out Loy, and loudly informing Danu that she was under arrest.

"She's unconscious!" Kali angrily retorted, her breathing so painful that she was grimacing with each gasp for air.

"Kal," Whit called, her gray eyes worried, "You're hurt."

She knew she was; her ribs were on fire. She didn't even bother trying to hide her agony as Whit's gentle hands separated her from Danu.

Above them, the shock giving way to rage, Loy let fly a string of curses. "Damn it. What is going on here? Why would Danu want to attack me?" Then her eyes narrowed and she shot a look of pure hate at Whit.

Whit scrambled to her feet, kicked the knife away, and leaned down to help Kali.

Baffled, watching Loy, Kali took Whit's outstretched hand.

The roar of voices began to drop, as all the women in the meal hall strained to hear this exchange.

"Can you stand?" Whit asked. At Kali's nod, Whit offered her arm, supporting Kali as she stood and then bent in half, gasping.

Clenching her hands into fists, Loy snarled, "The Danu I knew in Boudicca would have *never* tried something like this!"

Completely ignoring Loy, Whit steadied Kali with a hand on her elbow. "Send for a Healer," Whit ordered Fea, adding, "and put that damned gun away before you shoot someone!"

Undaunted, Loy went on, "The whole colony knows she's infatuated with you! She would do *anything* for you!"

Finally turning, Whit snapped, "*What?*"

Striding up to Whit, stopping inches from her face, the Fiscal Director hissed, "Because you couldn't stand a little competition, you've ruined this kid's life!"

Fuming, Whit retorted, "You're crazy, Loy." Then she swung back toward Fea. "I want an investigation into what happened here," she ordered. "And I want facts this time! Report directly to me and no one else."

Fea nodded toward Danu's still form. "What about her?"

"She needs a Healer."

"But it was attempted murder—we all saw it!" Fea returned.

"It wasn't Danu," Kali declared simply.

Everyone, even Whit, looked at her as if she were out of her mind. "It wasn't," Kali insisted. "Didn't you see her eyes?"

"Danu's under arrest," Fea stated obstinately.

Whit retorted, her voice rising, "*I* will determine who is under arrest, Captain Greenberg. Is that clear?"

Humiliated, the irate security officer nodded.

"Then carry out my orders, Captain!"

Fea slapped a hand to her heart in an embittered salute, but Whit and everyone else nearby heard her mutter under her breath, "You mean carry out your cover-up!"

Glowering, Fea radioed for a Healer, while Whit's attention again settled anxiously on Kali. Nearby, Arinna stared at the knife on the floor, as if in shock. Alborak knelt by Danu, touching her shoulder protectively as the crowd pushed in closer, murmuring angrily. Casting a wary glance at the women all around them, Lupa requested permission to call for a security detail.

Kali leaned against Whit, amazed, watching fear settle into the crowd and transform it into a mob. Distorting the faces, distorting perceptions, feeding on itself, making them angrier, uglier, spreading like wildfire in a dry grass field. Some were shouting at Whit, frustrated. Others were shouting rebukes at the women who were openly challenging Whit. And some were doing neither, too busy glaring at Danu with revenge in their eyes. Women were actually calling for Danu to be handed over to them, saying that they would personally teach her about crime and punishment.

Whit shouted a series of orders and the warriors in the crowd came slowly forward, moving with a marked reluctance. Finally, they enclosed Danu, Kali and Whit in a small, protective circle of gray uniforms.

Gazing about herself, her mind blurred with the pain in her side, Kali saw the women of Isis and barely knew them. *What is happening to us?* she wondered. *How will we ever build the colony together if there is so much hate among us, waiting for a target?*

❨ ❨ ❨

Late that evening, Whit crept into her bedroom by the dim starlight that was shining through the skylight above. Hovering over the slim form beneath the bedcovers, Whit listened to the soft breathing and sent a silent, intense prayer of thanks to Gaea.

She quietly sat on the chair nearby, unlaced and pulled off her boots, then stood again and wearily stripped. Kicking her discarded warrior's uniform aside, she longingly contemplated taking a bath, then decided she didn't want to take the chance of waking Kali.

Her ribs were bruised again and even with the pain-killers she had taken, Kali was liable to rouse if Whit wasn't careful. Neith said it was Kali's adrenaline, kicking in and negating dosages that would normally flatten anyone else. Three weeks ago, when the building had collapsed, the Healer had been shocked when Kali had not only woken, but had begun asking direct, lucid questions barely an hour after Neith had sedated her in the merchants' square.

Lifting the covers carefully, Whit crawled in beside her lover, sighing contentedly as she anticipated the long night of rest to come. Whit had only just stilled, when Kali rolled over and a warm, smooth arm reached across Whit's chest.

"What time is it?" Kali mumbled.

"After midnight," Whit returned. "Glad to see the medic got you home alright. I really wanted to come with you, but what with everyone ready to clap Danu in a containment cell...."

Kali shushed her with a finger on Whit's lips. "I understand—you're Military Governor." Then Kali whispered, "Tell me what happened?"

"In the morning, okay? I love you."

Moving to kiss Whit's cheek, Kali, moaned softly.

"Keep still, Kal," Whit entreated in an insistent whisper.

With a subtle, dreamily satisfying stroke over Whit's stomach, Kali asked, "What about Danu?"

"She has a broken wrist, but otherwise, she's fine. When she came to in the clinic, she didn't remember a thing about attacking Loy. She was astonished when I told her, very upset, very convincing. Albie, Neith and Lupa seem to believe her."

"Do you?" Kali whispered.

"Don't know. Sweet Mother, I'm tired. In the morning I'll tell you...."

Kali snuggled closer. "Did Fea arrest her?"

"No," Whit stated, yawning. "Loy is dropping charges."

Shifting her stroke, Kali sent her hand along Whit's side, over her breasts and then up along her neck. "Stay awake," Kali ordered in a low voice. "Why did Loy drop the charges?"

Whit shivered slightly, her fatigue moving aside as her body processed the summons it was steadily receiving. Desire came through her like puffs of wind in the trees on a cool summer night. "Several reasons," Whit breathed.

"Tell me."

"Lupa threatened to play up how Loy's been behaving. A thirty-one-year-old woman pursuing a diffident seventeen-year-old—it just wouldn't play well with the voters and the election is less than two months away."

"Good for Lupa," Kali chuckled, then shrank against Whit, stabbed with pain.

Turning to face her, Whit smoothed the golden hair back and crooned tender endearments until Kali relaxed again.

"What other reasons?" Kali rasped.

"Go to sleep," Whit pleaded.

"I will, I promise. I just want to know what I missed."

Grumbling about how stubborn Kali was, Whit elaborated on the events. "Arinna seems to think that Danu's our vandal—that Danu's experiencing psychotic episodes—causing accidents, setting fires—all the while hoping to be caught and stopped." Whit stopped, drawing a sharp breath as Kali's hand made another seductive journey over her torso. "So, Neith is going to arrange for a psychiatrist for Danu to see daily," Whit exhaled. "And Alborak has volunteered to act as a combination guard-attendant, responsible for Danu's actions."

"Even at night?" Kali demanded, her wonderfully pleasing hand pausing, betraying Kali's distraction.

"No, then she'll be with Lupa, much to Albie's disappointment."

Kali laughed, and again her amusement ended in a moan of pain.

"The rest in the morning," Whit said firmly.

"No," Kali answered, her voice soft and sleepy in the dark room. The restless hand renewed its wandering, only slower and moving in lazy circles over Whit's stomach. "Tell me what you think happened...."

Whit mumbled, "You *saw* what happened."

For a moment, there was silence.

"What if," the low voice was very faint now, the hand was still, "what if we only saw what someone wanted us to see?"

Suddenly, Whit was caving in; her mind became sluggish with exhaustion and her body seemed to sink beneath her, through the bed, going endlessly, heavily down. For a moment, her mind flickered, catching the question Kali was asking, considering it, and then Whit passed inexorably into the realm of sleep.

9

hit strode around the perimeter of the granite blocks, watching the crane lift another load of cedar shakes up to the roofers. The hot, mid-August sunlight beat down mercilessly, and even the brim of her warrior's cap did little to help shield her from the glare. Yet from what she could see, the Leader's House was progressing amazingly well. Despite the endless delays in June, the building was now more than halfway done and looked as if it might be the loveliest structure of all.

Whit paused as she came around to the front, admiring the sweep of the long porch, the huge cedar columns, even now being carved with a myriad of matriarchal designs by the artisans. Danu's interpretation of Maat's original plan was rising steadily before the colony's eyes. And as it did, the major government and business sectors of the city were nearing completion, too. A few construction teams had been released to begin building private residences, and as excitement grew over this development, Danu Sullivan was suddenly back in favor.

And I'm damn glad of it, Whit reflected.

Danu had come out of last month's bizarre assault on Loy with more than just a cast on her broken wrist; she had gained a reputation. Gradually, communal reaction to Danu had transformed from the initial fury of the meal hall into an awesome, if grudging, respect. It was as if studious, pensive Danu Sullivan had turned out to be someone else entirely—a scrapper, a woman who would not be trifled with. Also, without Lupa having to say a word, it seemed that Loy's behavior had long ago been noticed and remarked upon. Many citizens believed that, even though Danu had been wrong in losing control of her temper, the Fiscal Director had deserved the scare.

Looking around the Leader's House job site, Whit automatically checked on Danu's location and found her standing by a truck, discussing a blueprint with one of the electricians. Watching that rangy body lean against the vehicle, Whit pondered the fact that this young woman had attempted murder. It seemed so strange, so entirely out of character. Whit could almost, but not quite, believe Kali when she insisted that it had not been Danu at all, that some other force had caused Danu to act as its agent.

At any rate, it was now more obvious than ever that Danu was a genius; in addition to overseeing the government and business structures still underway, she was altering residential blueprints on demand, tailoring each house so that it revealed the uniqueness of its owner. In doing so, Danu was agreeably responding to the needs of at least a hundred women a day, and they loved her for it.

Early this morning, during the Directors' meeting, Whit had asked for a report on Danu's mental health. Both Lupa and Albie had related that in the last month Danu had been her usual quiet, intense self, functioning without incident. And Neith had confirmed Danu's attendance of the required daily psychiatric sessions, informing Whit that she'd have to speak directly to the Healer involved to learn more.

Taking off her hat—a lightweight, gray version of what the last century had called a "baseball cap"—Whit pushed her hair back off her brow, then settled the brim low. She sank her hands into her shorts pockets, and scrunched her toes in her hot, sweaty boots. Gradually, the noise and bustle of the work site around her faded. She fell into a vague, heat-induced reverie, feeling generally very pleased with things.

The merchants' sector was completed, and had turned out to be a delightful surprise: buildings full of interesting nooks and crannies, placed gracefully along straight, broad streets that led to the marketplace. In contrast, the business district was marked by sleek, contemporary designs, employing titanium sheeting and colorful concrete-vinyl slabs.

Among the various neighborhoods just beginning construction, the designs reflected the tastes of the women living in each quadrant. Some favored classic townhomes, while others were building small, heat-efficient bungalows. A group of forty or so talented carpenters had banded together; they were busily erecting stylish, endlessly eccentric Victorians, complete with turrets and gingerbread on the porches. A brick masons' guild had spent many evenings with Danu, telling her what they wanted and then conferring with her as she fashioned the necessary detail into blueprints. These last creations were like nothing Whit had ever seen before—fantastic, and yet charming, like small Gaudys lifted out of old Barcelona. And on the outskirts of each quadrant, placed along the huge, inner ribbon of communal park, sat sprawling, multi-roomed compositions of natural wood. In these halls, the children would be taught and counseled and cherished.

For Whit, the schools were the most important structures of all, for in them, the nation would hatch. Everything that Freeland had become was rooted in its educational system for the young. Their ability to deal with their diversities of race and ethnic culture were the result of growing and learning and working together from an early age. They had purposefully chosen to pursue unity by reveling in, and appreciating their differences.

Whit knew the reason for this. In the days after the Great Schism, when they were struggling to feed themselves, to pass on any knowledge preserved, to protect those still threatened by AGH, the women of Freeland had forged enlightenment into life-style. In Isis, as in the seven other city-colonies, schooling translated into chances, challenges, and endless opportunities to explore one's potential.

And these past few weeks, seeing the Leader's House taking shape day by day, had stirred Whit into thinking of Isis as more than a fuzzy dream. With these solid, granite blocks, a symbol of permanence was being assembled, and Isis was simultaneously transforming itself into a busy, thriving colony.

The Lumber Co-op was operating twenty-four hours a day, logging, cutting board, fire-treating the wood, then stacking it in the warehouse for use in the colony and also for sale to foreign buyers. Conversely, the first sewage-fertilization end-product had been poured into canisters and carried high into the mountains by jet transport. Hovering low over an old 20th century clear-cut, the transports had dumped the cans, then landed to unload the machinery and eco-balance teams. Bulldozers had mixed the clean, rich nutrients into the earth, and then teams of volunteers had sown the land with pine seedlings. Isis was already replacing every cedar, every fir, every madrone tree it borrowed from the forest that surrounded it.

Whit thought with satisfaction that the first Isis-produced food products had appeared the previous week: vegetables from the new hydroponic sheds on the outskirts of the colony, and brown bread made in the newly constructed brick ovens. They would probably always be transporting grain from Artemis, but now they were establishing a fledgling trading economy, bartering mountain trout and wool shorn from the colony-owned flock of sheep, for sacks of wheat. Many of these early cooperative concerns would later be supplanted with private enterprise versions of their function, but initially, they were colony-owned, collaborative efforts.

Later, if this incarnation was anything like the last, Isis would develop two major sources of commerce. First, computer research and development, leading to a market in high performance Molecular Memory Devices. And second, reclamation businesses: collecting the machines still salvageable from the era of dynamic manufacturing before The New Order Christians came to power and America went mad. After a general clean-up and repair, the machines would be modernized. Computers were often installed into them to mimic once human-driven operative responses. Through its smart-machines, Isis had once solved many of the problems arising from Freeland's essentially small population.

However, such industries demanded full time workers, and everyone was currently devoting their best effort to re-building Isis. Once the work force was released to private business, Whit had a feeling this experience of working together toward a common goal, building a colony, would make Isis a formidable society of businesswomen.

And then in the distance, Whit saw the sewage-fertilization crew crossing the busy construction site, arriving to set up the internal works. Pulling down her hat brim, she searched for Kali. When she saw her, Whit sucked in her breath, stunned by the visceral reaction that hit her. Construction boots, sleek, tanned runner's legs, baggy khaki shorts, and a loose, forest-green cotton shirt that was damp with perspiration and torn at the shoulder. The radiant, blonde hair was woven into a short, French braid, though several strands had worked their way free and hung provocatively over Kali's face.

She's sweaty and grubby and all I can think of is making love to her. Mother, I'm far gone this time. With a thudding heart, Whit dodged around a group of artisans who were arguing about the meaning of some symbol, and approached Alborak's team.

"How're the ribs?" Whit called out.

Kali cast her an exasperated look. "Fine."

Coming closer, Whit justified in a low tone, "I can't help it. I still worry about you."

"I was hurt in June, right before Midsummer," Kali reasoned. "This is August 16th! Tomorrow is Lammas!"

"But you re-injured your ribs while you were fighting with Danu...."

Squatting down, Kali took the end of a thick length of plastic pipe, and lifted it with a grunt. Alborak hurried over, took the opposite end and the two women lugged it to the steel tray that would lift a load to the second floor. Whit trailed after them, shaking her head.

"Okay, okay. You're fine," Whit chuckled, signing to include Albie, though she addressed Kali. She reached out and gave Kali's brown arm a squeeze. "And you have big biceps, now, too. Don't think I haven't noticed what an Amazon you're becoming."

Alborak struck a pose; her broad shoulders flexed underneath the sleeveless blue shirt, and her thin black trousers stretched with her stance. Artemis the Archer. Whit recognized it and broke into pleased laughter.

With a self-conscious blush, Kali smiled, then gave Whit a sportive push. "I'm tougher than you think!"

Grinning, Whit returned, "Oh, are you, now?"

As they began scuffling, arms and hands and feet moving to get a better position in the impromptu wrestling match developing between them, Alborak abruptly took them by the shoulders and shoved them apart. With a mock severe expression, Alborak signed to Kali, *Get back to work!* Laughing, Kali signed back, *You need to get laid!* Alborak's eyebrows shot up and Kali had a new wrestling partner, as Alborak's only aim in life seemed to be dumping Kali on her rear end.

"Gov!" Lupa shouted from over by the crane. "C'mere!"

Abandoning Kali and Albie to their sparring, Whit walked over to join her Deputy Governor. As she stopped beside Lupa, thankful for the cool shadow of the huge machine, Whit muttered, "You okay?"

Mopping her face with a bandanna, Lupa tugged at the collar of her khaki jumpsuit and started on about how the crane had broken down.

The machine had seemingly ceased functioning in the midst of transferring the last batch of cedar shakes to the roof.

"Where's the mechanic?" Whit asked, glancing around.

"I sent the one I had assigned to this job site over to the lumber mill. One of the saws jammed."

Looking up, squinting into the sunlight, Whit could see a tray full of wood shingles suspended at the end of the still cable. "Is it the synth-hydraulics?" Whit asked.

Lupa answered, "I don't think so. I just tried to soft-boot the crane program and all I'm getting is garbage. Look." Lupa moved aside and Whit peered at the small screen in the side of the motor housing. A random series of alphabet letters and numbers were rapidly appearing, accumulating in a running string of nonsense.

A faint memory stirred in the back of Whit's mind. In flight school, she had learned how engine programs could be interrupted, over-ridden by a renegade code. "Who's been working this machine?" Whit asked softly.

Scratching her silver-haired head, Lupa responded, "Half the colony. All the women like to sit in the saddle and get a grip on this big monster."

Climbing up on the dusty, thick, vinyl tread, Whit began scrambling up onto the deck of the vehicle. In the distance, she spotted Danu, in a white shirt, sitting on a truckbed with a woman on either side of her. They were going over a set of blueprints together.

"Who was the last to use it?" Whit asked. She made for the driver's seat without waiting for an answer. A strange, prickling uneasiness was spreading across her shoulders and back. "Who?" she demanded of Lupa, her voice sharp.

"Marpe, of all people," the Chief Builder snickered. "You should have seen her, dressed like a fashion-plate, perched up there, all prim and..." Registering Whit's tension, Lupa stopped, disconcerted. "What is it?"

Whit dropped into the compu-chair that ran the mammoth machine. "Was Danu over here earlier?"

Lupa nodded, saying, "She was checking on the instructions I gave to the electrical crew. She's concerned about the second-story wiring."

Adjusting the driver's screen to her view height, Whit rapidly typed standard operating commands into the computer panel. Nothing happened. "What about Loy?" she demanded.

"What?" Lupa's leathery brow furrowed with puzzlement.

"Was Loy near the crane computer?" Again Whit typed escape-program commands into the computer panel; the stream of unrecognizable data continued across the screen.

"Yeah," Lupa admitted. "She brought Marpe a canteen of water, then leaned against the machine in the shade here and gossiped until Arinna came by and talked both Loy and Marpe into helping her over there...somewhere." Glancing around, irritably, Lupa grumbled, "I don't know where they've gotten to, but they certainly left me in the lurch."

Frantically, Whit re-typed the commands for escape-program, then shouted to Lupa, "Renegade code! I have no idea how to break the sequence!"

Alarmed, Lupa didn't bother going to the ladder in the rear. She began climbing over the thick tread, determined to get her old, stiff body onto the vehicle. "Crash the program!" she panted.

"I'm trying! I can't seem to access it!"

And then, miraculously, the unintelligible data streaming across the screen stopped. There was an endless pause and Whit heard Kali's laughter in the distance. As Whit's head snapped up, she had a sudden premonition. "Kali, *move! MOVE!!!*" she shouted. No sooner had the words left her lips than the crane engine snarled to life in a surge of power.

Approximately twenty-five feet in front of the machine, Kali's face turned toward Whit, a brief question in her eyes, though she was already responding to the urgency in Whit's voice. Having traveled across the Wilderness together, they had bonds which grew directly out of shared trauma and danger. When Whit shouted to her that way, questions would wait. Kali was darting clear as the thick cable that ran up the neck of the crane moved quickly forward, gave a resounding jolt, and then ran quickly in the opposite direction.

The whole machine bucked, throwing Whit from the bucket-chair as the cable reversed itself again. Her cap was gone. She tossed her head to clear the hair from her eyes. Trying to regain her seat and send another escape-program message, Whit noticed Alborak still standing beneath the heavy tray of roofing material, the tray now dancing menacingly on a fraying tether. The crowd began screaming as everyone else at the work site understood what was about to happen. Alborak, unable to hear, unable to understand why Kali had bolted away from her mere seconds ago, finally followed everyone's gaze and looked up.

For an instant, Whit had a clear impression of how strong and beautiful this young woman was—the brown hair gathered in a long, shining pony-tail, her sun-bronzed, muscled arms, and open-legged stance. Then the cable jerked forward and back, and snapped with a dreadful rip that seemed to tear through Whit's brain.

Screams. Then a flash of white, launching from the right and thrusting in a blur across Whit's field of vision. The steel tray smashing straight to the ground and the explosion of small cedar missiles flying up and out as they burst their retaining bands.

Before she could dodge, one of the shingles soared into Whit's forehead, cutting her above the eye. Wincing, she was already moving to Lupa, who was howling from several slices on her arm and scalp. And as she cradled the trembling elder, Whit threw a verifying glance to where she had last seen Kali, and then didn't see her. Frantically searching, Whit spied her lover slowly uncoiling from a protective cower, no less than ten feet from where the tray had landed. *She tried to go back after Albie!*

The numbness vanished and a towering wave of relief hit Whit. *Kali is safe—thank you Mother!* And then, despair slammed into her. *Albie!* Whit let go of Lupa and forced herself to stand, craning her neck to see over the deck of the crane. She was suddenly sick with horror at what she feared she would see.

What she saw was the almost empty steel tray lying absolutely flat, the heavy cable coiled like a snake upon it. And on the other side of the tray, Albie lay in her blue shirt—feebly struggling to get out from under Danu Sullivan. Near them, several women seemed to wrench themselves out of their paralytic poses, as they hurriedly began clearing the half-load of cedar shakes that had been dumped over Danu's back and legs.

Whit dropped to the ground and then assisted Lupa off the big machine. Neith appeared with several warrior medics in tow. She snapped off an impressive barrage of triage commands and got the warriors setting up first aid stations. One of the medics saw the bloody hand Lupa held against her hair and took charge of the pale-faced woman. Then, glancing at the trickling gash on Whit's face, the youngster invited her to sit down, too. Whit refused, mumbling that she was okay and moving past them.

Seeing the crowd gathering just beyond the fallen tray, Neith made for the spot, shoving her small body roughly into the middle. Close on her heels, Whit followed, snagging Kali in the crook of her arm. They embraced as they moved, each desperate to see if Danu still lived.

Neith ordered the crowd back, cursing them like an old grain-swapper when they didn't move fast enough for her. Now that she had seen just who was lying there, Neith was rapidly losing her professional detachment. Whit barked some names and the beefiest warriors in the circle of women asserted their presence, clearing a perimeter by pushing back the more curious.

Signing quickly, Neith got Alborak to cease her panicky effort to crawl out from under her injured friend.

As Neith ran the somascanometer over Danu's back, Whit watched the white cotton shirt turn color. Hundreds of tiny cuts were oozing red, slowly staining the shirt. The crowd waited, murmuring worriedly. And then Danu lifted her coppery curls from Alborak's chest, caught sight of Alborak's startled face, and dropped her head down, again. Her back shook a moment, and everyone held their breath, until they heard her clearly. Danu was laughing like a madwoman.

Looking both delighted and annoyed, Neith promptly swatted her across the rump.

As a loud, hearty laughter rose among the crowd, Loy appeared, pushing into the center, furious. Approaching Whit, Loy demanded in a voice that carried, "Were you trying to kill them?! I never saw such reckless operation of a crane in my life!!"

The laughter died into silence and all eyes swung to Whit. Half of the stares, Whit couldn't help but note, had become accusing.

☾ ☾ ☾

Kali couldn't believe how easily Loy had cast blame on Whit. As Kali opened her mouth, intent on hotly denying the charge, the frozen silence was split by Lupa Tagliaro's harsh, disgusted voice. "Whit wasn't operating the crane! She was trying to interrupt the programming error."

The crowd around Neith, Danu, and Alborak parted and Lupa strode into their midst. Behind her trailed the earnest medic, trying to subdue her with a hand on Lupa's arm. The wounded older woman slapped away the attempted restraint. "The crane computer screen was all nonsense...a renegade code," Lupa announced.

Standing up, Neith grasped Lupa gently behind the neck and pulled her head lower, peering at the bloodied white gauze Lupa gingerly held in place. "I want to examine this," Neith told her gently. "Let's go to my clinic."

"In a minute," Lupa insisted. "Loy's got this all wrong and I'm a witness."

The medic pulled a large tool box over and Neith helped Lupa sit down on it. As Danu rose, watching Lupa's white face with deep concern, Neith informed her, "Don't go anywhere, Sullivan. I want to see your back, too."

Still angry, Loy demanded, "Renegade code?! That doesn't make any sense! How did a renegade code get into the crane system?!"

All the women in the crowd looked to Whit. Kali noted that the silent accusations were quickly being transformed into anxiety.

Narrowing her eyes suspiciously, Whit returned, "Good question."

"Military Governor," Loy threatened, "if you wish to avoid charges of reckless endangerment being filed against you, please explain to the people of this colony what occurred that caused you to nearly kill two women."

At that, Kali indignantly faced Loy, "She was trying to stop the machine!"

Loy ran her eyes over Kali, answering, "Sorry. You're her lover—your opinion is biased."

Kali snapped, fuming. "I can't believe you're *blaming* Whit! You have no authority, you have no evidence...."

Swinging around to the assembled colonists, Loy hissed, "This whole reconstruction effort has been plagued with unnecessary accidents!

Whitaker and Lupa Tagliaro have set a ruthless pace—one of inordinate haste! They are taking dangerous short-cuts, so busy fretting about winter and early snows that they are putting lives in danger! Danu and Alborak were nearly killed just now!"

"But we weren't," Danu stated, brushing dirt off her hard-foam cast.

"By sheer luck you weren't," Loy retorted. "Whit has been made responsible for our safety. And when a machine suddenly develops a lethal malfunction, I hold her accountable!" With a defiant look, Loy barked at Whit, "That's what we mean by Chain of Command," then turned and walked stiffly away.

Apprehensively, Kali glanced over at Whit. The smoke-gray eyes were leveled at Loy's back. "Captain Greenberg, I expect a thorough investigation. Report to me with your findings tonight at the Command Center."

At the edge of the crowd, big Fea Greenberg studied Whit impassively, then moved away.

Then, Whit quickly examined the strained faces in the crowd, as if deciding something. "I declare a temporary suspension of work on this site."

The crowd still stood there, grim and silent.

"We've all been working hard for months now. I think we need a holiday," Whit announced. "And as tomorrow is Lammas, please take the day to use for your own pleasure."

The women broke into grateful, surprised grins. Some turned to talk to a friend, some hustled over to ask a special woman to join them in some amusement.

Far in the rear, Kali spotted Arinna, already working on the crane computer, disassembling the metal housing with a motorized screwdriver. With a crushing hug and a very serious kiss, Whit reluctantly took her leave of Kali and went over to help Arinna.

☾ ☾ ☾

"So, what happened after they carted me off?" Lupa demanded, wiggling into a more comfortable position on the bed and ignoring Neith's admonition to lie still.

It was late afternoon, just before the dinner hour of the same day, and Danu was visiting Lupa in Neith's clinic. Lupa had developed chest pains shortly after the crane accident, and Neith had insisted that she spend the night under medical observation.

Covertly watching Neith, Danu described the rest of the day's events. "Whit tried to reassure everyone. Of course, Neith made me spend about a half an hour with my shirt off before...."

Interrupting, Neith murmured, "Before everyone agreed what a fine physical specimen she is," causing Lupa to laugh.

Going deeply scarlet, Danu faltered.

Neith studied the EKG print-out and remarked, "Don't worry, Danu. I'm not jealous just because you saved your other girlfriend's life in front of the entire colony." The wry smile that followed made Lupa laugh all the harder.

Danu fell silent, unsure how to reply. She had gone from famine to feast in the romance department; so far it was just a lot of hand-holding, earnest talks, and soul-shattering kisses, but she *was* seeing both Neith and Albie at once. Unable to make up her mind, she had delayed the decision inexorably. She truly liked and enjoyed each woman too much to stop seeing her.

Even now, with Albie's passionate thank-you kiss still tingling on her lips like a hot brand, Danu found herself picking at the cast on her wrist, gazing at Neith. The white medical coat fell to her knees, and khaki pants covered her legs, but the open-collared shirt beneath revealed enough of Neith's luscious mahogany skin to make Danu wish she could see more. It was all Danu could do to keep from reaching across Lupa and stroking Neith's neck.

"And so, what happened?" Lupa demanded, impatient with the etiquette of teenage love affairs.

Danu pushed a hand into her shorts pockets and resumed, grateful for the diversion. "After Whit gave us Lammas off, most everyone went and worked on other unfinished buildings in town. A few of the more suspicious ones waited until Whit told them about the nonsense data you two saw on the crane computer. She explained that sometimes a computer program develops a glitch, triggering a malfunction of the machine...."

"Bah!!" Lupa shouted, thumping the bed for emphasis. "It was a renegade code—a plant—specially coded information someone loaded into the crane's computer. Someone deliberately intended to override the original programming!"

In a very low, very cordial tone, Neith told her, "You must remain calm, Deputy Governor." Then the Healer fixed Danu with a quizzical look. "Whit doesn't think this 'glitch' was intentional, does she?"

Danu replied, "I think she was trying to allay fears."

"So do I," Lupa agreed. "Someone has caused a series of malicious disruptions. First the scaffolding mysteriously collapsing, then a building framework blown apart in the merchants' sector, then arson in the supply depot by the Leader's House—thank Gaea Albie and Danu were back there that day and put it out before the fire really got out of control."

Under Neith's penetrating scrutiny, Danu felt the blood rush into her face.

"And now the crane...." Lupa finished.

"What does Whit plan to do about this?" Neith asked, her soft brown eyes wide.

"Yes, what?" Lupa asked Danu. "Surely, Whit isn't still hoping to catch this devil herself?"

Meeting both their eyes, Danu stated, "Whit radioed me just before I came in. Lilith is due here tomorrow. There's going to be a full investigation."

Groaning loudly, Lupa thumped the bed again. "Which means more delays!"

With a sympathetic smile, Neith patted Lupa's arm. "It is just as well. You need a day in bed."

As Neith walked away, Danu stared at her retreating figure.

Giving a chortle, Lupa whispered, "I know who needs a day in bed—and it isn't *me!*"

☾ ☾ ☾

Across town, in the Cedar House, Kali followed up her day of work as a utility crew laborer with a meal and her usual schooling session. Still dressed in her dusty work clothes, Kali spent several hours studying, then took the last of her secondary school final exams. After filing the 21st century herstory test, she sat back in the compu-chair and closed her eyes, relieved and yet discouraged. There was still so much to learn.

She knew Whit would be in town until late, meeting with her Directors and the Chiefs. Today's crane accident meant Fea Greenberg was running yet another investigation. *Which means Loy is probably counseling Fea about likely suspects,* Kali thought glumly. *We'll be lucky if Whit isn't under arrest by morning.*

She turned off the computer and wearily walked to the doorway. Pausing there, she made herself focus carefully on closing the door and then engaging the DNA lock system.

Since she had checked the research files stored in her mother's computer a few weeks back and discovered the Think Tank Project in its entirety, Kali had become incredibly nervous about the lab's security. Whit said the data couldn't be housed in a safer place, but Kali wasn't so sure.

The Isis Cedar House had its own force field, which would be triggered by anyone attempting to break into the building. All the same, Kali knew that anyone in Isis could unlock the outer door by merely touching their fingers to the DNA plate; the entrance to the Cedar House was programmed to accept the DNA code of any settler in the colony. Only the lab door had a built-in code limit. The lab door would recognize the DNA codes of only two individuals: Whit and herself.

Kali walked along the dimly lit hallway, opened the door to the Council Room, and then passed through that spacious, shadowy chamber, listening to the echo her construction boots caused as she walked across the smooth, tile floor. Gazing into the darkened corners beyond the security lights, she thought she sensed the presence of another person. She stopped and stood there a few moments, listening with her mind.

Nothing.

Now I'm imagining things, Kali thought. Scratching her head, bewildered, she resumed her passage through the vast hall.

Once outside, she stopped beside the big motorcycle and rummaged in the saddlebag attached to the rear. Pulling out Whit's leather flight jacket, she slipped it on and then climbed aboard the bike.

As she rocked the cycle off its kickstand, she caught the edge of the coat collar with her chin.

The jacket smelled of Whit. Kali sat there for a moment, holding the soft collar against her nose, breathing in that distinctively sweet fragrance. Then, sighing, she started the engine and set off across the meadow.

Though it was only 8:30 p.m., a luminous blue-green twilight filled the western sky, silhouetting the fir trees which covered the ridge. It was mid-August now and the sunlight hours were lessening each day. Autumn was close—a month away, and Kali worried that winter would be upon them before they had managed to complete the really essential parts of Isis. Today's mysterious accident would only slow things down more.

Troubled as she was by the day's events, Kali was yawning as she aimed the bike toward the trail home. She was more than thankful that now all she had to do was stand in the shower, and then fall into bed.

☾ ☾ ☾

Styx looked up from the small camp fire she had built in the yard before Whit and Kali's house, watching the headlight flashing through the trees on the ridge. She waited patiently, sitting on her rock, as the motorcycle turned into the drive and purred toward her. In the glow of yellow firelight, Kali looked endearingly disheveled and tired. Dressed in work boots and baggy, khaki shorts, Styx recognized Whit's leather flight jacket hanging on Kali's more slender frame. Kali dropped a foot on either side of the cycle, bringing it to a slow stop and staring at her in surprise.

"I caught a ride out from the airfield with a supply truck," Styx explained, standing up easily and walking to her.

"What are you doing here?" Kali asked anxiously, dismounting quickly and knocking the kickstand down. "Is Lilith alright?"

Styx replied calmly, "Lilith is well." Opening her arms, she waited for Kali's greeting embrace before finishing, "It is *you* we are concerned about."

Stepping back, Kali's brow wrinkled with puzzlement, "Me?"

Nodding, Styx placed her arm around Kali's shoulders and led her over to the fire. "We heard about the crane accident. This is the third time that you've been involved in one of these bizarre episodes." Kali interrupted, trying to minimize the incident, but Styx waved her silent. "It seems too often for it to be mere coincidence."

Distractedly, Kali gestured toward the large granite home before them. "Come up to the house. You must be hungry or thirsty."

Turning and glancing at the dark windows, Styx returned, "In a few minutes. I had dinner, earlier, in Artemis." Her low voice soothing, Styx said, "It's a fine summer evening to be outside. And you and I need to talk, I think."

Unsure what that meant, Kali gave Styx a searching look.

"Lilith is helping Cimbri and Nakotah tonight," Styx continued. "As the new Leader and Deputy Leader of Artemis, they are presenting their first policy proposal to the Artemis Council. They will all join us tomorrow, for Lammas. Which allows you and me tonight to discuss our common idiosyncrasies."

Kali stepped away from Styx and held her hands over the fire, warming them. Warily glancing at Styx from the corner of her eye, she repeated, "Idiosyncrasies?"

"Cimbri asked me what I thought about the mind bond you two shared while she was taking care of your ribs, last month." Watching Kali swallow nervously, Styx elaborated, "She didn't mean to betray a confidence. She thought that by now you would have told me."

Kali bent her head, chagrined. Her golden hair, gathered back from her face in a tangled French braid, flashed in the firelight.

Quietly, Styx related, "She also mentioned that you're telepathic."

Kali cursed under her breath, "Shit."

Styx motioned Kali to sit down on one of the large granite boulders. Instead, Kali used her well-scuffed boot to restlessly kick loose some small stones beneath the grass.

Shrugging and sitting, herself, Styx remarked, "In many ways, you are still a child."

Lifting her head, Kali sent Styx a defiant look.

Styx studied Kali as she elaborated. "Maat was brilliant, brave, resolute. She valued the concrete, and had no time for the ethereal. How ironic that you, the child she produced, are steadily developing powers that she felt were beyond any human brain."

Heaving an exasperated sigh, Kali bent down and yanked out a tall stem of grass, inserting the tip in her down-turned mouth. "My mother would think me a freak," she mumbled, not looking at Styx.

Again, Styx shrugged. "Then I am a freak, too. I believe we have merely learned to understand a language of the mind."

Relaxing a bit, Kali tossed the grass stem aside, walked over and sat beside her. Styx's long braid was in front of her shoulder, and her large-knuckled, brown hands absent-mindedly stroked the black and silver threads.

"Why can I hear them thinking?" Kali blurted. "How do I make it stop?"

Styx put an arm around her, asking in a calming voice, "Do you remember hearing voices when you were little?"

"Only a few times. Mother didn't believe me when I tried to tell her. After a while, I didn't believe it either, and then I didn't hear with my mind any more."

Stroking her back, Styx murmured, "And in Elysium?"

Kali shrank down a bit, the stark fear flooding her at the mere mention of that land. "I heard the Regs. I knew what they wanted to do every time they looked at me." With a slight, involuntary shudder, Kali finished, "Only the AGH tattoo and the skin lesions Baubo caused kept them off of me."

"Tell me about Baubo," Styx prodded.

Facing her, perplexed, Kali admitted, "In those earliest days, the ones I can barely remember, I know I couldn't speak. Yet, she always knew what I wanted to say."

Styx nodded. "Did she train you—teach you to perfect these mind skills?"

"No. I'm positive about that. She worked me hard—that's all."

"Explain," Styx urged. "Worked you hard how?"

"Baubo had me work in the fields with my hand tools for hours, until I'd get dizzy, fuzzy-headed. Then she'd come and lead me to the shade trees. I'd lie down in the grass and she'd talk to me till I felt like I was floating. I think I slept...." Kali trailed off, pondering the sensual nature of that deep rest. "I had dreams of being free...of being home...though I had no idea where 'home' was." Blushing, Kali nearly whispered, "I had dreams of standing by a tall, dark woman's side, and knowing...she needed me."

"Trance-teaching. No wonder," Styx muttered. "You're opening like a California poppy touched by the morning sun."

"What?" Kali frowned, bewildered.

Fingering the coarse tassel of hair, Styx explained, "Baubo taught you to channel the psychic skills you were born with, among them, telepathy. And she programmed you so that the full range of these powers would unfold as you came home, as you learned to believe in yourself again."

Dumbfounded, Kali stared at Styx's wise Mayan face.

"Like it or not, Kali you're a telepath, if not more," Styx continued. "And there is probably not much more I can teach you, for I think you are far more gifted than I am."

Protesting, Kali sat up straighter. "But you're telepathic...."

"Not like you are," Styx stated gently. "I hear people I am close to, people I care for. Correct me if I'm wrong...but you hear just about everyone, am I right?"

With a tight nod, Kali rose, picked up a few small dry branches Styx had gathered earlier and tossed them on the flames. The fire crackled and leapt, lighting up Kali's sunburned, melancholy face.

Styx announced, "And I think you have many other abilities, waiting beneath the surface of your unconscious, ready to sprout. Baubo planted a rich field when she trance-taught you."

"But I don't want this!" Kali declared. "I don't *want* to hear people's thoughts! I don't *want* to know things without ever understanding how I know them! I want to be like everyone else!"

"By the very nature of your genes," Styx instructed, "you are never going to be like everyone else. You were given a gift, like Danu was given her architectural talent, like I was protected from a familial health weakness."

Kali's breath left her throat. "I know."

"Yes, you know," Styx consoled her. "And now you must do more than know. You must *use* your knowledge. Your mother never carried you. Your DNA was nurtured in a nutrient wash of your mother's own creation, and then you were placed in the Artemis Delphi unit. You were especially conceived to be who, and what, you are becoming."

After a moment, obviously struggling for words, Kali managed, "I'm not...crazy, then."

"No!" Styx huffed, mildly aggravated. "Pay attention! Your mother was attempting to expand your cognitive abilities, and in doing so she seems to have engendered some sort of paranormal sensitivity."

"Well, what am I supposed to *do* with it?!" Kali asked, bewildered. "I'm so out of control—just stumbling along...."

Firmly Styx counseled, "You will never control your gift without defeating the best part of who you are. You must, instead, learn how to focus and use your power."

Kali studied Styx, relieved to hear some explanation at last, while at the same time, almost instinctively doubting that something so far-fetched could be true.

Without saying a thing, Styx's reply sounded in Kali's mind. *It is true—you know it is true. And there may be others like us.*

Kali shook her head, skeptical.

The wise, dark eyes gazed at her, as Styx commented, "You must admit, someone seems to be going to a great deal of trouble to get you out of the way."

☾ 10

The next day was the "Feast of Bread," the August 17th celebration of the grain which was ripening into an abundant harvest. In Artemis, where grains were a vital crop, Lammas was full of meaning. But in Isis, with its glacially scraped soil, Lammas had always been primarily a day to celebrate good beer.

By mid-morning, Nakotah had landed the Leader's Swallow at the edge of the Isis airfield. As Cimbri and Lilith disembarked, an elated Nakotah waved at Whit from the cockpit, causing Whit to burst into laughter.

"Cimbri may have won the election for Leader of Artemis," Whit promptly told Kali, "but it looks like, as Deputy and partner, Nakotah won the aircraft!"

Styx left Kali's side and went to embrace Lilith, as the former Leader of Artemis whispered softly, "Oh, my dear, you were only gone for one night, but how I did miss you!"

And then they were all hugging one another and laughing. It had been a busy summer, and the six friends had seen each other far less often than they had intended.

As they walked from the landing strip to the large, four-wheel-drive troop transport, Lilith asked, "Anything new on the crane accident?"

Whit asserted, "According to Captain Greenberg's report, there are still no clear answers. All I really know is the obvious: the crane drastically malfunctioned." Her gray eyes serious, she addressed the entire group. "The machine, like most heavy construction vehicles, does not register a DNA code when someone accesses its programming functions. A fingerprint scan of the crane computer housing brought up the recent smudges of half the women in the colony. I have absolutely no hard evidence."

"But you do have a suspect in mind, I think," Styx guessed, her soft, dark eyes on Kali, who seemed unusually withdrawn and preoccupied.

"I can't prove a thing," Whit stated. "However, I'm hoping that Captain Greenberg will be able to turn up something soon."

"In the meantime," Styx announced to the new arrivals, "it seems that we'll be treated to some campaign speeches, today. Loy Yin Chen has challenged her opponents to attend a public forum in the meadow before the Cedar House."

"Oh, no," groaned Nakotah. "Not more speeches." She tossed her long braids over her shoulder and advised Whit, "There's nothing worse than having to listen to a campaign speech, except having to *give* one."

As Whit smiled in response, Lilith asked, "With all that's been going on, Whit, are you prepared to handle campaigning as well?"

Hesitating a moment, Whit finally said, "I'm ready, I guess."

Reading uncertainty in Whit's hesitation, Cimbri remarked, "That's probably what Loy is counting on. Your mind is everywhere except on the Leader election. She and Arinna have an advantage over you, there."

"What's this I hear about Loy making accusations against you?" Lilith asked Whit.

For the first time, Kali stirred out of her reverie and spoke up. "A month ago, when Danu attacked Loy in the meal hall, Loy implied that Danu had done it *for* Whit—to help Whit get rid of her competition."

Disturbed, Lilith inquired further. "Did she accuse Whit of putting Danu up to it?"

They reached the big troop transport and everyone began climbing in as Kali answered, "Not exactly in those words, but the intimation was there."

"Whoa!" Cimbri said, looking incredulous.

"And then," Kali went on, "after the crane cable snapped and the freight tray almost landed on Albie, Loy accused Whit of operating the machine in a reckless manner." She touched her lover protectively on the shoulder as Whit helped Lilith step into the truck. "But when Lupa told us about the strange programming code both she and Whit had seen on the monitor moments before the crane malfunctioned, Loy changed tactics."

"How?" Cimbri prompted.

"She made a far more accurate statement," Whit replied, suddenly grim-faced and frustrated. "Loy reminded the crowd that I am responsible for the lives and welfare of this community. With all these accidents and emotional disruptions occurring, it doesn't look as if I'm doing a very good job, does it?"

No one answered.

Everyone except Whit was in the large vehicle now. Stiffly, she climbed in beside Kali. Starting the engine, then shifting into gear, Whit muttered, "I hate politics."

From her seat in the rear with the others, Lilith watched Kali reach over and give Whit's knee a reassuring squeeze.

                    (((

As the transport vehicle drove over the smooth new road through the outskirts of the colony, heading toward the countryside, they passed a glum-looking Danu Sullivan wandering along the side of the road.

Whit slowed down and called to her, "Where are you going?" When Danu shrugged, Whit pulled the vehicle over and insisted that Danu get in beside Kali. "When you have a day off," Whit scolded, "you're supposed to celebrate and have fun, damn it."

And having said that, Whit seemed determined to keep her spirits up. Once they reached the granite house in the valley, she and Kali served the group a leisurely lunch of fruit, bread, and cheeses. Then, in the tradition of Lammas, Whit brought out the beer.

Raising her glass, she officially toasted Cimbri, the newly elected Leader of Artemis, and her Deputy Leader, Nakotah. While everyone echoed the toast, Cimbri and Nakotah laughingly embraced. Then everyone raised their cup in salute to Lilith, who was beginning her retirement.

At Cimbri's request, Kali took everyone on a walking tour of the large house. Somewhat embarrassed, she explained that with the time-consuming, tiring work of re-building the city, they had not spent much time furnishing or making their home comfortable. Except for the bedroom, with its huge bed, the dressers built into the walls, and the audio chip-player, the house was austere. Empty, uncarpeted rooms, curtainless windows, and echoing halls were all Kali and Whit had to show. The house had become merely a place to sleep, as they had fallen into a habit of taking their meals in the communal meal hall in town. The rooms of the granite house were bare and unwelcoming. With a smile, Lilith told Kali not to worry.

"Once the snow begins," Lilith comforted her, "you can spend months working on the inside of your home, just as everyone else will. Right now, you are all racing winter."

Whit, who had been trailing along at the rear of the tour, moodily silent, came to life again as they reached the porch. She began circulating among her friends, jesting and listening attentively, as if making another conscious effort to put aside her troubles.

For the next few minutes, Kali moved about, politely refilling cups. Leaning against the porch railing, Lilith was watching Whit intently. In a soft, white dress, Lilith looked serene in her first month of retirement. Yet those penetrating blue eyes were narrowed, determined, as if the elder had come on some unspoken mission. Almost without effort, Kali found herself delving into Lilith's thoughts, listening through the levels of mind-chatter in Lilith's busy brain. Then all at once Kali's focus was jarred by a warm tone breaking into her own mind.

You must exercise good judgement when using this trick.

Startled, Kali turned, met Styx's discerning dark eyes and realized Whit wasn't the only one under scrutiny.

With a short nod, Kali moved away, mortified. She had been going along for weeks, now, not allowing herself to notice how much she had come to rely on this obnoxious little invasion of privacy. She was constantly listening in on the thoughts of others. Ever since that building had dropped out from under her, burying her in debris, the mind-link had seemed an imperative asset, like an additional sense she could not explain or forego using.

Setting the pitcher aside, Kali realized that without effort, she was hearing threads of thought swirling all around her, clear as the voices in the air.

Danu's thoughts, alone, were blaring. A freckled hand dashed through red curls several times in succession, unconsciously displaying the habit she had picked up from working these past few months beside

Whit. Danu's thoughts were tumultuous; from what Kali could discern, Albie had extended an invitation to Danu only this morning; an invitation to sleep with her. Though powerfully attracted, Danu had asked for time to think and Albie had laughingly consented. And now—in the fickleness of the heart—all of Danu's thinking seemed to center on Neith.

On the steps, Cimbri sat, leaning against the large, white painted column, smothering a yawn. Her dark African skin betrayed a slight sheen of sweat, though she seemed comfortable in her loose orange-red slacks and matching shell. Her thoughts were meditative, focused on the quiet. Ever the sensuous woman, she was engrossed with listening to the finches cheeping in the meadow and smelling the spice of Queen Anne's lace in the warm breeze.

Whit stood beside Cimbri, looking marvelously fit in a well-pressed warrior's uniform. "I see Nakotah just had to try out the Leader's Swallow," Whit teased, referring to the silver, four-seat tilt-rotor Nakotah had landed so jubilantly at the airfield earlier.

Cimbri grinned. "She seems to think it's her own personal toy! She wants to fly it everywhere. I keep telling her it looks elitist, but you know 'Kotah...."

Whit laughed. After a slight hesitation, she asked softly, "Do you like the new job?" Kali noted that Whit was looking down at Cimbri with an almost tender concern. It was easy to see that they had been lovers, once.

They are so different from the way Whit and Loy are with each other, Kali observed.

With a smile, Cimbri returned, "Well, it's only been a few weeks. So far, I'm surviving. But being Leader is...different." As Whit grinned back, Cimbri finished, "You look wonderful, Whit. I think leading is good for you."

It's true, Kali thought. The summer's work had burnished Whit, leaving her like a smooth, round stone in a shallow stream. Strong as she had been before, Whit had grown stronger. Her rough edges had been smoothed down and the true integrity of her granite exposed. Her will had been forged by adversity, her resilience had endured both the obvious and the subtle tests of leadership.

Zealous backers had already long ago nominated Whit for Leader of Isis. Loy's name, and Arinna's too, had been on the ballot for weeks. The election was scheduled for early September, barely two weeks away. And with all the curious twists of fate that had occurred during the reconstruction of Isis, no one had any clear idea who would win.

Yet, at the mere thought of the election, a chill of foreboding settled around Kali's heart.

☾ ☾ ☾

Leaving the others on the front porch, Whit went to the kitchen at the back of the house, seeking a moment of peace before she faced the prospect of delivering a campaign speech to a meadow full of women, some of whom were disgruntled, disillusioned settlers. The back door was open, and Whit walked over and gazed out at the quiet August day.

Hearing a step, she turned and found Lilith almost upon her. "Only you could get this close before I heard you," Whit laughed.

"'A good warrior never turns her back to a door,'" Lilith admonished, chuckling. "Wasn't that your motto, once?"

Shrugging, Whit commented ruefully, "Too many doors to keep track of, these days."

"Come, Whit, talk to me," Lilith said gently, pushing the screen door open and leading the way outside.

Slowly, Lilith sat down on the top step of the smaller back porch. Whit sat beside her in the cool shade, then reached over and took Lilith's hand. She was wonderfully content in the company of this woman who had adopted her shortly after her own family had died in the fall of Isis.

Looking up, Whit noticed Styx and Kali walking through the wildflowers and tall, green grass on the side of the house. They seemed to be deep in earnest discussion.

Watching them, too, Lilith asked, "Is Kali alright, Whit? She seems...on edge."

Whit frowned. "Yes. I've noticed it, too. She finished her secondary schooling last night, but she won't let me tell anyone. All that work, even when she was exhausted from laboring on the utility crew, and she's still not satisfied."

"She measures herself against you," Lilith observed.

Knowing the truth of it, Whit kept silent.

Lilith asked, "How is she adjusting to life in Isis?"

Carefully, Whit considered the answer. She had known that Kali's need for exits—a door, a window, some escape route—had caused Kali to be placed on a utility crew, a crew that would usually be working in a wide-open building framework, not in a fully enclosed structure. But everyone had their little quirks. Whit, herself, liked to sit so that she faced the door of a room; her years of warrior training and her own time in Elysium had left her with that peculiarity. And though unsettled by it, Kali had weathered being caught in the blast and collapse of that building in the merchants' sector well over a month ago.

"All in all," Whit stated, "I think she's okay. Why?"

With a smile, Lilith remarked, "I have some news for you."

"Oh?" Whit was intrigued by the dancing blue light in Lilith's eyes.

"According to this morning's comline report, the citizens of Isis have made Kali the fourth nominee for Leader."

Whit blinked, stunned.

Lilith spent a moment studying Whit's face, the piercing blue eyes plumbing the depths of Whit's soul. "Will you be able to handle that?" Lilith asked.

Gripping Lilith's hand tighter, Whit looked back at her. "I serve the women of Isis," she answered, feeling a bit dazed. Then her eyes fell. She struggled to make sense of this news, adrift in uncertainty. Was her leadership being completely rejected? Was Kali's steadily increasing resemblance to Maat causing a nostalgic reaction of some kind?

"You realize, of course," Lilith's serious voice intoned, "that you two are now seen as a pair, as Cimbri and Nakotah are in Artemis."

"A pair?" Whit whispered, baffled.

"Yes," Lilith soothed, then removed her hand from Whit's grasp and slipped it around Whit's waist. "The citizens of Isis are not just looking for a Leader and a Deputy Leader. They are looking for two individuals who will work together as a team. No doubt those who nominated Kali have her in mind for your Deputy."

Relieved, Whit sighed, "Oh."

Her voice rising subtly, betraying the intensity of her feeling, Lilith finished, "But one day, Kali *will* be your equal, in all ways. And *then* what shall you do?"

"Help her," Whit returned. "As she has always helped me."

Saying nothing, Lilith pulled Whit into a sheltering, maternal embrace. After several minutes, Lilith pronounced, "You are worthy of each other, then. And worthy of the task before you."

☾ ☾ ☾

Thirty minutes later, shortly before two o'clock in the afternoon, everyone climbed into the transport vehicle and Whit drove over the ridge to the Isis Cedar House. As the transport wound along the smooth road, surrounded by evergreen trees, the vehicle was silent with the tension of its passengers.

Sitting down beside Whit, Kali reached over and took her hand. And Whit realized that while Styx and Kali had walked through the field of tall grass by the side of the house, Styx had been informing Kali of her recent nomination for Leader. All at once, as Whit met those deep, loving brown eyes, she was deeply glad for Kali. The P.O.W. who had survived so much, was about to stand for Leader, as her mother had once stood before her.

Nakotah began humming a warrior song about love and honor among women. Gradually, Cimbri, Lilith, Styx, Danu, Kali and then Whit herself joined in, until they were all singing the verses, uniting voices and souls in eloquent emotion.

Leaving the fir forest, the road rolled down to the edge of the meadow and the song drifted to a sudden close. In the distance, the large Cedar House stood, its tall white belltower clean and vibrant against the blue sky. And there in the vast meadow, approximately a thousand women sat on blankets, sharing picnic lunches, talking, waiting for the speakers to arrive.

For a moment, it seemed odd to Whit that there could be so many women in one place and no children in sight. And yet she knew that two weeks from now, after the election, the children would begin arriving, and Isis would be a full-fledged colony again.

Carefully, she steered the big transport vehicle along the paved road that led to the Cedar House. Women near the road saw Lilith and began waving, while some threw questioning looks at Whit, as if they still weren't sure what they thought of her. Then they passed a group who had no doubts about their loyalties. The women jumped to their feet, calling Whit's name and cheering.

Parking the transport near the edge of the forest, Whit hopped out and helped everyone disembark. Lilith, Styx, Cimbri and Nakotah spent a moment sincerely wishing both Whit and Kali good luck, trading embraces and short, encouraging remarks before setting off for the far side of the field. As visiting dignitaries, they would be seated in chairs situated close to the stage.

Nearby, a temporary automatic-camera tower had been erected to carry this debate on the comline. With a glance, Whit took in the two huge screens that had been assembled before the Cedar House, allowing the camera to magnify what some in the back of the crowd might have trouble seeing.

Like me sweating and scared to death! Whit couldn't help but worry. *I've never been much good at making speeches. Action has always been my specialty.*

Left standing alone with them by the transport, Danu Sullivan glanced shyly from Kali to Whit. "Just remember, no matter what anyone says about you, no matter how many things have not gone quite right—you're both responsible for bringing all of these women to Isis." With that, Danu made a sweeping gesture with her hand, and Whit really looked at the multitude of women before them.

They were laughing, dynamic, free women—all manner of races, all manner of ages and physical appearances, covering the hillside like so many wildflowers blooming beneath a summer sun. This was the population of Isis, and together, during the past four months, they had made a grand start on building the core of their city.

Moved beyond words, Whit felt the tears slide down her face, tears of reverence and wonder and joy.

Dashing her own tears away, Kali gripped Danu in a bear hug, then released her and strode purposefully toward the speakers' platform.

Danu turned toward Whit, extending her hand. Slowly, Whit pulled her into an embrace that felt oddly comfortable. Hugging Danu gently, Whit whispered in her ear, "Thanks for reminding me about what really matters."

They separated, each regarding the other with open, heartfelt affection. At last, Whit turned and marched toward the speaker's platform, where Arinna, Loy and Kali waited for her.

☾ ☾ ☾

Sitting there in the hot sunshine, fanning herself with Styx's bandanna, Lilith watched the candidates draw straws to determine the order of speaking. Then, the comline technicians bustled about, attaching tiny microphones to each candidate's collar and testing it for good reception, before leaving the stage. Arinna cleared her throat and her familiar voice was amplified by the speaker units which were mounted on the huge screens flanking each side of the stage.

After another moment, the Chief of Security, Fea Greenberg stepped forward and announced, "The first speaker will be Arinna Sojourner; the second, Tomyris Whitaker; the third, Kali Tyler; and the last speaker will be Loy Yin Chen."

Anxiously, Styx and Lilith exchanged an uneasy glance. They both knew that the last speaker always had the advantage of the last word.

Arinna stood before the crowd, arrayed in a smartly tailored, peach-colored suit. Raising her silvery voice, Arinna called, "If you elect me Leader, Isis will one day be a grand city, a shining star among colonies."

She went on like that for quite some time. While her speech was competent and delivered with great poise, Lilith found herself wondering exactly how Arinna intended to achieve any of these unrealistic visions. Arinna offered no ideas, no policies to consider. After twenty minutes of grandiose rhetoric, the crowd was stirring with a lazy irritability. It was too hot to be sitting in the sun listening to pipedreams.

As Arinna sat down, Whit stood and a hearty cheer went up from various bands of loyal supporters. Whit walked to the front of the stage, looking splendid in her neat, gray uniform, her glossy, dark hair shining in the sun. The crowd shifted expectantly, as if anxious to hear something of worth from one they felt sure would give it to them.

"We have come a long way," Whit began. She paused and looked around at them, appearing strangely calm, as if her mind was at rest. "Where there were ruins in April, there will be a city in September."

A murmuring response grew in the crowd; they were proud of themselves and what they had accomplished. Lilith mentally congratulated Whit for reminding them of that.

"However," Whit continued, "We still have a long way to go."

Some women loudly groaned.

"Yes, you are sick of me prodding you to complete more buildings, to achieve more goals, but there are children coming...."

The crowd was silent, now. Lilith could hear a joyous bird singing deep in the forest.

"...and we are responsible for them and for each other. I have put together some proposals concerning economic planning and city services, which I have filed in the comline system under my name. They are far too extensive for me to try to tell you about in a campaign speech. Instead, I think you may prefer to access them and evaluate these detailed accounts of my ideas at your convenience."

Women throughout the crowd were sitting up straighter, eyes riveted on Whit, plainly interested.

"I'd like to take this opportunity to thank you for your cooperation and hard work while I acted as your Military Governor. I am honored to know each and everyone of you." Whit paused again, her eyes passing over the crowd. With a smile, she finished, "And whatever else happens, elected or not, I am always at your service."

And then, Whit brought her hand to her heart, saluting them.

It was such an unexpectedly short and evocative speech, that the audience sat there for a moment afterwards, astounded, while Whit walked back to her chair and sat down. Then, the women of Isis were on their feet, returning the salute and applauding.

Thoroughly heartened by the cheers ringing out, Lilith turned to Styx and enthused, "I think she's turned their heads again!"

"We still haven't heard from Loy," Styx rejoined.

Nodding, sobered by that fact, Lilith watched Kali come to the front of the stage. In her sleeveless, mint-green shell and stone-gray cotton pants, her golden hair held back from her face by a French braid, Kali looked amazingly like Maat.

The similarity seemed to strike the older women in the crowd at the same time the realization hit Styx and Lilith. There was a noise like the surf upon the sand, as hundreds of women softly gasped.

Meanwhile, Kali herself looked a bit overwhelmed. She stood before a thousand women, her brown eyes wide, her hands nervously clenching and unclenching at her sides. Just as Lilith began to fear she would be unable to manage a word—let alone an oration—Kali called out to them. "There comes a time in each woman's life when she must decide what she believes in, what she will stand for...." She stopped as her voice trembled. With a stronger, second effort, she went on, "And what she is willing to *contribute* to grow freely in a free land."

The women in the meadow were silent, waiting.

"For us, here in Isis, that time is *now*. We are about to choose our Leader." Kali searched the sea of faces, pausing and locking eyes, speaking directly to one woman at a time. "Will we choose a Leader who dares to expect our best effort? Will we choose a Leader with written plans, proposing how to forge a robust economy, how to safely utilize our natural resources?"

Carefully, Lilith inspected the women near them. Kali definitely had their attention.

"Or will we choose," Kali continued, "a Leader who is too concerned with her own glory to think about the possible glory of Isis? A Leader who does not bother to find a way, because she is too busy finding fault. One who does not produce plans, but instead, ridicules the plans of others."

Behind Kali, Loy folded her arms across her chest, glaring at the slender, blonde speaker. A murmuring discussion began among the crowd.

"A woman who has never tried to grow," Kali stated forcefully, "because she has found it much easier to simply *cut down* anyone else around her who threatens to stand tall."

She stood there, gazing at them, prolonging the effect of those deliberately penetrating questions. Then slowly, Kali's eyes swept the crowd. She seemed to be looking into each woman's soul. Finally, she said, "I trust that your inherent wisdom and love for Isis will guide your decision." And with that, Kali turned and began moving back to her seat.

Loy stood and walked toward the front of the platform, scowling. She was unable to resist whispering as she came alongside of Kali, "Talking about *me*?" The sensitive microphone on her shirt collar caught both the words and Loy's defensive tone, broadcasting them through the speakers on the sides of each visual screen. As she heard herself, Loy's head snapped around. Alarmed, she became absorbed in checking the crowd's reaction. Kali continued past her, resolute and silent.

Bravo, Kali! Lilith thought, watching Loy searching her pockets for her notes, desperately trying to regain her composure.

Drawing out some small cards, Loy inspected them quickly, then challenged, "How can anyone even consider electing Whitaker as Leader, when this colony is still at the mercy of a malicious vandal?" She paused for dramatic effect, and re-pocketed the cards.

In the crowd, silence reigned.

Loy settled her lightweight black vest more comfortably over her satiny, white shirt, then launched her attack. "As Military Governor, Whitaker has been made directly responsible for our safety, our welfare. Yet we have had accident after accident, injury after injury! She is responsible...."

Someone in the crowd yelled, "What are *you* responsible for? What are *your* plans?"

Loy stopped, confounded. After casting a suspicious glance across the many women in the meadow, she renewed her speech. "Everything Whitaker has done...."

Another, different voice hollered, "What have *you* done?"

Fuming, Captain Greenberg rushed onto the stage to stand beside Loy. "There will be no heckling!"

Yet another anonymous voice called, "What are you, Fea—her guard dog?"

Enraged, Captain Greenberg scanned the laughing crowd, bellowing, "I'll get you, whoever you are, if I have to arrest half the women here to do it!"

Through tight lips, Loy indignantly ordered, "Go sit down."

"Let me handle this...." Fea retorted, still sweeping her eyes over the assembly.

"You big idiot," Loy snapped, trying to push her away. "You're just making this worse!"

Unaccustomed to being called a big idiot—particularly in front of an entire population, with a comline telecast catching the action as well—Fea shoved Loy's hands from her. "So, I'm an idiot, am I?" Fea retorted, instantly in a rage. "A few months ago, when you needed me, I was good enough to be your next Major! But only if I lent my authority to your tale about old methane pipes under the merchants' sector!"

A low grumble of anger followed that revelation, as women turned to each other in disbelief, discussing what they had just heard. The grumble quickly became a roar. Women were declaring their outrage, expressing their shock.

Fea had just publicly revealed that Loy Yin Chen had both meddled in a security investigation and extended a bribe. Lilith knew that any chance Loy might have had of defeating Whit in an open election had just evaporated.

Shaking her head in disgust, Arinna stood up and rapidly left the stage. Fea Greenberg followed her. Whit and Kali looked at each other, unsure what to do.

By now furious, Loy shouted at the audience, "It's not like it sounds! Let me explain!"

"Why don't you blame it on Whit?" someone called back.

The crowd began to laugh. Aghast, Loy stood there, her dreams of power disintegrating before her eyes.

"You don't understand," Loy began again, trying for a reasonable, professional tone of voice. "Captain Greenberg has somehow gotten an overly optimistic impression...."

The laughter turned into a scattering of boos.

"She was *lying*!" Loy flashed. "I never told her that...."

The boos grew in number and were joined by whistles and catcalls, until Loy was nearly drowned out.

Gathering her pride, Loy gave the crowd a look of unbridled hatred, then stalked majestically from the stage.

Amazed, Whit and Kali exchanged another look. Suddenly decisive, Whit flipped the transmitter switch on her microphone, turning it off, before leaning forward and doing the same thing for Kali. Earnestly, Whit demanded, "Why did you speak for me? You're a nominee, too. You should have spoken for yourself."

"What makes you think I didn't?" Kali returned, betraying with a small grin how pleased with herself she was.

Laughing appreciatively, Whit lovingly stroked Kali's cheek, then looked about them. They were the only ones left onstage. The audience was standing, milling about, folding up their blankets. "Well,

I guess Loy got what she deserved. Can't say I'm sorry." Then shrugging, she suggested, "Let's go home."

As they both stood to leave, the first cheers went up. Quickly, the reaction compounded, until all the women in the meadow were yelling and whistling their encouragement. The women of Isis were choosing their leaders with their voices, long before any ballot was required.

Proudly, Lilith stood in the circle of Styx's arm, yelling her head off, as Whit and Kali disappeared down the stage stairs.

☾ ☾ ☾

Much later that same afternoon, Danu stood in the broad doorway of the meal hall, searching for that distinctively lovely face. At last, she gave up and left the clamor of the communal dining hall behind her.

Dejectedly, Danu shoved her cast-free hand in the pocket of her khaki work pants and set off down the street. The buildings on this side of Isis were for the most part completed, and stood resplendent in new paint and early evening sunshine. Colorful flower boxes hung below open windows, windows which allowed the sounds of women's voices to echo into the paved street and embrace Danu with the vibrant sense of a new life.

The campaign speeches were long over and it was the end of the third and last dinner shift. Danu had been wandering aimlessly for hours. She hadn't seen Neith anywhere, and she found that she was tremendously depressed at not being able to find her. No matter how exciting the prospect of sleeping with Albie had at first seemed, there was a minor complication developing. Having Alborak would mean *not* having Neith, and that felt like it would be a tremendous loss.

How does Loy do it? How does she step from one woman's arms into another's, as if no matter how her body flamed, her heart never warmed?

Just then Lupa appeared, crossing the street from the modern townhomes and calling for her to stop. "Whatcha up to, kid?" the gruff voice demanded. The golden light of sunset fell on the frizzed gray hair, bathing Lupa in a kind of dazzling glow. With a start, Danu realized how glad she was to see her.

"Just walking," Danu answered, then shyly amended it. "I'm thinking over a proposition." She knew the older woman would be able to help her.

Lupa slipped an arm through Danu's, bumped into her shoulder companionably. "Gaea's gift at last, eh? Which one? Neith or Albie?"

With a slight stutter, Danu admitted, "O-One asked and one didn't. I guess the decision was made for me."

"Guess again, Danu," Lupa retorted, with a relentless grin.

Danu stopped, gazing distractedly down the street. At the corner, Albie was standing with the new Deputy Leader of Artemis, Nakotah Berry, and a group of carpenters. Albie was signing rapidly; it must have been a joke, for the women were laughing and clapping Albie's broad shoulders.

Beside her, Lupa prompted softly, "You know who you want, I think."

Nodding, Danu met Lupa's dark Mediterranean eyes. "I guess I'll have to try to explain this to Albie."

Lupa smiled. "That's the way of an honest woman, yes."

Danu laughed nervously, started to walk off, then stopped and waited for Lupa. "Aren't you coming?"

"I think I'll go look over the Leader's House site. Want to be sure we're ready for action tomorrow, in case we get the go ahead from Whit."

With a nod, Danu set off for the group of women at the corner, trying to figure out how to turn down a romp in one woman's bed, in order to try for an attachment with another's heart.

(((

As the sunset began to cast its luminous red glow in the west, Whit swung a long leg over her motorcycle and waved to Cimbri, Lilith, Kali and Styx, who stood on the porch watching her. She would only be gone for a little while, just enough time to feel the clean mountain air rush past her face, just enough time to ride the old highway to Mount Tahoma.

Having realized how close she was to becoming Leader of Isis, Whit was anxious to seal her intentions with a private supplication to the Goddess. Her destination was Selene's Altar, the towering rock face roughly fifteen miles from Isis. While Kali entertained their guests, Whit intended to meditate beneath the light of tonight's full moon. If she was going to stand for Leader, she may as well start the process with a spiritual devotion, requesting guidance and good fortune for the endeavor she was about to undertake.

The quiet cycle purred beneath her, and Whit leaned into the curving road, fluidly shifted through the gears, steering the machine toward higher elevations. She was sure she would be back before Kali even had time to miss her.

☾ ☾ ☾

Back in Isis, Lupa paced the yard in front of the Leader's House, examining the half-finished structure looming in the dimming light. Of all their work this summer, this was the best, she thought. The basic lines were so similar to what had once stood here, and yet the flowing expansion of Danu's design had lent the building a grace, a magnificence that felt inspirational.

In the gathering darkness of the shadows, closer to the house, Lupa thought she saw someone moving. Curious, she walked closer. The figure—a slender, womanly form—began running away. Instinctively, Lupa shouted for her to stop. Instead, the woman ran quickly into the darkening street and Lupa swung around, hesitating. She was torn between chasing the mysterious woman and running a standard safety check on the building. Her need to protect the building won out, and she dashed to the main doorway.

Lifting the radio from her belt, she barked out a message to the warrior security patrol, describing what she had seen and asking them to come immediately to the site. Lupa had no sooner slipped the radio back into place, when the explosion ripped through the building, and then through her.

She never heard or felt a thing, as the building buried her.

❮ ❮ ❮

The dust was still cresting in gaseous waves when Nakotah dashed up to the ruin of the Leader's House. As the members of the security patrol arrived, confused and demanding to know what to do, Nakotah decided for the sake of order to stand in for their chief, Captain Greenberg. She dispatched a search party, hoping against hope that Lupa Tagliaro was not beneath that pile of rubble. Within the flattened structure, various boards flickered with the first, small flames of an erupting fire. Quickly, electro-torches were driven into the glacial silt that formed the ground here, and frantic women began poking through the outer edges of the wreckage.

With a commanding voice, Nakotah shouted orders and had the area cordoned off. The tremendous noise of the explosion had quickly brought a crowd of shocked and questioning onlookers, a crowd that kept growing. Nakotah wanted an organized search by selected members of the security patrol before the small fire already underway engulfed the rest of the rubble. While other security warriors kept the crowd under control, Nakotah grouped the searchers into a long line, which began moving forward together, kicking tentatively through broken stone and lumber. Nakotah steeled herself for what she felt sure was to come. And then, out of the corner of her eye, Nakotah saw Danu Sullivan duck under the rope and promptly get seized by a particularly large sergeant.

"She's okay," Nakotah called. "Let her through."

In the surreal, flickering light of the growing fire and the glaring electro-torches, Danu ran over to Nakotah. "Where's Lupa?" she demanded in a strangled voice.

Just then the cry went up. The security patrol had found someone. Danu tried to join the rush of warriors, but instinctively, Nakotah held her back. Neith nimbly raced by them, over the fragments of fallen stone and splintered board. Panicking, Danu began to fight for free passage and Nakotah gave the girl a rough shake.

"Spare yourself," Nakotah stated, her voice breaking with the despair she felt.

Highlighted in the harsh, white light of the electro-torches, Neith was kneeling beside a bloodied, stocky form, mechanically going through her emergency medical procedures. Then she abruptly stood and backed away. In a low, quavering voice, Danu and Nakotah both heard her say, "It's no use."

With a heartbreaking wail, Danu broke from Nakotah's arms and sprinted forward. Close enough to see, she skidded to a halt. She had only wanted to say good-bye to Lupa, to the brusque, cantankerous woman she had come to love and respect. What confronted her there in the jumble of debris was oozing red pulp wearing the remains of Lupa's clothing.

She knew she was screaming, but couldn't make herself stop. Then Neith was grabbing her, wrestling her away, murmuring in her ear. And Danu clung to her, sobbing, as they blundered away into the darkness.

(((

Kali was trying to concentrate on being a good hostess, mixing a vegetable salad for the guests that lounged in her kitchen. Lilith, Styx, and Cimbri seemed pleasantly satisfied with their tea and brown bread with honey, talking quietly of the latest events during Cimbri's tenure as Leader in Artemis. The homemade pine table and chairs she and Whit had been making do with, had seemed like wealth to Kali, used to having no access to wood of any kind in Elysium. But she could hear Cimbri's opinion of the rough-hewn carpentry work, and felt a bit embarrassed by the furniture, now.

As Kali approached the table with the bowl of salad, she felt a flare of annoyance with Whit for abandoning her like this. Still convinced of her ineptitude with these social affairs, Kali sat down silently and watched her guests serve themselves. After several anxious glances at the closed kitchen door, Kali at last rose and went to open it.

She stood in the threshold a moment, sensing something. *Danger. I can smell it, taste it. But where? How?* Perplexed, she turned away, then stopped. Inexplicably drawn, she turned back to the open door.

Styx stood up and moved toward her. "What is it?"

Kali shook her head, staring at the last of the sunset, at the deep turquoise creeping into the sky above the pink and yellow wash of light.

And then came the loud, ground-shuddering thud of a large, distant explosion. They all looked at one another, too surprised to say anything, until the follow-up, a smashing psychic blow, hit Kali.

With a cry of pain, Kali was doubling over, dropping to her knees, as if the impact destroying Lupa would destroy her, too. She was buffeted with an insight that shredded her as a knife whittles wood. A grief and fear she hadn't known since Elysium overwhelmed her.

She wasn't sure how long it went on, but at last she felt as if she were surfacing from a long, cold plunge in churning water. She was gasping, shivering, desperately trying to reorient her senses. Gradually she became aware that Cimbri was holding her, speaking to her, demanding something from her. Nearby, Lilith was crouched on the floor with her arms around Styx.

Reaching out, clasping Kali's hand, Styx croaked, "Focus!"

The room swam around her. Mentally, Kali tried to push away the surging force that pressed in around her, and failed. "Focus!" Styx implored. "We are under attack! You are the stronger one! Fight back!"

As if spurred on by Styx's words, the unseen power struck at Kali. A vice-like grip seized her lungs. Suddenly the kitchen, the friends around her faded into blackness. She couldn't breathe. She was lost to confusion, pain, sheer terror; she was helpless, held captive. And through the blinding hail of emotion, she suddenly saw Whit astride her motorcycle, traveling the old, crumbling highway toward Selene's Altar.

And Kali knew then, that as surely as the moon would rise tonight over Isis, Whit was marked for death.

☾11

*I*t was just a little after 9 p.m. when Whit turned off the old American highway and aimed her motorcycle up the rutted trail to Selene's Altar. The moon was still too low in the sky to light her way, but her headlight was strong and cast a beam far ahead. Slowly, the machine rolled along, climbing the steep, dark path. Occasionally the vinyl tires slipped on smooth rocks already slick with evening dew. After a long, bumpy ride, Whit approached the summit. She dropped her feet on either side of the machine and braked at the end of the trail. With a flick of the wrist, she cut the motor and just sat there.

The wind up here was stronger, colder. The sun had departed; a royal blue sky still held the last radiant brilliance of the passing day. In the west, the aquamarine and pink horizon silhouetted a vast, timbered mountainside. In the east, Mount Tahoma sat, an enormous, ghostly, lavender presence beneath a full, huge, impossibly white moon.

Whit took a deep breath, dismounted from the bike and set the kickstand. Pulling her leather jacket closer about her, she left the bike and strode toward the cliff's edge, about forty yards away. Fearlessly, Whit stopped at the brink. Buffeted by the wind, she stood looking down at the dark fir forest and the glint of a river far below, before sitting on the hard ground. She leaned back on her hands, gazing up into the deepening blue of the night, noting the indigo color, watching the glimmering stars begin to burn with their distant fire. Every once in a while, the fir trees rustled softly, or a surge of wind brought the sound of the river flowing far below her lofty perch.

Whit arranged her denim-clad legs in the lotus position. She straightened her back and wiggled until she was sitting comfortably. Placing her hands on her knees, she inhaled deeply, tasting the chill air, feeling the air circle in and fill her lungs. After a long moment, she exhaled, consciously stilling her mind, banishing the flitting, busy thoughts. She disciplined her breathing, as Kali had been teaching her to do all winter.

She could almost hear Kali speaking in her ear. *Clear your mind. Take a deep breath. Hold it. Reach with your soul.* Whit looked up into the sky, concentrating on her effort, methodically repeating the process.

Whit prayed, *Mother, use me as you will.*

Time passed. The moon rose higher, grew smaller, but its intense light did not diminish. Instead, the moonglow seemed to blaze down harder, burning through her clothes, her skin. The moonlight seemed to consume her. It was magical and all-encompassing. Unbelievable as it seemed, she was sure she felt the universe moving through her.

Kali's final directive, the last part in the pattern they had often followed together, echoed in Whit's mind, a potent memory. *Soar.*

At this point, Whit usually lost her concentration, while Kali would go on sitting there, eyes closed, never revealing what happened for her during those sessions. Whit, however, would suddenly become acutely conscious of a tickle behind her left knee, of a particularly important task she had forgotten to do—until that very moment. Or she would find herself entranced by Kali's still, relaxed posture. Sometimes she would rise and quietly leave the room; other times, she ended up gently grabbing Kali, kissing and stroking her, finishing any semblance of calm for both of them.

In short, Whit had been unable to master meditation.

But strangely, tonight, Whit *was* prolonging the inner quiet. She closed her eyes, concentrated, and willed it with all her being. *Soar,* she told herself.

Easily, smoothly, she felt herself rising, flying. The valley below the cliff stretched out like the view from the Swallow, and Whit felt her being fly through the night toward Isis.

Mother of the Earth, Whit prayed fervently, *make me fit, make me strong. Let me nurture the women of Isis, as they nurture me.* She seemed to rise higher. Like an osprey finding an eddy of air, she stretched her soul and rode the zephyr effortlessly, circling above Isis. Far below, the lights of Isis gleamed like stars on the ground. *Her place, her people, back in the mountains, where they belonged.* Even in the midst of this astounding union with the spirit forces of nature, she had Kali at the forefront of her thoughts. *Gaea, bless Kali, the one I love beyond all else.*

(((

The grip on Kali suddenly eased. With a shuddering groan, she drew in sweet air and opened her eyes. She was perspiring profusely. Her hair was damp, her shirt wringing wet. Exhausted, she slowly tried to sit up and Cimbri promptly assisted her.

"What happened?" Cimbri hovered, watching her.

An arm's reach away, Styx breathed heavily, still cradled in Lilith's arms. Lilith gazed at Kali, eyes wide, and said with wonder in her voice, "You were both wild, battling, as if...." Faltering, Lilith stopped.

Quietly, Styx asserted, "There's another one."

Cimbri drew back. "Another what?"

"Another Think Tank innovation," Styx gasped, "...another one...someone who is stronger...."

"She means stronger than me, I think," Kali interpreted.

And then Cimbri was staring at Kali, as if a whole other woman had materialized before her. Grimly, Kali answered, "Yes. I suppose that's what I've been trying to avoid dealing with all along. Please don't look at me like that—like I'm some mutant."

Shamed and yet, still puzzled, Cimbri answered earnestly, "I'm sorry. I've always been strongly opposed to DNA manipulations, except in the cause of preventing needless affliction. But I'm missing something here. What does the Think Tank Project have to do with this?"

Looking around herself furtively, Lilith interjected, "You felt what was in this room—that cold, repulsive horror...." Shuddering, Lilith licked her lips, then began again. "Do you believe in what you just experienced?"

Cimbri evaded the question by focusing on Kali. "Explain what just happened here. I'm at a loss."

Massaging her limbs, Kali murmured, "It is rooted in science, and always has been. It's the unmeasured potential of the human mind, beyond all self-conceived or imposed barriers, where spirit becomes pure energy."

Styx interrupted brusquely, "There is time for explanation later." She reached over, stroked Kali's hair back from her face. "You fought off whatever it was, but I sensed someone near the end, helping us. Who? And who was our attacker? Why did it happen?"

"I don't know," Kali moaned. She leaned forward and gripped her head. "I feel so stupid, so ignorant. And now there is someone out there, using her psychic skills like a battery of deadly weapons and...." Despite her effort to stop it, a sob tore out of Kali. "I don't even know who she is!"

Holding her, Cimbri soothed, "But its alright. You and Styx are free of...Gaea, what was it?"

"No," Kali cried, "It's not alright. Lupa is dead!"

Shocked, the others all stared at her.

"And Whit, oh Goddess," Kali whispered to herself, "I've got to find Whit!" With a rough shove off the floor, Kali was up. The three women rose to stop her, but Kali was already through the kitchen door, running into the night.

☾ ☾ ☾

Whit! Stop that! Protect yourself!

Whit's soaring over the valley abruptly ceased. With a resounding jolt, she felt herself sucked backwards into her body. *Was that Kali I heard?* Incredulous, she shook her head, feeling dazed by the dazzling moonglow. *No, that's impossible.* Then immediately she reconsidered. Everything else she had experienced tonight had been impossible, so why should a message from Kali be so unreasonable? After all, there was no one on earth with whom she felt closer, and it often seemed as if Kali read her mind.

*Whit! Get off that cliff! Come...*And then the message ended, as a door slammed in mid-sentence ends a voice calling from another room. The quiet of the night took on a muffled, enclosed vibration, as if someone had just lowered a plexiglass dome over this part of the world. Whit's years of warrior training had long since left her with inner antennae, an awareness of impending peril. And this strange stillness rang with menace.

Moving quickly, Whit scrambled back from the cliff face, sending a few loose rocks rolling toward the edge. She raced to her motorcycle, jumped into the saddle, and snapped the kickstand up with her boot. As she reached for the starter, a sudden blow across the back of her head sent the moon and stars into a swirling black sea. She felt herself tumble from the bike, roll onto her back. She lay there, insensible, paralyzed.

Slowly, her eyes focused on tall, narrow spires, glinting in an unreal light. After an immeasurable delay, she knew what they were: silver fir trees, standing tall and timeless in the moonlight. Whit moved slightly to see what was happening. Her vision blurred with the excruciating blast of pain that glance cost her, but she saw enough to know that Kali's warning had been accurate. In the moon bright night, another motorcycle was visible at the edge of the forest, and a woman clad in black leather pants and jacket was suddenly standing at Whit's feet. Through slitted eyes, Whit watched the woman kneel down, grip her boot, and with a grunt begin dragging Whit toward the cliff edge.

Yanking her leg free, Whit drove her other heel into the woman's knee, bringing her down with a snap of cartilage and a violent thump. The woman screamed in pain. Whit began half-crawling, half running away, too blinded with head pain to fully stand. She had almost made it to the woods when she shot a look back over her shoulder and was astonished to see the injured woman behind her spring to her feet.

"You cannot run from me, Whit," an eerily familiar voice called. "I have come back for justice."

Whit's pain-muddled brain made her halt. She paused, swaying on unsteady feet, suddenly overwhelmed with a dreadful horror.

"Turn and look at me, Whit," the voice entreated. "You remember me: the woman you killed with your bare hands...."

Like a moth which can not keep from flying into the blazing light that will mark its death, Whit turned to face her enemy. And as she swiveled about, her worst fears were realized. There in the moonlight stood Branwen Evans, smiling, her neck still oddly bent from the assault she had suffered at Whit's hands nine months earlier. Aghast, Whit shuddered with horror.

The woman walked easily toward her, showing no trace of the destructive kick Whit had unleashed on her knee just moments ago. And as she came closer, Branwen was crooning, "Come, Tomyris. Let me repay you. Let me take you into the Mother's sleep, into the end of all suffering."

Trembling, Whit couldn't take her eyes from the fair face, the light brown hair and smiling eyes. *Oh, Bran. Forgive me.* An ice-cold fear sliced through her, pounded into her veins. Closing her eyes against the fierce headache that threatened to split her completely in half, Whit felt close to fainting. The woman reached out, grasping Whit's sedation gun and lifting it from the holster.

Wait a minute. I have a headache because someone hit me on the head. Whit stared at the apparition before her, the woman she was so certain was Branwen. *Ghosts don't hit people.*

The thought hit her like a bolt of lightning. Whit concentrated on the possibility that what she was seeing might not be true. She looked with amazement as, shimmering, like heat rising from a landing strip tarmac, the image before her wavered. Then, all at once she was not looking at Branwen. The neck was slender, straight, and unharmed. And...oh, Goddess, the face belonged to Arinna Sojourner!

"So you have finally managed to see your real opponent," Arinna chuckled. "You are harder to frighten than most, aren't you, Tomyris?" And then, snapping the weapon's gauge to lethal-force, she pointed the short, dark pistol barrel at Whit.

Horrified, Whit staggered away from the tree, into the clearing before the cliff. Arinna moved after her dragging her leg, her knee obviously severely damaged now that the illusion had been shattered. "Come, Whit, don't fight me. I *must* and *will* kill you. Don't make it harder on yourself."

Whit's mind went into overdrive. A swift evaluation of all the accidents at Isis rapidly spun through her brain. Arinna had been wandering around Isis on Beltane, alone and out of sight, and later that night the scaffolding had fallen. Then, the explosion in the merchants' sector that brought the building down. *Where was she that time?* Whit couldn't remember. *Did she set the fire in the re-cycling bin? And Danu's strange madness—could she have managed that?* Then her mind was on the crane, with its renegade program. *Lupa said Arinna was there, talking to Loy and Marpe!* But Whit had a hard time continuing this line of thought. Her head hurt too much to think any of it through. All Whit really understood was that Arinna was trying to close the distance between them, and Arinna had just announced that she intended to kill her.

Grasping the back of her neck, nearly staggering as she continued to back away from her deadly opponent, Whit demanded, "Why the hell are you doing this?"

With cold, simple logic, Arinna stated, "Loy will be elected Leader of Isis. And I will rule with her, as Deputy. It is our destiny."

"If it's destiny," Whit attempted to reason, "then you don't have to interfere. Isn't that so?"

Arinna explained, "I am weaving the destiny *I* choose. Oh, we both already know how the Leader election will go, don't we?" Arinna laughed, a clear, bell-like sound. "Especially after today's fiasco—with that fool Fea unable to endure a minor insult.

"According to town gossip, you will be elected Leader of Isis, despite my clever efforts to undermine progress and thus discredit your beloved and competent image." Arinna shook her head, marveling at Whit. "You have a formidable will and substantial charisma. You have overcome every roadblock I devised."

How can she think Loy still has a chance? Whit thought.

As if in answer, Arinna informed her, "I had to skip dinner and do some damage control, so forgive me if I'm irritable. Dear Fea was a bit stubborn at the end and resisted writing the suicide note in which she apologized for her slanderous blunder."

Feeling stupid with pain, Whit wasn't sure she had accurately caught Arinna's meaning. "Suicide? Fea?"

Ice-cold green eyes pierced Whit. "Seems she told a vicious lie in a fit of temper, and then was overcome with remorse when she realized she had ruined a friend's career. They'll find poor Captain Greenberg dangling by the neck in one of the newer building frameworks, strangled by a thin, but adequate length of construction rope...."

"Sweet mother," Whit breathed, sickened.

Arinna gestured with the gun, signalling that she wanted Whit to move closer to the cliff edge. "But I am losing patience. You have become an impediment, and must be removed."

"Killing me won't change anything," Whit counseled, thinking of Kali's nomination to the field of candidates.

Arinna peered at her, murmuring, "Believe me, Kali won't be able to take your place."

The hair stood up on the back of Whit's neck.

Arinna dragged herself inexorably closer, smiling cruelly, despite the obvious injury to her knee. "Your death must seem completely accidental, my dear Whit." Feigning sudden anguish, Arinna stated, "A miscalculation of how close you were to the cliff." With a sinister laugh, she ended, "Don't worry, Kali won't grieve long."

Bending over, Whit waited with bated breath until Arinna came into range, determined to go down fighting. Instead, Arinna stopped, just clear of where Whit guessed she could reach with a snap-kick. Motioning toward the cliff edge with the pistol once again, Arinna warned, "Oh, no you don't."

Baffled, Whit sluggishly swayed out of her wobbly stance. Once more, she tried to reason with her executioner. "Arinna, does Loy know about this?"

"Enough, Whit," Arinna snarled. "Move."

As Whit stumbled forward, Arinna lurched along behind her. The injured leg only seemed to make it awkward for her; there seemed to be no real pain involved, which perplexed Whit no end.

Arinna murmured, "Too bad you wouldn't leave the illusion intact. Your compliance would have made the ending so much easier."

Whit's aching brain shook off the pounding throb long enough to examine that strange remark. *Why did I see Branwen instead of Arinna? What trick of the mind was that?* And then the answer was so clearly there in front of her. *Arinna caused me to see what I saw, until I questioned it, and broke the illusion.*

"Well done, Governor Whitaker," Arinna remarked, laughing softly, maneuvering a little farther away from Whit.

She's reading my mind! Whit suddenly noticed how far Arinna had already herded her, how much closer to the edge she was. Her head ached miserably, she was half-blind with pain every time she tried to fully stand. *Don't think—she's reading it—using it!*

Unexpectedly, Whit tripped on the stony, uneven surface and went down. She hit the ground beneath her with a thud. The wind was knocked out of her and she lay there, face down, powerless. She heard Arinna dragging her bad leg, closing the space between them.

Kali's voice intruded, delivering a firmly authoritative order. *Roll left!*

Whit responded automatically, as if she were still in warrior boot camp. She quickly rolled her body into Arinna's legs. The force sent her toppling over Whit.

Run! Run! Kali commanded.

Drawing on her last bit of strength, Whit obeyed, listening to her lover's voice though her lover was nowhere in sight.

She can't hear me! I've blocked her—like she's blocked me for months, now. I'm coming, Whit! I'm coming!

As Whit penetrated the edge of the forest, a blast from Arinna's gun hit a tree twenty feet to Whit's right, causing it to explode in a white spray of sparks. Plunging on, Whit crashed into the thick underbrush, then stumbled and collapsed. Dragging herself behind a massive, fallen log, she lay there breathing rapidly. Feeling fairly well hidden in the darkness, Whit finally allowed herself to peep over the edge of the log. In the moonlight on the cliff, Whit could see Arinna hissing with pain, moving her hands over her leg. The words the woman began to utter were a rhythmic force in the night, hypnotic and ancient. *Is that Celtic?* Whit wondered. As the pain in her head swiftly receded, Whit knew what she was hearing was a chant to heal.

And then Arinna stood, and the chant shifted into another lyric. Whit sat there, straining to hear her, caught before she knew the ruse. "Come into the moonlight, by my side. You cannot run, you cannot hide. Come to me, come to me, Tomyris!"

Whit found herself walking out of the darkness, bathed in moonlight, all the while her mind was shrieking *No!* But her body obeyed the inexorable command and steadily moved toward the shimmering vision on the cliff. With a lethal smile Arinna crooked a finger at her, opened her arms invitingly. Walking slowly into that embrace, Whit groaned, feeling the last of her own will being sucked from her.

With a sweet, horrid certainty, Arinna pulled Whit's head down and kissed her. Then there was a voice in Whit's mind, coaxing her into returning the intimacy. "I should have tried this sooner," Arinna commented, her voice deep and powerful. "It's no doubt how Kali caught you, whether she knows it or not. You cannot resist a Siren, can you Tomyris?"

Dumbfounded, Whit tried to move, to thrust Arinna away from her, and found she could not.

Taking Whit's wrist, Arinna slowly twisted the arm behind Whit's back. "You hurt my leg," Arinna confided, slowly forcing the arm up. "I had to focus most of my power on blocking the pain."

Whit opened her mouth to cry out.

"I haven't given you permission to speak," Arinna whispered.

And with those words, Whit had no voice. Sweat sprang out across her brow. The power Whit felt leaning into her increased unbearably, and Whit realized that this smaller, physically weaker woman could easily break her arm. *But how? She's stronger than a Reg—and this is no illusion!*

Below Whit's shoulder, Arinna chuckled, "And now, shall I show you what I can do, once my energies are not fractured into a hundred concerns? Shall I show you what Kali's mother created in that lab of hers, before she learned to fear the DNA manipulations?"

Whit shook with agony, her shoulder muscles vibrating like harp strings.

Abruptly, Arinna loosened her grip. As Whit's arm slipped down, Arinna shifted her hold, turned Whit to face her. "Kali and I are just alike, you know," Arinna confided, staring into Whit's eyes with malice. "Both Think Tank Babies, both products of the greatest enhanced human intelligence experiment ever attempted. The paranormal outcome was an...unexpected bonus, shall we say?"

Enmeshed in Arinna's power, Whit stood there, unable to do more than blink. *She's got to be psychotic,* Whit decided.

Well aware of Whit's conclusion about her sanity, Arinna threw back her head, laughing for several minutes, wildly amused. Then, sobering, Arinna proclaimed, "Oh Whit, you are so predictably *ordinary*! Must I explain everything?"

Confounded, Whit watched the glittering green eyes narrow.

"Do you have any idea how many times I've tried to break into Maat's lab? Do you really think I was tutoring Kali through secondary school courses all summer out of *kindness*?"

"With you out of the way, I shall have Kali serve as my DNA key. With her code, I'll gain entrance to that lab, gain access to Maat's computer and find her precious mother's buried files on DNA manipulation. And while Loy guides Isis into its commonplace, mundane little future, I will be raising the future of Freeland, cloning myself, re-creating the Think Tank project in a sealed, top security lab. The girls I produce will be forced into accelerated growth, trance-taught and steroid-fed as they incubate. I promise you that in five years, I will have a mighty army of paranormal warriors, and *I* will rule—first Isis—then Freeland—then the world."

Whit stood there, reeling with what she had just heard. Her initial suspicion—that Arinna was psychotic—was gone. The woman was a diabolical genius. Every word Arinna had just uttered echoed a report Whit had read long ago while she was writing a paper in college.

Maat Tyler had produced the report shortly after she had discontinued the Think Tank project. In it, Maat had discussed her fears regarding the unanticipated outcomes of intelligence enhancement research. One of the results that had perplexed her was the seemingly amplified powers of good and evil, within the person possessing extreme intellect. Searching her memory, Whit remembered that Maat had written specifically of two little girls in her study: one who used her gifts with goodwill and affection, and one who used her gifts to ruthlessly secure a dominant position over others.

"Yes," Arinna murmured, "I frightened Maat. She placed me in the care of two psychologists, and sent me to Tubman. Maat made sure I was kept far away from her Kali, lest I overpower her and make her my first disciple. You will at least be spared seeing *that* come true, Whit."

Internally, Whit was screaming for release. So much was suddenly horribly clear! All along, Arinna had been planning to take control of Kali, take control of the Think Tank files stored in Maat's lab computer. Arinna was going to set in motion a fiendish plan that would probably end up enslaving all of Freeland. And Whit couldn't do a thing to stop her, let alone manage to avoid her own death.

"Now, come with me," Arinna crooned slipping her arm around Whit's waist. "Give me your will. Let all those frantic, useless thoughts just drift away. I'll take care of you." And then a primordial language, one Whit recognized and yet had no name for, flowed over her, calming her, spellbinding her. And Whit felt Arinna's presence fill her completely.

Slowly, they walked to the edge of the cliff and stood looking over, down into the forest and winding river, far, far below. Whit stood there, unafraid, and completely defenseless, as Arinna nudged her toward the very lip of the cliff.

☾ ☾ ☾

As Loy brought the tilt-rotor round the mountainside, Kali gasped. She spied Whit and Arinna standing together on the precipice. "Now do you believe me?!" Kali demanded.

Startled at the sight, Loy didn't answer.

"Do a fly-by! Buzz them back!!" Kali shouted. When Loy didn't bank down immediately, Kali grabbed the stick and slammed the small copter into a port dive, straight at the cliff face.

Loy shrieked, snatching the controls back from Kali just as the Swallow swooped by the mountainside, missing the edge by barely ten feet.

"Land! Land!" Kali hollered. She looked behind them and saw Whit still standing at the edge of the cliff, while Arinna scurried toward the trees, then paused to watch the little helicopter.

"Damn!" Loy yelled back. "You're crazy! Why did you bring me here, anyway?"

"Because there's a sociopathic monster down there—your lover! Kali declared, her brown eyes flashing. I've brought you here because you're the only one that may be able to convince Arinna that her plan won't work, simply because you won't go along with it. You've got to convince her to give it up—to just leave—before she kills Whit. Now land, or I swear I'll crash us!"

Confused and annoyed, Loy punched the vertical descend switch and dipped the craft lower. "What are you talking about? " she shouted angrily at Kali. "What plan? I don't even know how I got into this!" she fumed. "One minute, we were arguing and I was telling you 'no,' and the next minute I was in this copter, flying like a bat out of hell!"

"There's no time now for explanations. Just *land*!" Kali snapped back at her.

Swiftly, expertly, Loy brought the craft to a gentle rest on the rock ledge, unwittingly placing the copter between Arinna and Whit. Impatiently, Kali thrust the hatch back and vaulted from the machine. Loy stayed in the cockpit, gunning the soft, rumbling engine, and glaring.

Dashing over to Whit, Kali grabbed her by the hand and pulled her back from the cliff's edge, toward the copter. As Kali tugged Whit around the tail section, intent on getting her on-board, Arinna suddenly appeared, barring Kali's way with her body.

Kali came to an abrupt stop. Whit, completely dependent on Kali's impetus to move at all, took one more step and bumped into the frantic young woman.

Grabbing Whit's arm, Arinna shouted above the low engine noise, "Kali, I see that the moon makes your magic grow like yeast. Not only did you break my binding spell, you have managed to summon Loy and have her pilot you here!" She laughed as if this were an entertaining surprise. "And blocked me all the while! I have not had such a well-matched game in years!"

"Get out of our way," Kali commanded, her voice loud and determined.

"You cannot stop me, you know," Arinna snarled, her dark hair blowing wildly in the wind.

Shifting to see what was going on at the rear of the aircraft, Loy called, "Arinna, what in Gaea's name are you doing?!" She left the engine on and leapt from the craft.

"There's no need for you to involve yourself," Arinna insisted. With a nod at Kali, she crooned, "Leave that one here and I'll take care of everything."

Apprehension flooded Loy's expressive face. "What are you saying? Take care of what?" She walked closer.

In a fierce, steely tone of voice, Arinna commanded, "Just get in the Swallow and get the hell out of here!"

Anxiously, Kali almost spoke up, then decided against it. By now, she thought she could predict Loy's response to a direct order.

After staring defiantly at Arinna for a long silent moment, Loy's gaze moved to Whit. The gray eyes were glazed, unfocused. Arinna's hand lightly held Whit's upper arm. "What have you done to her?" Loy shouted above the whirl of the rotor blades.

"Nothing for you to be concerned about," Arinna retorted. Then her tone deepened. "Leave us alone, Loy. I can handle this."

Loy stared at Arinna, then vigorously shook her head, as if clearing it.

"Why must you be so stubborn, Loy?!" Arinna hissed. "Take my advice. Leave Kali. Go back to Isis—you *will* be Leader."

With great effort, Loy stated, "I won't let you hurt Whit." Some of the words were slurred, but her voice was strong and heartfelt.

"You won't?" Smiling malevolently, Arinna considered Loy with rueful eyes. "Do you really think you can stop me, my little puppet?"

But Kali had registered the dangerous undernote in Arinna's reply and began to subtly move. As she was swinging around to face Kali, Arinna missed Loy's look of rebellion. Clumsily, obstinately, Loy threw herself into Arinna, breaking Arinna's hold on Whit's arm.

Suddenly, with lightning speed, Kali grabbed Whit's hand and made a run for it.

Flattening Loy with a sweep of one arm, Arinna harshly commanded, "Stop!"

Kali's feet slammed to the ground as if rooted. Beside, her, Whit was frozen in mid-stride, her face blank, devoid of expression.

Arinna turned, focusing her fury on the woman at her feet. "Hear me, Loy! I *gave* you power over me! I allowed you to possess my body, but you are *my* plaything now, and you will not interfere in this matter!"

For the few seconds that Arinna was distracted, Kali found herself whispering the spellbreaker chant. Somehow, almost instinctively, she knew the words to the ancient rhyme, without any idea how she had acquired the knowledge. She listened with amazement as they flowed from her mouth in an ancient rhythm. All at once, Kali's feet were free. Blinking, Whit heaved a deep sigh, then rubbed her hands over her face wearily.

Arinna's voice seemed to fill Kali's ears. "I believe you are pulling knowledge from my brain, and then using it against me...."

"Arinna, you should leave while you can," Kali advised. "The warrior women of Isis are already searching for us. Loy won't allow you to make her Leader; she's self-serving, but she'll never be an accomplice to murder. She's as stubborn as Whit. Your power won't twist either of them to your purpose; it just makes them puppets. And as for your schemes of creating a Think Tank dynasty, forget it. There are no DNA files. My mother destroyed them."

"You're lying," Arinna charged.

With all her will, Kali blocked Arinna's assault on her memory. "I'm not!"

"Well, I'll have *you*, then!" Arinna proclaimed. "You saw those files, you worked on those projects...."

"I was a child!" Kali snapped.

Responding to the anger in her voice, Whit turned a bewildered face to Kali, the gray eyes still unfocused.

Swallowing, Kali finished quietly, "And after the mind-drugs the Regs used on me I can barely remember basic schooling, let alone genetic engineering files."

"All the same, I must bond with you and examine your unconscious." Gracefully, Arinna advanced on Kali, murmuring words, rhythmic enchantments, catching Kali off guard. The stars above were swirling. Dimly, she was aware that Arinna had gripped the collar of her shirt and was dragging her toward the small helicopter. Though she resisted Arinna with every cell in her body, her deadly enemy was gradually overwhelming her.

Then, seemingly out of nowhere, a military jetcraft arced across the western sky, flying low and fast. And Kali knew. *It's Nakotah. She's using a heat-seeking scanner—searching for us!* Emboldened, Kali made one last mental push and forced Arinna's tenacious will from her mind.

"No!" Arinna cried, distraught at Kali's success. She spun around, torn between objectives, knowing she only had a few moments to act. *Escape? Stay? Kill everyone?* Kali heard the thoughts with a chilling realization: Arinna was panicking.

"Go," Kali urged. "Get away. Come back for me later, if I'm so damned important."

In one decisive move, Arinna released Kali's collar and darted to the plane. Kali collapsed to her knees, exhausted from even that brief contest of wills.

Climbing into the cockpit, Arinna laughed contemptuously at Kali. "Oh, I'll be back for you, have no doubt. We are sisters, your mother's creation, and we belong together."

Raising her arm, snapping her fingers, Arinna brought Loy to her feet. Loy threw one dreadful, terrified look at Kali before the shutters came down and her dark eyes went horribly blank. Loy shuffled to the aircraft and began climbing into the cockpit.

"Don't take her!" Kali entreated.

With a melodious laugh, Arinna replied, "She has earned her fate, don't you think? She who has played with the affections of so many, will now be my toy. I shall free her when I tire of her service." Laughing wickedly, completely delighted with herself, Arinna settled Loy into the seat beside her and slammed the hatch closed.

The wild, spectral laughter was still ringing in Kali's head, an unwanted telepathic connection, as the copter lifted from the cliff and rose into the southern sky.

❨ ❨ ❨

Later that night, after Nakotah had found them and taken them back to Isis, Kali and Whit stood wearily on the tarmac of the airfield and recounted their unbelievable tale of sorcery and sabotage. The hundreds that had gathered to meet them listened, alarmed and distressed, then broke into angry reaction, shouting for Arinna's arrest and punishment.

At last, Whit waved them silent and informed them, "There shall be no pursuit, at least until we can figure out how to oppose her." Warriors in the multitude began protesting, and Whit shouted vehemently, "I will not send you to do what I could not do."

Beside Whit, Kali amended firmly, "This is *my* confrontation. Arinna is the product of my mother's experimental research, as I am, myself. It is my duty to destroy the madness my mother inadvertently created."

Exhausted, dizzy with fatigue, Whit merely shook her head in refusal. "You aren't doing this alone, Kal. I won't let you."

The crowd around Nakotah's jetcraft waited, silent, realizing this had gone quite suddenly from a spontaneous public strategy session to a private discussion between lovers.

Kali faced Whit, resolute. "I have to. Isis needs you now more than ever. And Arinna is no Regulator that you can out-fight or out-think. She's a *power*. Her psychic talents are finely honed and she has unfathomable resources. She's misusing the powers of Wicca, invoking spells for her own warped objectives."

"How can *you* fight her, then?!" Whit demanded, the emotional catch in her voice betraying how much she feared what Kali was proposing to do. "You're a raw talent! You don't know any spells!"

Kali responded, "I'm going to do what I can! And I'm the only one who can challenge her without...ending up like Loy."

The night wind stirred, caressing Kali's golden hair. That familiar jaw was set and the dark brown eyes shone with purpose. *Always so brave*, Whit reflected. And as moonlight glimmered in all the watchful eyes on them, Whit obeyed her impulse, leaned forward and kissed Kali hard.

For a second, Whit felt Kali's stiff reserve, and then, Kali melted in her arms. Women were cheering, encouraging her, as Whit stepped back. Kali blushed, as much aroused as she was embarrassed.

All at once, Lilith and Styx appeared, pushing to the front of the assembly. Authoritatively, Lilith pronounced, "That's enough for tonight. They must rest. We meet tomorrow at 9 a.m. in the Cedar House." Taking Whit in one arm and Kali in the other, Lilith began shepherding her daughters away, toward a nearby electrobile.

"You both look like you can barely stand," Lilith worriedly informed them. "Styx says your contact with Arinna has drained you. Come, we'll take you home."

"I can't," Kali argued. "I have to...."

Opening the car door for Kali and Whit, Styx soothed, "You're worn out, Kali. And there is much you must learn before you confront Arinna Sojourner again. As it is, we are incredibly lucky that she gave up trying to master you and took Loy, instead." Observing the enormous yawn that Kali suddenly gave, Styx finished, "You need to sleep and heal yourself."

Grumpily ducking into the car, settling on the seat beside Whit, Kali muttered, "Alright, I'll sleep." She leaned her head against Whit's shoulder and closed her eyes. "And leave in the morning," she mumbled.

Moving into the front seat, beside Lilith, Styx chuckled. "No, not so fast. You will be trained first."

"Trained?" Kali's head popped up. "By who?"

"Me, of course," Styx returned. "I was not Baubo's apprentice all those years for nothing. I was never her equal in the practice of Witchcraft, but I know enough to put you on an equal footing with Arinna."

Lilith started the car and drove away from the airfield, following the road that would wind through Isis and then to Whit and Kali's house in the countryside.

"Training will take time," Kali countered. "I don't have any to spare."

Rubbing her eyes, Whit muttered, "Kali, you can't face her unprepared."

"Whit, she's going to...."

"Kal, she nearly defeated you!" Whit yelled. "I was out of it up there, but I saw her take you by the collar and drag you away from me! You just barely managed to hold her off—and next time she'll be ready to circumvent that. I won't lose you to her! I *won't!*"

Ferocious, Whit embraced her, and they stayed that way, silent, huddling together as Lilith drove through the moonlit night, carrying them home. They were passing through the streets of town, the windows of the many residences glowing with lamplight, when Kali shook off the dozing state that had been enfolding her, and quietly asked Lilith to stop the car at Neith's clinic.

"What are we doing?" Whit asked, following Kali out of the car, to the door of the clinic.

Kali gripped her hand. "Lupa is here."

Grimly, Whit nodded, understanding.

Together, they all walked in to pay their last respects. In the hallway, Lilith and Styx trailed slowly behind, allowing Whit and Kali to outdistance them.

Tears in her eyes, Lilith whispered, "I fear for them, Styx. "Arinna is like nothing we have ever known."

Somber, Styx said softly, "Lupa gave her life for an ideal—a colony where free lesbians could build their homes, create their families, and live peacefully and harmoniously together." Nodding her head at Whit and Kali, Styx explained, "*They* are an example of that ideal, Lil. Their love for each other is their strength, their sustenance. With all of her magic, Arinna did not overcome them."

"By the love of the Goddess," Lilith murmured.

"More than love," Styx stated firmly, "They are Freeland warriors. And they, thank Gaea, are our future."

The End

About The Author

Jean Stewart was born and raised in the suburbs of Philadelphia. She grew up loving any and all sports, enthralled with nature and music. She spent years trying to achieve her childhood dream of reading every book in the Swarthmore Library, and is now afflicted with a voracious appetite for books.

She has taught school, coached hockey, lacrosse, and basketball, driven a truck and supervised railroad freight—all while writing books in her head. She is currently working on another novel—as usual.

She lives near Seattle, in the Pacific Northwest, with her life-partner, Susie.

It is her heart's desire to live long enough to see a woman elected President of the United States.

She has been quoted as saying, "If you find Whit or Lilith or Cimbri admirable, then strive to be like them. Become a Leader, yourself, and we'll turn America into Freeland."

If You Liked This Book...

Authors seldom get to hear what readers like about their work. If you enjoyed reading this novel, why not let the author know? Simply write the author:

Jean Stewart
c/o Rising Tide Press
5 Kivy Street
Huntington Station, NY 11746

Future Sequels to the Freeland Warrior Series

Why not write and tell Jean Stewart what you would like to see happen in Freeland, Elysium, or perhaps on Earth, as the Freeland society develops and moves into the 22nd century? What kind of world do you envision? What do you want to see happen to your favorite characters?

Remember to look for the sequel to <u>Isis Rising</u>!

Write:

Jean Stewart
c/o Rising Tide Press
5 Kivy Street
Huntington Station, NY 11746

MORE EXCITING FICTION FROM
RISING TIDE PRESS

ROMANCING THE DREAM
Heidi Johanna

This imaginative tale begins when Jacqui St. John leaves northern California looking for a new home, and cruises into the seemingly ordinary town of Kulshan, on the Oregon coast. Seeing the lilac bushes in bloom along the roadside, she suddenly remembers the recurring dream that has been tantalizing her for months—a dream of a house full of women, radiating warmth and welcome, and of one special woman, dressed in silk and leather.... But why has Jacqui, like so many other women, been drawn to this place? The answer is simple but wonderful—the women plan to take over the town and make a lesbian haven. A captivating and erotic love story with an unusual plot. A novel that will charm you with its gentle humor and fine writing.

ISBN 0-9628938-0-3;176 Pages; $8.95

YOU LIGHT THE FIRE
Kristen Garrett

Here's a grown-up *Rubyfruit Jungle*--sexy, spicy, and side-splittingly funny. Garrett, a fresh new voice in lesbian fiction, has created two memorable characters in Mindy Brinson and Cheerio Monroe. Can a gorgeous, sexy, high school math teacher and a raunchy, commitment-shy ex singer, make it last, in mainstream USA? With a little help from their friends, they can. This humorous, erotic and unpredictable love story will keep you laughing, and marveling at the variety of lesbian love.

ISBN 0-9628938-5-4; 176 Pages; $8.95

EDGE OF PASSION
Shelley Smith

The author of **Horizon of the Heart** presents another absorbing and sexy novel! From the moment Angela saw Micki sitting at the end of the smoky bar, she was consumed with desire for this cool and sophisticated woman, and determined to have her...at any cost. Set against the backdrop of colorful Provincetown and Boston, this sizzling novel will draw you into the all-consuming love affair between an older and a younger woman. A gripping love story, which is both fierce and tender. It will keep you breathless until the last page.

ISBN 0-9628938-1-1; 192 Pages; $8.95

RETURN TO ISIS
Jean Stewart
The year is 2093. In this fantasy zone where sword and superstition meet sci-fi adventure, two women make a daring escape to freedom. Whit, a bold warrior from an Amazon nation, rescues Amelia from a dismal world where females are either breeders or drones. Together, they journey over grueling terrain, to the shining world of Artemis, and in their struggle to survive, find themselves unexpectedly drawn to each other. But it is in the safety of Artemis, Whit's home colony, that danger truly lurks. And it is in the ruins of Isis that the secret of how it was mysteriously destroyed waits to be uncovered. Here's adventure, mystery and romance all rolled into one.

Nominated for a 1993 Lambda Literary Award
ISBN 0-9628938-6-2; 192 Pages; $8.95

FACES OF LOVE
Sharon Gilligan
A wise and sensitive novel which takes us into the lives of Maggie, Karen, Cory, and their community of friends. Maggie Halloran, a prominent women's rights advocate, and Karen Weston, a brilliant attorney, have been together for 10 years in a relationship which is full of love, but is also often stormy. When Maggie's heart is captured by the young and beautiful Cory, she must take stock of her life and make some decisions.
Set against the backdrop of Madison, Wisconsin, and its dynamic women's community, the characters in this engaging novel are bright, involved, '90s women dealing with universal issues of love, commitment and friendship. A wonderful read!

ISBN 0-9628938-4-6 ; 192 Pages; $8.95

LOVE SPELL
Karen Williams
A deliciously erotic and humorous love story with a magical twist. When Kate Gallagher, a reluctantly single veterinarian, meets the mysterious and alluring Allegra one enchanted evening, it is instant fireworks. But as Kate gradually discovers, they live in two very different worlds, and Allegra's life is shrouded in mystery which Kate longs to penetrate. A masterful blend of fantasy and reality, this whimsical story will delight your imagination and warm your heart. Here is a writer of style as well as substance.

ISBN 0-9628938-2-X; 192 Pages; $9.95

Danger in High Places
An Alix Nicholson Mystery
Sharon Gilligan

Free-lance photographer Alix Nicholson was expecting some great photos of the AIDS Quilt— what she got was a corpse with a story to tell! Set against the backdrop of Washington, DC, the bestselling author of **Faces of Love** delivers a riveting mystery. When Alix accidentally stumbles on a deadly scheme surrounding AIDS funding, she is catapulted into the seamy underbelly of Washington politics. With the help of Mac, lesbian congressional aide, Alix gradually untangles the plot, has a romantic interlude, and learns of the dangers in high places.
ISBN 0-9628938-7-0; 176 Pages; $9.95

CORNERS OF THE HEART
Leslie Grey

This captivating novel of love and suspense introduces two unforgettable characters whose diverse paths have finally led them to each other. It is Spring, season of promise, when beautiful, French-born Chris Benet wanders into Katya Michaels' life. But their budding love is shadowed by a baffling mystery which they must solve. You will read with bated breath as they work together to outwit the menace that threatens Deer Falls; your heart will pound as the story races to its heart-stopping climax. Vivid, sensitive writing and an intriguing plot are the hallmarks of this exciting new writer.

ISBN 0-9628938-3-8;   224 pages; $9.95

SHADOWS AFTER DARK
Ouida Crozier

Wings of death are spreading over the world of Körnagy and Kyril's mission on Earth is to find the cause. Here, she meets the beautiful but lonely Kathryn, who has been yearning for a deep and enduring love with just such a woman as Kyril. But to her horror, Kathryn learns that her darkly exotic new lover has been sent to Earth with a purpose—to save her own dying vampire world. A tender and richly poetic novel.   *ISBN 1-883061-50-4; 224 Pages; $9.95*

How To Order:

Rising Tide Press books are available from you local women's bookstore or directly from Rising Tide Press. Send check, money order, or Visa/MC account number, with expiration date and signature to: Rising Tide Press, 5 Kivy St., Huntington Sta., New York 11746. **Credit card** orders must be over $25. **Remember** to include shipping and handling charges: $4.95 for the first book plus $1.00 for each additional book. *Credit Card Orders Call our Toll Free # 1-800-648-5333.* For UPS delivery, provide street address.

Our Publishing Philosophy

Rising Tide Press is a lesbian-owned and operated publishing company committed to publishing books by, for, and about lesbians and their lives. We are not only committed to readers, but also to lesbian writers who need nurturing and support, whether or not their manuscripts are accepted for publication. Through quality writing, the press aims to entertain, educate, and empower readers, whether they are women-loving-women or heterosexual. It is our intention to promote lesbian culture, community, and civil rights, nationwide, through the printed word.

In addition, RTP will seek to provide readers with images of lesbians aspiring to be more than their prescribed roles dictate. The novels selected for publication will aim to portray women from all walks of life, (regardless of class, ethnicity, religion or race), women who are strong, not just victims, women who can and do aspire to be more, and not just settle, women who will fight injustice with courage. Hopefully, our novels will provide new ideas for creating change in a heterosex-ist and homophobic society. Finally, we hope our books will encourage lesbians to respect and love themselves more, and at the same time, convey this love and respect of self to the society at large. It is our belief that this philosophy can best be actualized through fine writing that entertains, as well as educates the